Snakepit

MOSES ISEGAWA was born in 1963 in Kampala, Uganda.
He now has Dutch nationality and lives near Amsterdam.
This is his second novel.

ALSO BY MOSES ISEGAWA

Abyssinian Chronicles

MOSES ISEGAWA

Snakepit

PICADOR

First published 2004 by Alfred A. Knopf
a division of Random House, Inc., New York
and simultaneously in Canada by Random House of Canada Limited, Toronto

This edition published 2004 by Picador
an imprint of Pan Macmillan Ltd
Pan Macmillan, 20 New Wharf Road, London N1 9RR
Basingstoke and Oxford
Associated companies throughout the world
www.panmacmillan.com

ISBN 0 330 41996 X

Copyright © Moses Isegawa 2004

The right of Moses Isegawa to be identified as the
author of this work has been asserted by him in accordance
with the Copyright, Designs and Patents Act 1988.

Originally published in the Netherlands as *Slangenkuil* by Uitgave De Bezige Bij,
Amsterdam, in 1999. Copyright © 1999 by Rien Verhoef.

1 3 5 7 9 8 6 4 2

A CIP catalogue record for this book is available from
the British Library.

Printed and bound in Great Britain by
Mackays of Chatham plc, Chatham, Kent

Snakepit

One
In the Air

B at Katanga did his first and only job interview inside a military helicopter, the missile-laden Mirage Avenger, owned by General Samson Bazooka Ondogar. In the years to come, his first impression of the machine would repeat itself in his mind like a leitmotif. The thing looked surreal, the spinning blades like whirling knives, the sun's rays its only decoration. The military-green colour gave the monstrosity the look of a toad, some creature made for children to play with, or to dump things in. He had the sense that it would not take off, or if it did, that it would drop them in the lake. It reminded him of his return from Britain a fortnight before. Entebbe Airport had been empty, his plane the only plane on the tarmac, aside from the Learjet belonging to a famous astrologer. Since the coup, air traffic had dried up, except for the weekly Libyan and Saudi flights which brought supplies and a few intrepid passengers. For a moment, it felt as if the Avenger had been dispatched to take him to exile.

He remembered waking up early that morning with the feeling that his life was about to change in some major way, and showering for a very long time, as if shedding his skin, and putting on his best suit. He remembered leaving his friend's house with the belief that the time had come to rise and face his destiny. It was as if the ground were shifting, making things rock and vibrate. He remembered arriving at the Parliament Building and standing at the gate, in the shadow of the massive statue of Marshal Amin Dada. The statue resembled the hundreds of its replicas stationed in towns all over the country. He remembered the big dark Boomerang 600 which picked him up, the door held open by a soldier, and dropped him at the Nile Perch Hotel.

On the way to the hotel the events of the past weeks had rolled through his mind. A month ago he had completed his post-graduate degree at Cambridge University in Britain and decided to return to Uganda to seek his fortune. So much had happened during his time away. Fifty thousand Indians and 180,000 Africans from different countries had been expelled, leaving many places open in the civil service. It seemed that flag independence was giving way to economic independence, and he wanted to be part of it. He remembered the euphoria and uncertainty which had marked his arrival, the application letters to government ministries and parastatal organizations, and the encouragement from family and friends. Now he was on his way to meet the Minister of Power and Communications in the sanctity of his favourite toy, the Mirage Avenger. It looked almost too good to be true. He remembered exiting the car and walking on the red carpet to the steps, the wind in his face, all kinds of thoughts in his mind. Inside, he walked through a corridor to a comfortable compartment. The background was dominated by a huge portrait of Marshal Amin making the salute, huge fingers jutting, the medals on his chest shining. There were files on a table, a battery of golden Parker pens, a black telephone, and a general's woolen hat.

Suddenly, General Bazooka's imposing frame obstructed the light. He had emerged from another compartment and stood erect in an immaculate uniform adorned with medals, a gleaming holster at his side, a swagger stick in one hand. He measured Bat up for one long moment before stepping forward, bending a little and gripping his hand in a crushing handshake which was meant to show him who the boss was. He sat down with a grin on his face, commented on the fine weather, patted his hair, strapped himself in the seat and gave the order to take off.

"I am sure that we are going to have a very good working relationship. You can tell a man by the way he shakes hands. First, I am taking you on a tour. If at the end you are unimpressed, then I will interview somebody else. But I have never been wrong in my estimation of a man."

"Thank you, General."

The Avenger took off precariously, like a creature off balance. It veered to one side, then the other, making the shrill noise of a tormented beast. Bat looked out and saw the city fading under him, reduced to a patchwork of coloured roofs, cut by the road network, dotted with treetops. A church steeple loomed in the distance, menacing like a spear sharpened to impale condemned sinners. For a moment he thought about the astrologer's Learjet and he wondered whether the man had also been interviewed in the air. From what he had heard about the sensational spread of astrology in the country, and the evidence of it he had seen in the newspapers, he concluded that if astrologers built churches the skyline would be crowded with their spires. His mind wandered and he remembered stories about British tycoons who held business meetings in private jets, aboard yachts or from inside golden coffins. It struck him that the General might be playing at that kind of eccentricity in a bid to impress or intimidate.

"The most beautiful city in the world," the General said emphatically as if anticipating stiff opposition.

Bat did not agree, but said nothing. He looked out the window as if to confirm his views.

"Do you know why? It is because I own a fifth of it. I own a fifth of everything in this country. That comes down to about four million people, ten million fishes, two thousand crocodiles, twenty islands and much more. You can imagine the feeling. There is nothing like it, I can assure you," he said, looking outside for a long moment, as if to make sure the city was still there, a smug smile on his face.

On any other day, Bat might have panicked, but today he was determined to succeed and was not going to let anybody stand in his way. A man who openly boasted about owning a fifth of the country could be managed. All it took was studying his ways, finding his weaknesses, and going around him.

"Right now I am looking for somebody who is hungry and dedicated. Loyalty is paramount and disloyalty a cardinal sin. This government hates half-measures, I can assure you. You have it all or you lose the whole lot. You are either in, or out in the cold. It has taken me twenty years to get where I am and I like it. If you are ready to work hard, I guarantee you the fulfil-ment of your dreams," he said sombrely.

"I intend to do all I can for the good of the ministry," Bat said, looking the man in the face.

"I am flying you to Jinja to the source of the Nile. It is where I grew up. It is also my headquarters."

Bat opened his mouth to say something, but the General cut him off.

"Flying makes a man a god, I can assure you. It is only from above that you can appreciate the taste of power and the size of the job at hand. As the boss of the Anti-Smuggling Unit, I deal with smugglers. Aided by the CIA, Kenya is destabilizing our country by encouraging those bastards to ferry coffee to her borders. They use my islands as their bases. I am going to crush them all and pin every dung fly on a stick up the ass. Where do you come into the picture? By taking care of business at the min-istry," he said, pointing at Bat with a very long finger. "When everything is running smoothly, I will concentrate on cleaning out my islands. I have given those bastards enough time and warning. From now on it is going to be shoot first, ask questions later. There are undermining our economy. They want to ruin us. Do you know that Rwanda is now listed as a coffee-exporting country? Whose coffee does it export? Our coffee channelled through Kenya. I believe that the time has come to take the war to the Kenyans. I am going to ask the Marshal to authorize me to bomb some of their islands. Take the responsibility for the ministry from me and see what I will do."

"I will do my job to the best of my ability, General."

For the first time that morning Bat felt relaxed and he started to enjoy himself. I have a job, I have a job, I have a job, he said under his breath. My dreams are about to come true. My gamble on returning home is about to pay off big-time. He made quick calculations in his head and realized that his financial worries were over. He felt so excited he wanted to scream out loud. He could hardly wait to get started.

"Most intellectuals are abandoning us, I can assure you," the General began. "I am sure you have met some of them in Britain. I am not intellectual. I don't understand what they think and I don't care. I am interested in results, facts. Do you see the Owen Falls Dam below us? And the famous Nile? Some intellectuals say that this is not the source of this river. That it begins somewhere in Rwanda. What difference does that make? It is splitting hairs, I can assure you. I expect you to keep this dam running, supplying us with electricity at all times. Every time the power fails in my home, I will hold you responsible. I want you to keep the phones working, the mail delivered. I am not interested in details, but in results, progress and commitment. It is a mess in the ministry and nobody knows what to do. I place all those educated and non-educated bastards in your hands. You are free to fire anybody, any time, anywhere. If anybody gives you grief, report him to me and the bastard will lose his neck, I can assure you. My trust never comes cheap. Earn it."

"You can rely on me, General."

Bat did his best to appear calm and collected, but behind his mask of seriousness he was savouring this moment. The river Nile looked so white, so glorious as it pushed its way north through the rocks, bushes and forests. Lake Victoria beckoned in the distance. He experienced a moment of pure contentment. Here in the air, with no troublemakers in view, with the power to hire and fire faceless minions, it felt wonderful. He could wave his wand and all the backlog and the mess at the ministry would froth away. He hadn't been this happy in the last two years. Everything seemed to have been building to this moment, his triumphant entry into the bastions of power.

"If you have any questions, call me. Bureaucrat One, your immediate boss, can answer some questions. But he is just a figurehead. You are the one I will be watching. The tour is over. A mountain of work is awaiting you at the ministry, I can assure you."

THE HELICOPTER DROPPED the General at the headquarters of the Anti-Smuggling Unit and took Bat back to the city. He savoured the luxury and wondered what Damon Villeneuve, his only British friend, was doing. Damon wanted to become a politician and had asked him to stay in Britain. But Bat had known that Britain would make him wait for years if it was going to yield success to him. He wanted to return home where jobs were waiting, where he would be somebody, where his expertise was really needed. He had wished Damon much success. He thought about Mr. and Mrs. Kalanda, the friends who had put him up for the last two weeks. There was another friend, a professor at Makerere University. They were all going to have a big drinking party. Now that he had a job and good prospects for the future, he felt even closer to them.

The Avenger landed behind the Nile Perch Hotel. Bat could see soldiers in the distance keeping guard, patrolling the grounds. His eyes swept over the beautiful greens, the well-tended trees and hedges. He liked this hotel, its four floors, the laid-back greyish colour and its aeroplane windows. Heads of state, ambassadors and foreign dignitaries had slept there. He might also spend a night there some day, for the hell of it. He didn't like the sight of soldiers, but this was a military government. He would have to get used to them. The fact that he had just been with a general made him feel a degree of contempt for these privates and corporals and sergeants whose futures looked bleak, whose lives meant little. The fact that he was not a politician filled him with confidence. I am indispensable, yes I am. Each successive government will need my services. All I have to do is do my job well.

The Boomerang took him back to the Parliament Building. He looked at the magnificent edifice, its murky history hidden behind a friendly ivory exterior. He walked through the yard, his shoes crunching gravel, and headed for the main gate. Governments were sworn in here, under the arch, near the trees where the new statue loomed. The colonizers had stood here on their last day in power. Milton Obote had stood here on his first day in office. Marshal Amin had also stood here on his first day as head of state. Somebody else was bound to stand here for his presidential inauguration. This was Bat's first day as Bureaucrat Two in the Ministry of Power and Communications. He crossed the road to the ministry headquarters, to his new office, his entry witnessed by the glum soldiers on guard, cheered on by the pebbles under his shoes.

GENERAL BAZOOKA had carefully studied Bat's file and had been struck by the fact that although they were born in the same month in 1938, their lives had taken completely different routes. Bat seemed to have cruised through life like a powerful machine oiled by the privileges of his birth. It made the General look back, a rare occurrence, and trace his dramatic rise to power. He kept thinking that in this race the last could indeed come first, and vice versa.

His grandfather had been a traditional warrior turned colonial soldier, in the days when Captain Lugard was fighting wars in the name of the Imperial British East African Company. He had fought numerous battles for the King's African Rifles, and his bones lay somewhere in a valley or atop a hill here in the south. The General's father had followed in his father's footsteps and joined the army. He ground out his life as a sergeant, further promotion blocked by his limited education.

General Bazooka had always been aware of the burden of third-generation offspring. From early on he was determined not just to aim to survive, but to prosper. He wanted to leap-frog his way to the top. The biggest roadblock for him had also been education. He remembered his father's booze-induced outbursts. He remembered how the old man blamed him and his mother for taking all his money. He had not liked being blamed for exhausting the resources spent on his father's irresponsible habits. It made him decide to look after his overworked mother. He could not bear the sight of her standing in green swamp water up to her thighs, her back bent, her left machete arm rising and falling, harvesting papyrus reeds. He could still see her splitting the stems, the knife travelling lengthwise with blinding speed. He was afraid that she would cut off her finger or that the sharp reed edges would split her forearm from palm to elbow. He could still see her sewing the dry shrunken reeds together into mats, cutting off the edges and rolling them into cylinders. He could still see her putting the load on her head, braving the sun or the rain and walking the countryside in search of customers. At each stop she would ease the load to the ground, undo the string and spread out the heap of mats for viewing. Then she would roll them again, tie them and put them on her head, sweat running down her back.

General Bazooka had grown up very conscious of the privilege enjoyed by the southerners, their thin presence in the army and their domination of the civil service. They always seemed to be doing the easy part. They always seemed to have everything he dreamed of: the power, the houses, the cars, the land, the style. They were the majority, the dominant culture which everybody else tried to emulate. The schools were full of their children, the hospitals their brothers and sisters, the clergy their uncles. He dreamed of taking what they had. He had always known that salvation lay in the very place his ancestors had sought it: in the barrel of the gun.

He had always felt wounded when his father accused his mother of sleeping with the southerners she sold mats to. These fights mortified him; his parents seemed to be ignoring the real enemy. The fights were always over money. His father wanted all the earnings from the mats to go to his pocket despite the fact that he hardly bought anything for the house. His mother refused. General Bazooka decided to solve the problem. He started doing odd jobs after school. He washed cars, mowed grass in rich neighbourhoods and off-loaded coffee at nearby ginneries. He stole things from the shops where he occasionally worked. He attacked civilians and drunkards, and he wondered why his father would not use his gun to enrich himself instead of whining. He kept going to school despite his hatred of it. At school the social contrasts irritated him. The children of the mayor of the town were brought to school in a chauffeur-driven Boomerang 500, the car of his dreams. The show of wealth would make him think of the most important event in his life: the coronation of the kabaka (king) of Buganda in 1942, the beginning of his fixation with kings and his dreams of becoming a prince. The coronation had also been his father's fondest memory as a soldier. The old man would reminisce about standing on guard, enjoying the glamour, the pageantry, the music and especially the gun salutes.

With Bazooka's education and fanatic drive, the army could not ignore him. He showed a genius for all things military. He was, above all, fearless and serious. He revelled in the discipline, the hierarchy and the obsession with detail. He adhered to the hard rules of reward and punishment with missionary zeal. He got promoted quickly. His talent for football made him popular. He avoided drinking, smoking and laxity, the unholy trinity which ended careers before they began. He was stationed at Entebbe at the time, not far from the military airport. He and his friends occasionally did window-shopping in town. One wanted a green bicycle, the other fine clothes. They were good men but they lacked ambition. In those days he liked socializing with civilians even though he was hurt by their disregard for his achievements. They did not think much of soldiers in general. They thought of the army as a leper camp, patronized only by the sick, the outcasts.

He told his friends that he would be the first sergeant to own a gold-plated Oris Autocrat wristwatch with a round face and luminous hands. They laughed at him. Autocrats were worn by bank managers, generals, doctors, people in higher leagues. It was at a party that he first saw this watch of his dreams, gleaming on the wrist of a young man of his age. A doctor, lawyer, pilot? He almost had a fit. A month later, on Christmas Day, he stalked his quarry. The Autocrat would be a wonderful Christmas gift. He caught up with the man at one of those parties which sprouted everywhere on religious holidays. People were in a good mood. They had saved all year long in order to enjoy and indulge themselves for this once. The euphoria was contagious. Bazooka stood a distance away, hardly able to resist the temptation to rip the watch off the man's wrist and dash away. The gold had probably been mined in South Africa or Zaïre, exported and then worked by skilful Swiss hands. The man had probably bought the watch in London. Many died mining gold; many died wearing it, he mused grimly. At ten o'clock he made his move. He joined the group at the table and said to the man, "The Autocrat or our lives."

"Over my dead body, you stupid goat-fucker," the man replied angrily, drunkenly.

"Well and good," said Bazooka, removing a stick grenade from his pocket. He unscrewed the cap and held the pin. "Nobody moves. The Autocrat or our lives."

The four other men in the group begged the man to surrender the watch, saying things like, "Our lives are more precious than that piece of junk," "Think about our wives and children," "Don't do this to us." But the man refused.

Bazooka ordered two men to remove the watch by force and hand it over to him. In the ensuing scuffle the grenade went off. Bazooka barely managed to dive out of harm's way. The explosion rocked the place, blowing limbs and clothes off people. Prize in hand, momentarily deaf in one ear, he made a speedy return to base. News of the incident was reported in the morning paper: THREE KILLED IN GRENADE ACCIDENT. His friends called him General Oris.

"I will make general one day," he said grimly. They did not laugh.

He continued to excel. His big break came when he unearthed a plot to kill two British military instructors and three African officers. A friend alerted him. He handed over the names, the details of the plot. Under interrogation the plotters confessed. The ringleaders were shot; Bazooka was promoted.

He distinguished himself in combat, fighting like a devil, planning with genius. The sixties, with their profusion of armed robbers, were a boon. He was put in charge of the Armed Robbery Cracking Unit. The capital city and the entire Central Region came under his command. He led operations against heavily armed car-thieving rings and wiped them out with a minimum loss of men. He tackled kondos, the armed robbers who terrorized households, by luring them into traps and ambushes and destroying them in do-or-die shoot-outs. He usurped police powers, taking the war to the criminals and undermining the credibility of the institution, rendering it helpless.

At the zenith of his power, he was made a full colonel and he met General Idi Amin, Commander of the Ugandan army. It was love at first sight. In Amin he saw a leader under whom he could rise to the very top. Amin, for one, recognized his potential, his future useability. In addition to the rest of his functions he was made head of a mobile brigade that carried out secret operations for Amin. He was sent to secure the South-western Region, where the January 21 coup found him. He took over the big towns of Masaka, Mbarara, Fort Portal and Toro. He locked up uncooperative army commanders, blocked roads with battle tanks and killed troublesome people. The mayor of Masaka, a staunch supporter of a recently fallen leader, was made to smoke his own penis before his body was dragged through the streets of the town.

Bazooka had fond memories of those pre- and post-coup days. It was like a dream, the way one government crumbled and another one ate it up, sprouting, spreading like a devil mushroom to fill the void; the adrenaline, the testosterone, the euphoria, the sheer terror of it all . . .

It took General Bazooka some time before he decided on how to handle Bat. On the one hand, he wanted to sabotage and destroy him; on the other, he wanted to give him a chance to prove or damn himself. He considered bugging his house with the help of Russian friends. But to what effect? Did he expect Bat to go around the house shouting anti-Amin slogans? The most effective way might be to put him at the mercy of Victoria Kayiwa. Two southerners destroying each other would be entertaining to watch. Victoria would do.

BAT'S LIFE CHANGED almost overnight. A week after his interview he moved into a government villa at Entebbe, thirty-two kilometres away from the seat of government in Kampala. The house was built on a hill overlooking Lake Victoria and was serviced by a gardener, a cook and a watchman. It had a red-tile roof, huge windows, heavy oak doors, a long curving driveway, a flower garden and trees all the way down to the lake. To the north was the golf course, the Botanical Gardens, the zoo and the civilian and military airports. To the east, the new State House, a Catholic church and the town centre.

Bat cherished every moment of his new life. The first thing he saw in the morning was the lake in the distance, and a sky with intimations of the day's fine weather written across it. It was a postcard picture of beauty which never failed to captivate him. A number of colonial officials had occupied this house in the forties and fifties, although there was no physical evidence of their having passed through. In the garage he had a green racing Jaguar XJ10, a car which reminded him of London, Cambridge and his postgraduate dreams. He had bought it from a departing expatriate. In the first week, he cleaned it himself, soaping and rubbing it down, dusting the carpets and greasing the nuts and bolts. Villeneuve used to sing the praises of the Bentley, but Bat found it too thick, too big-bottomed to make an elegant driving machine. The Jaguar was smooth, lean and mean—in other words, perfect. There were two other XJ10s in the country, both owned by generals. For that reason, the soldiers at roadblocks never stopped him and some saluted when he passed, which sometimes made him laugh.

At Makerere University, Bat had taken mathematics and economics. He had continued with the same at Cambridge, ultimately majoring in mathematics. He had chosen those dry subjects from the very beginning in order to combat his impulsiveness, an instinct that had compelled him, back in his secondary school days, to write a letter threatening to kill a boy who had refused to give back his transistor radio. Bat's father had lent him the radio, which had been in the family for twenty years. He, in turn, had lent it to the boy who had convinced him that he needed it badly and would bring it back soon. The boy, however, refused to honour his promise. As a result, Bat's father refused to give him pocket money. In an unthinking moment Bat wrote the fateful letter. A few days later a police detective visited his father at his coffee ginnery. Bat and his father reported to the nearest police station. He faced seven years in prison. He was scared shitless. He had had no intention of effecting the threat he outlined in the letter. Luckily, his father knew somebody in the police force and they escaped after paying a large bribe. The radio was returned the same afternoon; everybody was embarrassed, as it looked old and not worth such bother. From then on Bat decided to gain control over his life. He kept few friends and so had little trouble from the outside world.

Now as he sat in his office overlooking the Parliament Building, he marveled at how quickly his life had changed. How apt his choice of mathematics had been! It seemed as if these days every student wanted to study languages and history, probably because they were cheaper and one needed fewer books and none of the very expensive apparatus the sciences could not do without. Yet every employer seemed to be crying out for scientists, engineers, economists and mathematicians, and the ministry was no exception. Here the situation was exacerbated by the large presence of Amin's uneducated stooges. These former butchers, garbagemen and loafers held on to power by surrounding themselves with yes-men and throwing violent temper tantrums. These were men who could hardly multiply ten times ten. You had to write out the numbers in words for some of them to do it. Bat did his best to keep out of such people's way, but now and then they cornered him and asked very dull questions about policy issues, the mechanics of running the ministry, things they would never understand even after a hundred lectures. They came to him for help to open bank accounts in the local Commercial Bank. They relied on their thumbprints in order to make sure that nobody would forge their signatures and swindle their money, or because they were afraid they would forget their own signatures. A few came to ask how to open bank accounts in Switzerland, Libya or Saudi Arabia. He turned them away.

Given the state of affairs, it was a miracle that the government was running at all. The little success there was was a testimony to the resilience of the intellectual element that did work behind the scenes and in secret, men and women continually frustrated by Amin's stooges, who did not give a damn if it all went up in smoke, as long as they were not caught in the crossfire. Operating in the midst of such scum, Bat sometimes felt like a herdsman in charge of perverse pigs, dangerous and bad-tempered animals which shat everywhere and could snap and bite at any moment. His main task was to call for the modernization of the ministry. He wanted to purchase new equipment for the dam, the telephone network, and to train more engineers and specialists. He kept making recommendations and pressing for change. General Bazooka listened carefully, but he often replied that there were no funds. No funds when military hardware kept arriving in the form of new MiG 250 fighter-bombers, Russian TX 3000 battle tanks, AK-57 assault rifles, to mention but a few. While Bat waited for funds, he concentrated on reorganizing the ministry, weeding out unnecessary posts and cutting down on the red tape, which clogged the whole system and made the ministry less effective.

The evolution of a daily routine pleased Bat very much. He woke up early each morning, drove to the city, outraced most cars on the way, and arrived at his office with the high of speed still fizzing in his blood. His day was dominated by dictating letters, attending meetings, and poring over documents. He ate his lunch at his desk, except when he had to attend a luncheon with dignitaries, and drove his team like they were a pack of donkeys. After a twelve-hour day he would drive home to rest. Twice or thrice a week he would go to Wandegeya to meet the Kalandas and the Professor.

Mr. Kalanda worked in the Barclays Bank, his wife in the Uganda Commercial Bank. He was an old university friend with whom Bat used to share a room on campus. They used to do many things together, including double-dating. Between them they had financed three abortions. Now and then, Bat wondered whether Kalanda had told his wife all about their campus escapades. It had been Kalanda who had advised him to try the Ministry of Power and who had read him the rules of survival: "Keep out of politics. Keep democracy and human rights outcries on a tight leash. Keep your passport with you at all times."

Mrs. Kalanda was a fine cook, and she would often prepare something delicious to go with their beer. They would sit outside on the veranda and talk, argue, joke and watch night fall. If there was no shooting, they would stay there for hours, relaxing, enjoying the cool, scented evening air. If rifles started popping, they would hurry inside and Bat would depart when the commotion ended.

Bat received many invitations to weddings. Preparing for and attending weddings had become the number-one pastime in the land, rivalled only by séancing. The ruling class of soldiers, pirates, gangsters and hangers-on showed a huge passion for it.

The fact that many of them were Muslims, allowed to marry four wives, and that they had plenty of money to throw around, meant that there was no shortage of big wedding feasts. Nowadays, a man's worth was measured by the number of guests invited to his wedding, the length of the bridal train, the number of bands which played on the day and the bulls butchered. There were weddings which lasted weeks, as the celebrations moved from the husband's family to the bride's family and back, attracting carousers like flies on rotting fruit. Eating, as a sport, flourished, and no wedding was complete without a group of men vying to put away amazing heaps of offal, roasted lamb and goat, gigantic Nile Perch fish cooked whole and huge platters of cassava, sweet potatoes and matooke. The sight of gluttons masquerading as competitive eaters and ending up drooling, vomiting, and getting their stomachs pumped, became part of the spectacle. Wrestling, for one reason or another, had become an integral part of such occasions, with armies of pseudo-wrestlers moving from wedding to wedding, their oiled bodies on display.

There were many weddings Bat attended because General Bazooka or Bureaucrat One had no time and sent him in their stead. It was at one such gathering that he met Victoria Kayiwa. The reception was in the Nile Perch Hotel gardens. The afternoon was dying away, slowly letting in a cool evening. Bat was nursing his drink while listening to an army officer with bad breath who was going on about CIA infiltration and sabotage, and how all missionaries were secret agents stringing for foreign countries. He had tried to attract her attention on two occasions, but each time she had been talking to a bullish general with medals down to his knees. In fact, he had gotten the impression that she was the wife of a general. For many of these northerners a young southern wife was a status symbol to go with the six-door Boomerang 600 or sporty 300 break horsepower Euphoria. The staunch polygamists often paraded their harems, led by fellow northerner first wives and flanked by the younger southern trophies. Finally, he saw her walking towards him out of the corner of his eye. She was impressive, with a lean, tubular frame that made her cow most women. He could see her breasts swollen under the red cloth of her dress, her thighs carved by the long, flowing garment, her head carried by a long neck. As if on cue, the officer who was lecturing him slipped away, making her arrival all the more pleasing. There was a preliminary exchange of greetings and banter, during which both of them knew that something was going to happen between them.

"Which security organization are you representing tonight?" Bat said lightheartedly.

"Are you accusing me of being a spy, sir?" Victoria said, looking Bat straight in the face, the corners of her mouth forming a smile.

"Otherwise, what would you be doing here amidst this sleaze?" he said, making a sweeping motion with his glass.

"I was invited just like you, sir. This is beginning to sound like a police interrogation," she complained with a face that showed the opposite emotion.

"It is a police interrogation. These days one has to move like a snail, with the antenna up, picking up all the necessary signals for survival," he replied, smiling.

"You are right, sir," Victoria said, draining the last of her drink.

"What are you drinking?"

"Soda, just like everybody else."

Bat signalled a waiter to bring her a drink. His stomach felt heavy with the Pepsi he had been drinking all afternoon to combat the heat and for lack of any alternative. He watched as she picked a glass with care and raised it in a modest toast. To us, to danger, to adventure, he said under his breath, feeling a sweet recklessness rising inside him. He wanted her, this mysterious girl, and he was ready to take the risk. He didn't see much of a future with her, not with somebody floating in these murky circles, but she had to be a terrific fuck, a good way to relieve the pressure of work. After hours of poring over dry material, digesting estimates and mathematical projections, he needed to revel in unreason, and indulge in a bit of impulse. He craved intoxication, real physical satisfaction. What speed could not massage away, a thick crotch might.

"Where do you live?"

"In the city, like everybody else," she replied, looking at him over the rim of her glass. "How about you, sir?" she said, baiting him with yet another sign of respect—after all, he was a big man.

"Entebbe, by the lake, near the State House," he said with boyish airs, unable to resist this opportunity to show off. It actually felt good although it was obviously overkill.

"It sounds very exciting."

"The setting is so aesthetic," he said, enjoying yet another boast and realizing that, because he was unable to boast to the Kalandas, this young woman was a perfect victim.

"Ah, that sounds like the name of a car," she said, looking pleased with her retort.

"Never mind," he said, knowing well that he was talking to a social climber. It suited him perfectly, for the last thing he wanted was to talk about work or academics with somebody who had been to university but had failed to amount to much. She had probably been to secondary school, judging from the way she spoke, which was fine by local standards. "I am thinking of leaving."

"It figures if you live so far away."

"Not necessarily. I drive very fast. It is just that I am tired of this company and the soft drinks."

"I would not blame you, sir."

"Do you need a lift or do you drive your own Boomerang?" he said, smiling and thinking about how white her teeth were. He wished his teeth sparkled like hers.

"A lift would be just fine. I happen to be a woman of modest means."

"You ought to listen more carefully to the radio. They say everything is possible and that everybody can become stinking rich in this country."

She emitted a sudden gut laugh, as if something had got stuck in her throat, and her body quivered. Watching her gave him a strong erotic pang. Her mouth reminded him of Mrs. Kalanda's: eager, suggestive, packed with a big tongue.

Night had fallen very quickly and the motley congregation was disbanding, with the wrestlers getting dressed, the musicians packing up, the eaters groaning somewhere in the grass and the invited guests leaving amidst waving and cheering. As Bat removed the keys from his pocket, Victoria remarked that she had never seen such a beautiful car. Don't lie to me, he thought. What about the other XJ10s owned by the generals? Have they never given you a lift?

Inside the car she said that she wanted to see where he lived. He touched her hair, to send a clear message to her, and he was pleased that she did not make any sound or effort to resist him. To test her he swung the car violently and took off at high speed. He waited for her to ask him to slow down, but she said nothing. You must be used to the reckless driving of the soldiers or whoever gives you lifts, he thought to himself. I am impressed.

CAUGHT IN THE HEADLIGHTS, Bat's house looked like a precious parcel sitting on its wraps. He looked at it again, admiring its spacious garden, the view it commanded and its big windows, very proud that his very first house was not a dim little affair with an iron roof, but this gorgeous edifice. The fact that there was a beautiful woman beside him, awed by his achievements, made the moment very moving.

As they enjoyed a nightcap, sitting on the sofa and looking out on to the garden, and later when they were in bed, Victoria felt something new, as if she was on the threshold of a new beginning. I can feel it in my bones, she said to herself, yes I can. The fact that this rich man has taken the time to please me, instead of just aiming to fuck and ejaculate, roll over and snore, is a good sign. I am surprised by the way I feel because I originally came here to do a job and play a role. I have participated wholeheartedly in the sex, reaching orgasm easily. That is always a sign. My body and mind felt open to him. He could penetrate right through me. For the first time in two years my dream of having a child may be about to be fulfilled.

In the past two years Victoria had slept with many men who had met a bad end, some of whom she had even advised to flee for their lives. Sex had been nothing but an extension of her work, a tool like a gun or a knife. But it felt different now and she wanted it to stay that way. For that to happen she realized that she would have to disobey General Bazooka, who had sent her to track Bat and bring him to a hard fall. As she lay next to Bat, her hatred for the General rose up in her bosom like a wave crashing on the shore. She wanted to get back at him for derailing her life and turning her into a monster. She wanted to turn her life around and leave behind the madness of the State Research Bureau. All I need is a good plan and a way to Bat's heart, she said to herself.

Victoria was awake to see the day breaking for the first time in many months. She saw the lake and the trees and felt a sense of beauty and a wish to prolong the experience. The lake evoked tender feelings in her and gave her the urge to burst into song. She wanted to share her feelings with Bat but checked herself; it was too early in the game to rhapsodize about the lake or any-thing else. She watched him going to the bathroom, towel round his waist, his slippers slapping muffledly, and wondered what he was thinking. Does he know who I am? He reminds me of many men who walk unwittingly to their death, to torture, to imprisonment. Instead of the cold detachment I usually feel after completing a job, I feel unhinged, doubtful.

On the way to the city they talked sporadically. He let her know that he had enjoyed himself.

"It can be lonely in such a big house," she observed, looking out the window at the roadside scenery of market stalls, houses, cyclists and pedestrians going to work.

"I don't mind," he said almost absentmindedly.

"Most of your colleagues are married," she heard herself remark.

"It is a job they do better than me. I don't have the time to put in the extra hours in addition to my work."

"Maybe you have not yet met the right woman," she suggested, wondering if she was pushing things too fast. He said nothing, and she felt a sharp stab of pain in her breast. Was this outright rejection? She had the giddy feeling of being cast back into the sleaze she was trying to escape. She waited for him to say something about the weather, the road, work, or the statues of Amin, in vain. He kept chasing cars, overtaking them and grinning. In the city, he dropped her off at the Ministry of Works headquarters, and as she watched the car disappear, she was gripped by panic. What had felt like the beginning of redemption the night before had now turned into despair. The blades of violence flashed and beckoned maliciously. She felt herself sinking back into the decay she had just emerged from. How am I going to get hold of him again? How long would this have to go on?

Victoria came from a well-to-do family of textile importers. Her mother and father used to work together. They had been good parents, ever generous and attentive to her needs. Sunday used to be the highlight of the week. Everybody in the family would dress smartly and head for church, where her parents had special seats at the front, since they were pillars in the local Protestant community. Her father's family was well read: there was a doctor and a judge. Her aunts had married powerful men. At school she had suffered from a lack of motivation; it seemed as if there was little to struggle for. Her looks proved to be another distraction, as she believed that she was better than everybody else. She found it hard to apply herself to the duty at hand when her looks fetched her so much attention. Discipline became a problem and it was easy to cheat. Her father urged her to work harder, and she lived with the fear that he would find out that she cheated. In between, she dreamed of wealth, a house in the hills, and holidays abroad.

Then an incident to do with her parents' business turned her life upside down. Customs officials found a box of rifles in a container of imported fabric. Her parents knew nothing about the guns. Her father was arrested, interrogated, and imprisoned. Expensive lawyers failed to secure his release and the business suffered. Letters of credit were withdrawn. Her mother was threatened and she finally closed the business, with the belief that they would reopen as soon as her husband was freed, since he knew no failure. He never got out and the family had to move. Victoria was devastated. She fell into the company of bold but aimless girls, who went out with older men who drove Boomerangs and Euphorias, and had money to spare and appetites to satisfy. One such man took her virginity. She enjoyed the money but hated the wrinkles and the paunches and her self-hatred grew.

In the midst of her pain and confusion, she met Colonel Bazooka. She waved down his Boomerang one day and was surprised to see a soldier in a crisp, medal-festooned uniform. She was struck by the lean, disciplined, affluent air he had, and she could see that he was different from other men she knew. He was a northerner to begin with, a creature of people's fears and prejudices.

He liked her youth, her looks, her boldness and her spoiled manner. She was a southern dream. He was used to picking these girls up, but there was something about this one, a connection they made somewhere in the gut or the brain. Under her brittle shield of boldness was aimlessness, a yearning to be led and moulded. The defencelessness, the emptiness, and the loss showed behind the eyes. The head of the Armed Robbery Cracking Unit never failed to read the signs. He had a highly developed sixth sense, which was the very reason why he was still alive. The affair went on for months, and the more he feigned disinterest, the more she surrendered to him. Her mother finally found out about them. Ground to a pulp by worry, she handled it in the way she knew best. She issued an ultimatum. Drop the soldier or cease to be part of the family, she said.

"How could you do this to us? How could you do that to your

father? A soldier! A northerner! Have you no sense of who you are?"

Victoria replied that there was no longer any family since her father's disappearance. She further made the naïve mistake of betraying her mother to her lover, and the head of the Armed Robbery Cracking Unit exploded with anger.

"Who does she think she is? Doesn't she know who the boss is in this city?"

"Don't take any notice of her, please," she begged, down on her knees.

"Your people are living too far back in the past. We, the military, are the new royalty, the kings and princes. We do what we want. Your people should get that into their thick heads. The very same people who sold out to the British and let their king and their chiefs lead them to oblivion, but still have the nerve to feel superior! I will teach them a lesson."

"Please don't do anything to her, I beg you."

"Are you telling me what to do? You! Are you like the rest of your family?"

"No, I am not. I just don't want anything to happen to them," she said with tears streaming down her face.

"Get out of my sight before I cuff you," he roared, his eyes popping out of his head.

Something did eventually happen to Victoria's family. They were attacked by men in civilian clothes driving an unmarked Euphoria. They were beaten, stripped of every penny, made to beg for their lives and warned to leave the city as soon as possible. They disappeared in the maze of villages in the countryside and never returned.

Colonel Bazooka took Victoria and there she was, confused as children of privilege are when deserted by fortune, defenceless in a hostile world without a road map or course of action. He found it thrilling to roll brats like her in the gutters that they believed destiny had spared them from and set apart for the others. He had done it time and again and it still felt good. At this juncture he revealed that he was happily married to a tribes-woman with whom he had three beautiful children. She was deeply hurt as, no matter what she did, a good Protestant girl eventually got married to a man in a monogamous relationship, as concubinage was both sinful and sacrilegious. Her confusion and guilt came out in the urge to compete, to be what he wanted her to be, in the hope that she would supplant the first wife, whom she imagined to be old and worn out. What she did not know was that there was no competition. Wife Number One was unassailable. Queen to all latecomers, she got first priority in everything.

For a time they lived in a senior army quarter. On weekends they would go out to drink, as he enjoyed showing her off. During the week she kept house, which she did badly due to lack of experience. The food got burned and she cut her fingers and she did not know how long to cook the meat or how to wash clothes properly. He realized that violence would not achieve anything and he hired help.

He had a plan worked out for her. If she conceived, he would keep her as a second wife to bear him children with some southern blood in them. If she remained barren, he would enroll her in the State Research Bureau and use her as a decoy. He would only have to anger her to unleash the beast inside. A beautiful decoy would do wonders trapping rampant southern subversives.

To start with, he began to reveal to her what he did. He told her about army operations to curb robbery. He told her the number of people he had killed, how interrogation and extraction of information proceeded. He frightened the hell out of her because till then she had a black-and-white picture of good and evil wherein she believed deep down that bad people were totally bad and good people totally good.

After a year without her conceiving, his patience ran out. He had risen higher and was now in charge of the South-western Region, and his sense of power had reached mammoth proportions. He took her to different towns, and she saw how both civilians and soldiers respected and feared him. There was something mesmerizing about his demeanour. He was like a god, an apparition, a natural phenomenon. He enjoyed the adulation, and in his good moments he said that she had brought him good luck. In his bad moments, however, he accused her of being barren. He asked her if she was doing it intentionally so as not to have a child with a northerner.

"I need a child before I die. I have many enemies. I want to make sure that when the moment comes, I have a successor. There are big plans ahead with very bad odds. I don't want them to proceed before you are pregnant."

The gynaecologist found nothing wrong with her. The Colonel started having violent outbursts, wearing her down to a frazzle. He made her confess to earlier affairs and said that her earlier looseness made her barren. He started using military tactics to intimidate and control her. He would ask for tea and then smash the cup against the wall saying it had been dirty. He tinkered with guns, putting the barrel in his mouth and firing empty chambers. She would plead and cry and beg, but he would ignore her and continue firing away. When she was almost out of her mind, he would open the clip and drop the only bullet on the floor. Sometimes he asked her to pull the trigger when the gun was in his mouth.

"Do you mean to say that you have never thought of killing me?" he would roar. He would go on till he had forced a confession out of her and then say, "If you kill me, my soldiers will burn the whole town to the ground."

He would take a rifle and start shooting in the back garden till the whole place smelled of gunpowder and was filled with smoke. He would enter the house and spit on the barrel to show how hot it had become. He pressured her till she reached snapping point, ready to do anything to improve the situation. Then he announced his plans to her, saying: "I saw the killer instinct in you the first time I saw you. You are going to make a perfect decoy. You are going to rise to the top of the Bureau. Everybody is going to bow down to you. The Bureau needs beauties like you. It is too full of ugly men and unsightly women. Hold your position and they will eat your shit. If you show them fear, they will make you eat theirs, and you don't want that to happen. Every time you feel afraid, think about your father. Avenge him." Afterwards his mood would change and he would cuddle and tickle her. Through her tears she would start laughing, grateful that the danger had passed.

After the coup of 1971 he took her to a training camp where she stayed for months and they tried to break her down and reprogramme her. They began by shaving off her hair, burning her clothes on a bonfire and giving her military fatigues. Her name was replaced by a number. They verbally abused her, the word "turd" being one of the softer varieties of insult they hurled at her. They exhausted her body and mind with tough military drills till she felt like fainting. Food was deplorable, accommodation even worse. Trainees were made to sleep in holes for days, to camp in bushes. They chanted Amin's praise songs like mantras for hours on end, and they were made to pledge undying love and loyalty to him. At the end of the course they took the oath of obedience and allegiance at a graduation parade attended by army officers and the State Research Bureau's bigwigs, and were let loose on the world.

If Victoria thought she would get off lightly, she was wrong. Her first assignment was to frame a woman doctor, accusing her of supplying drugs to dissidents. She knew that it was a test to see if she could do in a fellow southerner. By taking the oath she had already crossed the line, and all she had to do now was to bury her conscience, that feeble agitator, under an avalanche of rage. One evening they attacked the woman who was going to die "while attempting to escape." She and her two children were made to lie on the floor. She was then dragged to the bedroom, made to cough up every cent and valuable item, and was shot. For Victoria there was a burst of fear, then euphoria. There was a flashback to her days of victimhood and a feeling of freedom and of being above both divine and human law. The sweetness of unreason drowned out any feelings of guilt. The woman's body stopped twitching and groaning; silence descended like a curtain; the gun smoke drifted; the drug wore off slowly. The partial deafness Victoria felt was a salient reminder that something had happened. Now and then the blast of the guns seemed to be banging in her head like trapped thunderclaps.

The Colonel, shortly afterwards promoted to major-general, was delighted and took her back to the city. He found her a job with the Ministry of Works. As lovers, they were finished, although he still kept an eye on her. Victoria endured periods of personal hell: diarrhoea, black-outs, searing pains, flashbacks. She tried to erase it all with alcohol, in vain. She realized that the General had used her and then cut her loose. She wanted somebody to talk to but could not trust anyone. She thought about running away, but where could she hide? The General's spies were everywhere and if caught she would most certainly be killed.

As the situation deteriorated, she pined for somebody to love. Her failure to save her father still dogged her. She wanted a man to reassure her that she was still human. She was tired of not being able to hold on to anything of value. She wanted a child although she doubted whether it would happen. Certainly not with the intellectuals, traders and bureaucrats she was sent to lure to death or destruction. The more she thought about it all, the more she believed that Bat was her godsent deliverer.

BY RISING to the heights many had expected him to attain, Bat had become a force in his family. He attracted visits from relatives who travelled to the city in search of jobs, loans, recommendations and connections. He did all he could to deal with this new popularity. He thought about investing money and using the profits to help such people and about involving his brother and sister in the scheme. But when he approached them, he met with disappointment. His sister was too busy with her nursing job to take on any other responsibility, and his brother had no interest in a regular job. He earned his living by exploding fireworks at wedding feasts and, when he felt like it, he repaired cars and nursed dreams of participating in the East African Safari Rally. Bat tried to talk to him but failed to change his mind. He felt angry with and afraid for his young brother. He finally scrapped the project, having reached the conclusion that business did not run in the family.

Not long after, he received the news that his sister had found a suitor. It struck him that she had grown up and was no longer a girl to be protected and told what to do. The news seemed to ambush him, and when she came to inform him in person, he found it hard to be genuinely cheerful. The fact that the suitor was a former clerk turned town planner left him reeling.

"Town planner?" he said, shaking his head a few times and almost whistling with sadness. "In this day and age! Most towns are just shrinking and dying. The few that are expanding are doing so without plan, spontaneously like a colony of mushrooms. What is he left to do?"

His sister, whom everybody in the family, including Bat's parents, called Sister because from the age of five she said she would become a nursing sister in the biggest hospital in the country, calmly, almost emphatically, said, "It is his occupation."

Bat had always assumed that she would marry among his former schoolmates, university graduates turned lawyers, doctors, heads of parastatal or private companies. There was also the Professor with his sickly wife. Maybe he would divorce and marry Sister. Bat felt that Sister owed it to herself to get a man who would look after her capably. She seemed to have thought about it too, and perversely settled for this town planner, a time-waster in Bat's book. It is his occupation, Bat thought unhappily. Accepted, full stop. No room for argument or compromise. Take it or leave it, Big Brother. He had already lost her to this mediocre man. He suddenly felt very distant from Sister, all past warmth and affection eaten by a blaze of anger, the goodwill turned rancid.

"Where do you plan to live?" he asked for lack of something better to say in these matters of the heart, of feeling, and of little logic.

"We plan to move to the country after the wedding. The need for nurses is acute in rural areas."

Where no sane person wants to go, Bat wanted to say, where you shouldn't waste your talent and energy, where career chances are dim. How about living in one of the towns the bastard planned to build out of ether? I always had the perception that you were dynamic, visionary, calculating, but the evidence here is different, demoralizing. I see resignation with the missionary spirit thrown in to sweeten it up. Are you so deep under the influence of that old narcotic, love? Has it juggernauted and crushed your judgement out of shape?

At Cambridge, I wrote you a few letters telling how tough my financial situation was, how rich some students were, how I had to wash dishes to make ends meet. I had not written out of self-pity but as a warning about the dangers of poverty. Now it is evident that you took nothing to heart and don't see marriage as an investment. You obviously have other values. You probably despise me for working with scum as I do in order to break the yoke of poverty.

"What have dad and ma said about this?" he said to break the train of thoughts.

"They are overjoyed. Father can't wait to hold his first grand-child."

"I am happy for you," Bat said, trying to put on a cheerful face.

"I am happy to hear it. When your turn comes, I will be happy for you," Sister said, beaming, joy suffusing her face.

You should be so lucky, he thought. After making my money I will just get the hell out of this country.

They talked about family, their young brother Tayari, the wedding plans, and finally Bat offered to take her out to eat. He drove her round in his XJ10 looking for a decent restaurant. His gloom lifted, and he realized that he could not control his sister's life, that he had never intended to. His affection for her slowly returned and he wished her well.

SISTER'S HOPE THAT the two most important men in her life would get on well, and produce a close-knit unit, did not materialize. The meeting between Bat and Mafuta Mingi was an uphill battle. At the end of the day, Bat failed to hide his feelings about his future in-law. He was a big overweight man with a paunch. In one so young, the paunch seemed to indicate a sedentary indolent life of overindulgence. Mafuta Mingi arrived dressed in a bad suit and was obviously uncomfortable with himself. Bat's villa, the staff, the sumptuous surroundings and especially the lake view reminded him of his first wife. He had a knack for getting women from well-to-do families. He always seemed to overreach himself, with the result that he had never been fully accepted by his in-laws.

He found Bat distant, almost cold, with the demeanour of somebody who is being cheated out of something very valuable. This was not at all the kind of reception he had envisioned, considering his father-in-law's demonstrated enthusiasm and his future wife's warm personality. Why was this man so unreachable? Mafuta now preferred the other in-law, the mad pyrotechnician. His impression was that the fellow had a death wish or some other difficult relationship with life. Tayari hardly bothered with words, but he had offered to make a fireworks display for the wedding. Mafuta would have preferred to ignore Bat, but given his position in the family, it seemed impossible.

Sweating under his armpits, Mafuta started going on about his work, how he had manoeuvred his way into town planning. He talked about the bureaucratic maze in the planning department, which had turned into a cesspool now that no more towns were planned and everything seemed out of control. He talked about how plans kept getting lost, how the Health Inspector offered dispensations against the advice of planning experts,

how applications kept going round and round till officials got
their bribes. Bat eyed him keenly, as if gauging whether he was
sane enough to be entrusted with his sister's life and welfare, and
when the monologue ended, he made no comment. Mafuta was
a brave man; he swallowed his discomfort and talked about wedding plans. Sister watched the two men and felt hurt, and pow-
erless to change the situation.

At the end of the visit Bat offered to drive the guests to town.
Mafuta was determined not to hate him and decided to accept
him as he was, although he knew they would never be friends.
In a way, he admired Bat's sense of independence. It made him
want to fight back, and the best way was to enter the business
world and crank up a few deals quickly. After all, this was the
get-rich-quick era. Winners in this new rags-to-riches world
passed them on the way, cruising in their Boomerangs and
Euphorias, flying Avenger helicopters. It struck Mafuta that he
was Bat's age. He did not want to lag behind. His in-law's success
reflected badly on him, as if he had wasted his life, as if he had no
imagination. He really wanted to be part of the action.

Mafuta was suddenly afraid of a repeat failure. He had begun
his forays into the marriage business by bagging a princess, a
woman faintly related to the kings of Buganda. The princess had
been bred with the view that everyone had to worship her as a
matter of course. At first, Mafuta had found it romantic to indulge his wife. He brought her breakfast in bed; he made sure
that everything was ready for her when she woke up. He found it
manly to put up with her raspy tongue, and swallow chidings
about his being a commoner, unfit to marry a princess. He liked
to hear his wife bemoan her fall from grace, the collapse of royalty. He liked to hear stories about life at the minor court where
she grew up. The king used to visit thrice a year and stay for a
month. The attention would shift to him; the place would crawl
with chiefs, nobles, soldiers, musicians, eunuchs, peasants. Every
courtier would bask in reflected glory and forget the feuds and
the schemes till the king left.

Mafuta felt proud to have a piece of the royal family under his roof. He eagerly sank into debt in order to maintain the lifestyle the princess wanted. He sold his share of his father's land, against everybody's advice. He enjoyed the drama, the status. He liked the fact that she always spoke in plural—"Mafuta bring us our handkerchief," "Mafuta, we have a headache"—because he felt included in each and every sentence she uttered. He seemed to hire new cooks and housegirls every week, because she kept firing them as soon as they arrived. Nobody was good enough, clean enough, efficient enough.

It amused him that the princess was so rude because hubris ran in the royal family. Up until the turn of the century, the king used to own everything in his kingdom. If you so much as looked at him aslant, your eyes could get pulled out right there by the bodyguards. At His Majesty's whim, your limbs could get hacked off. Big chief or commoner could be stripped to the last penny. Princes could also get away with just about everything, except planning coups or trying to rape the royal harem. The exploits of princesses were no less colourful, albeit less well documented. Over the years, the powers of the royals had been neutralized by the British, local politics and the army, but in the eyes of stalwart monarchists, the royals could still do no wrong. Mafuta saw himself as an extension of this incredible group of loyalists for the king.

It had only occurred to him much later that one never went to bed with history or the royal family, but with an individual, and this individual's very healthy sex drive had to be serviced dutifully. Sex, like food, was not asked for but demanded, and princesses never got ridden or fucked; they fucked and rode the shit out of you. Mafuta lay on his fat back every night and was ridden like a donkey to kingdom come, whether Her Highness was bleeding or not. Half-hearted erections would never do. The royal orifice entertained only sufficiently stiff dicks. He resorted to taking aphrodisiacs, very bitter stuff extracted from the bark of certain trees. He was gripped by performance angst and often lost healthy erections. He would lie there and wonder when he would stop being an extension of the peasantry and become a man. The constant rape of the self in service of aristocracy began to take its toll. The relationship seemed to have been going on for so long that he knew he would miss his princess if it ended.

Then one day he met Sister at a bus stop. She had two large cardboard boxes full of supplies she was taking to the village. She looked like somebody not used to the city and in need of help. He asked her the time, where she was going, the school she attended, why she had chosen nursing. When the bus came, he lifted her boxes and in the process popped two shirt buttons. He pointed at his hairy belly, drummed on it and they both laughed. She felt at ease with him and liked his deep voice, his sense of humour, his friendliness. They agreed to keep in touch. She provided him with something to do at work. Instead of planning gargantuan fantasy towns powered by solar energy, he wrote her letters professing undying love. He talked about his marriage, the mistakes he had made in life, his willingness to change and spend the rest of his life with her, the mountains they could move together. They started meeting regularly, going to films, dances and the Botanical Gardens. The proof that Mafuta had fallen in love was that he shamelessly told her everything the princess made him do. It poured out of him as never before, and he gobbled her sympathy avidly. Where other men would have lied to look good and tough, he just gushed like an overfull bladder. Everything—including the soiled sanitary napkins she left all over the place. He mimicked her, "Royal blood, commoner. Preserve it for posterity, Mafuta." They would both collapse with laughter. Sister hoped that he would remain this open, this predictable, after marriage, and she felt proud that she had supplanted a princess.

Sister now reminded Mafuta of those days to cheer him up after Bat had dropped them off.

"What do I need a princess for when I have you right here?" he said proudly, patting her back.

BAT SAW VICTORIA on and off; she somehow seemed to be there when he needed her. Her relationship with the General was dead, the only bond remaining being a lukewarm threat of violence if she strayed too far, for he had verbally released her. She started spending three days a week at Entebbe, reluctantly reporting to the office. She harboured dreams of spending the rest of her life with Bat. The fact that their relationship seemed to have developed by itself, without much effort on her part, made her feel that it was preordained. After all, she hadn't written Bat any letters or sent him gifts or done any of the crazy things women do to trap men. She just appeared at the right time, and he seemed to have taken her the way one took a gift, without prying too much. She had accompanied him to a few official functions, and waited for rebukes from the General, which never came.

The meeting with the Kalandas had been less successful. They were too educated, speaking in what sounded like tongues to her. They discussed economics, high finance and banking and lost her. Mrs. Kalanda had not helped matters either. Never, for once, did she revert to women's affairs. She kept up with the men till Victoria felt disgusted, stranded. She regretted the premature end to her education. She suddenly felt afraid that Bat might drop her because of her lack of education. Midway through the meeting, she tried to cut off the field by asking Mrs. Kalanda about politics. It was a no-go area for obvious reasons; nobody crossed it with strangers. Mrs. Kalanda rudely shut her up by saying that politics was the domain of spies and did not interest her at all. Victoria felt as if her cover had been blown. She apologized and asked for a glass of water to calm her nerves.

Later that evening Mrs. Kalanda told her husband that she did not trust Victoria. She even suggested that Bat should let somebody check out her background.

"The number of women in the State Research Bureau is staggering. Housewives, teachers, nurses, bankers, you name it," she said, shaking her head sadly.

"Are you calling her a spy?" Kalanda asked amusedly.

"She is a woman without history. She is like a butterfly; nobody knows where she came from. She appeared out of the blue at a party. What would stop her from flying away without a trace?"

"Do you mean to say that she is a gold-digger?" Kalanda said, remembering his campus days. Even then Bat knew how to choose good-looking women; Victoria was no exception. The way she rolled those big eyes!

"Maybe worse," Mrs. Kalanda replied worriedly.

"How does one tell Bat something like that?" Kalanda mused, his mind still preoccupied with Victoria's body. He liked women with a wild streak; he had not had any in a very long time. He wished he could have one, to while away the boredom that comes with married life and guaranteed pussy. He hoped Bat was having a wonderful time.

"You have known him since God knows when. If he won't listen to you, he will listen to nobody."

"He is not defenceless. I am sure he is minding his step."

"You are too complacent," Mrs. Kalanda said loudly.

"The woman is in love as far as I can see," Kalanda remarked languidly, as if thinking back to the heady days of fresh love; "you only had to see the way she kept sneaking looks at Bat."

"Maybe she went to acting school," Mrs. Kalanda said, raising her voice once again.

"Take it from me, my dear. Bat is all she is thinking about."

Kalanda never got around to asking Bat directly to check out Victoria's background; Bat knew very well the kind of people he worked and dealt with. To put his mind at ease, he asked whether Bat would tell Victoria about, say, a secret deal or fortune.

"Are you out of your mind?" Bat said, laughing. "What one hand does the other must never know."

VICTORIA GOT VERY INVOLVED with Sister's wedding. She attended many of the endless meetings which preceded weddings. For her it was never boring; she was connecting with the living, people preoccupied with everyday things, not abductions or other grisly affairs. It helped her combat her paranoia, since these people tried to be as oblivious to government goings-on as possible. She envied them their clean record and the fact that they had no nightmares rooted in harming other people. She prayed for pregnancy, for marriage, for life. If General Bazooka is happily married, and has been for years, and most people in the Bureau have families, why aren't things working out for me? She prepared for the wedding as if she were the bride. She bought a very beautiful gown and looked more desirable than she had ever been. On the big day, the church reminded her of her childhood before the catastrophe. She could hardly take her eyes off the bride and her groom. She kept thinking, Next time I will be the centre of attention.

Months into her assigned official task, she reported to the General that she was not getting any viable information from Bat. He asked her to keep at it. She had now become used to Bat's ways. After a very long day, he did not want to talk about work. When prodded, he would ask her to talk about something else, or throw a temper tantrum, leaving her on the defensive, begging to be forgiven. His finances were another restricted area. If she wanted money, he provided it without question. She had no way of making him talk if he was not communicative. She sometimes followed him to the lake, hoping that the waves and the wind would make him open up. He would sit on a rock, feet in the water, and let the waves do the talking. She was left with two choices: either to fabricate information or to let the General fuck himself.

GENERAL BAZOOKA GRUDGINGLY ADMITTED that Bat Katanga was the best employee he had ever had. It hurt to see how excellent his future prospects were. It was hard to tell how he had cleaned up the mess in the ministry. Whenever information was required, Bat or his team had it close at hand; whenever something needed to be done, they knew who would do it best and how long it would take him. His spies at the hydro-electric dam, which supplied the whole country with electricity, told him how well things were running. Much as he appreciated this level of efficiency, he felt it reflected badly on his position as overall boss of the ministry; it made him feel vulnerable, needful of this man and his talents as never before. How he would have loved it if a tribesman, a man he could trust 100 percent, had been the agent of this change! All this hurt very much because Bat was still uninitiated and had not pledged personal allegiance to me, his boss, his minister. He always talked about serving the government or the people, as if they, the leaders, his masters, weren't people, as if Bat were an elected official, not somebody chosen by him. He was still the Cambridge graduate full of British airs, driving a British car, oozing sophistication. He had yet to inhale the stench of decay, which every true follower had to imbibe before being trusted, accepted. Apart from his academic aptitude, what had he ever done to deserve his fortune? News had already spread among ministers that he was an organizational wizard, and a few generals had talked about poaching him, moving him to their ministries for at least a year each. They even talked about tossing a coin or rolling the dice to find out who would get him first. The dice! He swore he would never allow that. He was sure some of those generals had consulted astrologers, possibly the Unholy Spirit himself, and had been promised success. But he would never let them take Bat away from him. If it came to that, they would all lose him. He knew that many generals were jealous because only recently Marshal

Amin had singled out the Ministry of Power as deserving of special praise for showing improvement.

General Bazooka had other worries too. He was consumed with the task of retaining Marshal Amin's favour and trying to rise in the hierarchy of power. Before and after the coup, it had been very easy to divine what the Marshal thought and wanted. But over the years, with mounting international pressure and local discontent, the Marshal had become more fickle, paranoid, unpredictable. He had increased the power of the Eunuchs, the presidential bodyguard that surrounded him at all times, and it was now much harder to make an appointment to see him, or to get him on the hotline. I shouldn't be one of those made to wait, the General said to himself aloud, pacing up and down his office.

Over the years, the army of presidential astrologers, witch-doctors and soothsayers had increased fourfold. Some generals blamed these people, especially their leader, Dr. Ali—alias God, Jesus, the Unholy Spirit, the Government Spokesman—for the Marshal's unpredictability, but General Bazooka knew better. The uncertainty in the air created fertile ground for astrology and all kinds of witchcraft to flourish. He didn't hate Dr. Ali, with his enormous power, his Learjet, his Armani suits, his closeness to the Marshal. He just envied him, knowing how frantic the Marshal became when the runt stayed away longer than expected. In his book, Dr. Ali was the third-most-powerful man in the land, despite the fact that he was a foreigner, outside of the government and the armed forces, and he visited the country only ten times a year.

The General found it hard to discredit the man; he was the only astrologer who had predicted things which came true. He was the only person who could walk into the Marshal's office any time of day or night without an appointment. He was the only person in the country whose life was guaranteed because nobody, least of all the Marshal, dared kill such a powerful astrologer. What made matters worse was the fact that the man was incorruptible. He had all the money in the world, for he worked not only for Marshal Amin but also for President

Mobutu of Zaïre, Emperor Bokassa of the Central African Republic and General Bohari of Nigeria. In all the past years, General Bazooka had had one séance with him, paying a cool ten thousand dollars, and only recently he had heard that the Marshal had forbidden the astrologer from seeing generals or anybody else in the government.

This was a sign that the Marshal had become more fearful and distrustful of everybody. He could understand what the Marshal was going through. Both phantom and real coup plots were on the increase. It was hardly possible to tell which was which. Backbiting among the generals had also become worse. Factions of all kinds mushroomed almost daily, each demanding attention and ascendancy. The rivalry between the army and the security agencies, especially the State Research Bureau and the Public Safety Unit and the Eunuchs, did not make things easier. Amidst this volatile mix were the so-called presidential advisors. It was wisest to trust nobody. If it had been in the General's power, he would have deposed and shot all faction leaders, merged the security agencies and restored order. He even advised the Marshal to do so, but he had refused. The confusion mounted.

In spite of all this, General Bazooka knew that the real powder-keg in the house was Western Europe, namely Gross Britain and the USA. These two countries had slashed aid to Uganda. They kept sending spies or phantom spies, one hardly knew any more. They destabilized the economy by encouraging coffee-smuggling through Kenya. They encouraged Kenya to embargo Uganda's goods at the seaport of Mombasa. They campaigned against Uganda abroad, laying phantom crimes at the Marshal's address.

The Marshal had become increasingly aware of the vacuum in his support system, namely failure to formulate a suitable policy in relation to these states, and he blamed the generals for it. General Bazooka found the accusations unjust, even though he sympathized with his leader. At cabinet and Defence Council meetings, the Marshal had developed the habit of throwing obnoxious temper tantrums, banging tables, firing guns, cursing and accusing everybody of sloth and redundancy. These blanket accusations hurt and worsened the divisions. General Bazooka was aware that the Marshal's behaviour was a preamble to some action he could not divine. Was the Marshal about to hire some Libyan and Saudi advisors? Weren't there enough of these already? There was mounting panic among the generals. The last thing anybody wanted was another influential foreigner in the mix.

General Bazooka's guess was that the Marshal was going to promote an insignificant but highly educated southerner to a very important position. He believed that the Marshal was stalling because he was embarrassed by his decision. It had happened before. Some generals claimed that it was not a southerner, but a black American. He still remembered Roy Innis and his promises to send black American experts in medicine, education, business management and technology who never turned up. General Bazooka did not know whether to succumb to the generals' sense of relief, stemming from the fact that a black American civilian would not be hard to manipulate or frustrate. He would get a palatial home on a big hill, a fleet of Boomerangs, bodyguards, the royal treatment. His bodyguards would not be hard to bribe for information. And if he became too troublesome, he could always be disappeared or thrust into a car wreck. I hope that the generals are right, General Bazooka said to himself, although the scenario does not solve my problem of wanting to get closer to the Marshal.

THE ARRIVAL of the British delegation which would change things for good was a mediocre affair, almost as unremarkable as the recent departure of Dr. Ali's Learjet. General Bazooka would have missed it had he not been the Minister of Power and Communications. He attended the reception because these idiots, or snakes, as the Marshal called them, claimed that they could sell the government top-quality communications equipment without having to go through the maze of international protocol. General Bazooka did not like the idea very much because Copper Motors did the job well when it came to importing British goods, legally or illegally. Why introduce another group from the same country? And if it was a question of the new snakes undercutting the old crew, why not simply press Coppers to lower prices? If the arrivals had been Germans or Canadians, it would have made sense: diversification. The General sensed personal vendetta. Somebody at Coppers had probably displeased the Marshal.

The delegation confirmed his worst fears: it looked anything but impressive. Men going to cut million-dollar deals should dress with style. Ooze a bit of class. Not this crew. They turned up in badly creased suits and tired suede shoes. He noted that the eldest, a man in his fifties, with a large balding head and bushy eyebrows, had not even bothered to wear a tie. How the Marshal had agreed to meet people in this state of disrepair defeated him. It infuriated him that this old snake talked to the Marshal as if they were best friends. He kept sticking his large hands in his pockets, brushing back wisps of invisible hair on top of his head and rocking with laughter. At one time it looked like he was going to pat the Marshal on the arm or stick his finger in his belly.

A friendly presidential aide had informed General Bazooka that the unkempt crew had arrived two days before and had stayed at the presidential lodge in Nakasero. He smelled a rat. The Marshal wasn't somebody who took to people easily, except in some unique cases. General Bazooka started suspecting that maybe the Unholy Spirit had something to do with this crew; maybe he had consulted omens and advised the Marshal to receive them. By the look of things, it might have been love at first sight. He remembered how he himself had impressed the Marshal so strongly back in the sixties. He had heard that the Unholy Spirit had made the same impact. This white snake might also have scored in the same fashion. He suddenly felt an

attack of fear and a massive jolt of jealousy. He hoped that nothing would come of the delegation.

The reception turned out to be as disorganized as the hairs on
the old man's head. He never got the chance to talk to the group
properly; neither did he wish to. He would leave the details to
Bat, if it came to that. To kill time he nursed a drink, talked to a
colleague or two and was relieved when the Marshal asked for
silence and made a clumsy speech. The only noteworthy point
was the invitation to a cocktail party in two days' time, which he
extended to everybody. It was to take place at Paradise Villas, a
presidential resort somewhere on the shores of Lake Victoria.
He knew that there was momentous news in the offing because
Marshal Amin used the place exclusively for special occasions.
Later he heard that ambassadors and other dignitaries had also
been invited. The next day a spy in the Ministry of Foreign
Affairs informed him that the delegation had left for home.

On the big day, around one hundred dignitaries attended the
function. The West Africans stood out in their colourful, stylish
garb, which resembled very voluminous cassocks or billowing
nighties. The rest wore tuxedos, safari suits and gowns. There
was a profound air of prosperity; every hair seemed to be in its
proper place; every shoe polished to a high shine. Heavy watches
glinted on hairy wrists, women's jewellery flashed and winked
ad lib. An undercurrent of expensive perfume wafted in the air,
accompanied by classy modulated laughter. General Bazooka
was proud to be among these people, feeling like a child at a big
wedding feast full of music and goodies. Such moments made
the bothers of staying in power worthwhile. He looked at his
gold-plated Oris Autocrat and smiled with satisfaction as it
reminded him of the path he had travelled to get here.

Today was a special occasion, and his mother had agreed to
come along. Normally, she kept away from government functions. In her old age all she wanted was a quiet contented life.
She felt grateful for the prosperity that had come her and her
son's way. The General had given her a business in Jinja. She
imported and sold fish nets and money was rolling in. He had

also built her a villa in Arua, and her family took care of it for her. Once a month he visited her and she cooked his favourite meal, millet bread with fish, and they reminisced, laughed and enjoyed their good fortune. "Do you now and then think about the leeches and the snakes in the swamps where you used to cut papyrus reeds?" he would ask with a faint smile on the corners of his mouth. "Every day, every day, my son. I am so happy it is all in the past. If only your father were here . . ." Sometimes he brought the children along, because he wanted them to have a close relationship with their grandmother.

As a rule, she never asked about his work. Sometimes he told her about what went on in the corridors of power, but she never fished for details, rumours. It seemed so petty, so unimportant. In the past she also never asked what her husband did or had done. Men did what they had to do to provide for their families, and the wives brought up the children the best way they could and tried to be good wives, kind, understanding, supportive, tolerant of their husbands' weaknesses. Her only regret was that her husband had not lived to see his son in glory. Alcohol poisoning had claimed him. She now lived with another man, whom the General accused of exploiting her. She looked at her son in his beautiful uniform with the glittering medals, and they both smiled. She felt proud to have been invited, a fitting honour for a mother who had seen the General when he was still snot-nosed.

There were many generals and their wives who came from her region and spoke the same language. They treated her with the respect she deserved and listened to her with bowed heads and fixed smiles. She admired the well-dressed women; they reminded her of what she might have looked like had her beginning been so auspicious. What did it matter now? They all ate from the same table now. By the look of things, her son could only go higher. His was one of the best-performing ministries; the fight against smugglers was going well. The Russians had promised to give him ten more speedboats, which would ease the task of combing the lake of that lice. He had invited her, because he had heard from a presidential aide that the Marshal was about to promote a number of high-ranking officers. My son is going to become a full general, she said to herself. A full general before reaching forty!

The day could not have been better. The weather was fabulous, with a clear blue sky, mild sunshine and a slight wind that kept the heat down. The lake shimmered in the distance, little waves corrugating its surface, the horizon a faint brown line drawn across its extreme periphery. It changed from blue to grey to green as if somebody were pressing buttons from above. There was a boat race, a spectacle of coordination, timing and precision. Traditional dancers pranced and swayed to the music, their voices rising and falling in unison. Quick short speeches sped one after the other, as if everybody wanted to rush to the shattering climax.

Turned out in a spotless military uniform, Marshal Amin took the stage. He launched a tirade against the racist South African regime, the Americans, the British and the Israelis. On the home front, he slammed the military top brass for inefficiency, overindulgence, corruption. "I have found a miracle cure for those ills," he said dramatically. From behind the marquee Robert Ashes emerged. Marshal Amin gave a sign, and the dignitaries began to clap.

Robert Ashes had had a haircut for the event, and the straggling hairs round his ears and the back of his head were now in line. He was dressed in a nice suit with shiny shoes and a red tie. He walked with the confident air of a man ready to go into action. Marshal Amin announced that he had put Ashes in charge of the Anti-Smuggling Unit, effective immediately. He hugged him, as if to emphasize his words.

General Bazooka could hardly believe his eyes or ears, and the obscene hug in front of him seemed to last for an hour. He did not know whether to howl, or hang his head in shame. He flew into a silent rage and his lower lip quivered. He wanted to kill the white man on the spot. How could the Marshal do this to him? Without as much as a warning! In front of his mother!

My home area, he said to himself, my beautiful islands, handed over on a plate to that snake! The whole of Jinja, the northern shores, my waterfalls and crocodiles too!

Marshal Amin later cornered him with his mother, introduced Ashes and ordered General Bazooka to show his successor the ropes. General Bazooka hated the white man's smirk, his teeth, everything about him. He had no intentions of going anywhere near him, except if he was going to kill him, which he intended to do. He wanted Ashes' tongue, eyes and penis in a jar. The last time he made a man smoke his penis had been in 1971; three years later Ashes was going to become the second. It would pacify the generals humiliated by his arrival and promotion, and he would reclaim mastery over the lake and his beautiful islands.

"You are still a cabinet minister," his mother said in an effort to comfort him. "Don't worry. Look on the bright side. Now you have time to concentrate on the ministry, your family and other duties."

General Bazooka was too angry to answer.

ROBERT ASHES HAD originally come from the Industrial Northeast, born in Newcastle, Great Britain. His father was a dissatisfied factory manager, his mother a gentle housewife. The only thing his father failed to dominate was his drinking and his temper. Everybody called him the Weatherman, agent of doom and gloom. There always seemed to be something wrong at the factory: strikes, unmet quotas, cash-flow problems, fewer orders. Home was just an extension of his office, and the ways which had taken him from the assembly line to the top, he espoused there. Ashes later learned that his father was not his biological father, and that the Weatherman was frustrated by his failure to have a son from his loins. By then, Ashes had decided to leave anyway; he had no intention of working in factories, mines or docks. He craved freedom, adventure, not bullying bosses and claustrophobia. Before leaving, he decided to put his parents out of their misery. The house went up in beautiful flames. His parents were injured but they survived. He hitch-hiked to London before anybody began to ask questions.

War was in the air and Hitler's name was on people's lips. Ashes drifted and finally became a courier in the underworld: liquor, drugs, dirty money. There was robbery, extortion, arson and racketeering. At nineteen he enlisted and was rewarded with proper military training, discipline and a wide knowledge of arms. With his characteristic fearlessness, he made an excellent soldier. He was sent to North Africa and fought against the remnants of German forces. Africa was a revelation: the space, the skies, the sand, the opportunities. He was later transferred to East Africa, stationed in Kenya. The Coast was a dream, a tantalizing morsel bringing to mind the escapades of hedonistic gangsters. The Kenyan Highlands, the mountain ranges, a vision of majesty. For the first time in his life, he thought there might be a God. He knew that he would return some day. With the cash and freedom to enjoy all of it. He gradually got bored because there was no fighting. He still wanted to be in the thick of things, to garner more experience; he wanted to leave the force a honed fighter, a one-man army.

Back in Britain he asked to be discharged as the war had ended. Many of his former colleagues were dead or maimed; together with the few he could find, he entered the construction industry with a vengeance and used his skills to extort, kidnap and amass a fortune. American aid was flowing into the country, and it was a wonderful time for those with the will to fight their way up the hierarchy of their chosen trade. With time his wanderlust rose and his life seemed too predictable, too easy, smelling a bit like his father's past of petty bossing and bitching. He was itching to return to Africa and he flirted with the idea of becoming a pirate. A friend pointed him to the possibility of becoming a mercenary, hiring himself to the highest bidder as a military instructor to sprouting terrorist or guerrilla groups.

He enlisted to take the fight to the Mau Mau in post-war

Kenya; it was his kind of thing: the hunter and the hunted, the vague lines between right and wrong. The frightened whites and the agitated blacks turned him on. He loved the interrogations because they reminded him of the underworld he knew so well. He pulled teeth and nails, and sliced kneecaps; he got the name the Guardian Angel. In his book, both sides were right and that made it fun. He secretly admired the stubborn resistance of the Mau Mau, especially because when he was young, he had heard the Africans described as cowardly and unable to fight. These blacks were fighting a modern European state to the death, and he thought he would have done the same if he had such beautiful mountains to defend. It was ironic that he worked harder now and saw more horrors than he had during the war. Immersed in the fighting in Africa, the World War seemed very far away. What had it been about? Freedom? Camps? Totalitarianism? Democracy? Or money?

Yes, money. The fight against the Mau Mau was fun, but there was no big money in it. Part of him was spoiled now and he craved thousands, hundreds of thousands. He wanted out; let the blacks and the whites settle their problems. At about that time, a British intelligence officer offered him the chance to become a spy. He could go to Rhodesia, Namibia, South Africa. Southern Africa beckoned because of the diamonds and gold. A deal or two and he would be done. The end of the sixties found him in South Africa, the beginning of the seventies, in Rhodesia. The fighting was good, the diamond trafficking legendary. The celestial trinity of danger, death and money was as seductive as ever. He took his time and made one big haul. A kilo of uncut diamonds landed in his hands after a year's planning, and then there was a monstrous shoot-out. He was shot in the leg, and he crawled and limped past corpses, and wandered for four delirious days. At one time, he even vowed to stop with adventure-seeking. A white farmer picked him up in his tractor, and later he was flown to South Africa, where he fell in love with Cape Town: its magnificence, its history, its wine. A year later he flew to London.

It was in London that he heard of Amin, a real animal. He started collecting newspaper cuttings about him. He went to the library and looked for more information about Amin and Uganda, reading Winston Churchill, Speke, Burton, Baker and Stanley. Gradually, his resolve to stop running after adventure slackened, and he now craved a massive fix, one last fling. Uganda seemed like a very good spot for it. His burgeoning plans were, however, poisoned by the mass expulsion of expatriates in 1972. He went to the airport and refugee camps, looking for eyewitness accounts of what was happening in Uganda. He was convinced that he would be the lion-tamer, the man to control Amin and enjoy that peculiar brand of fame. What he needed was a plan. He roamed the streets of London in a daze. He tried the British Embassy; they did not need him. He tried five missionary societies, both Catholic and Anglican; they rejected him. He became depressed, redundancy gnawing at him. Hijackers, terrorists, Cold War–mongers, were all having their time in the sun, yet life was passing him by and he was not becoming any younger.

The Irish Republican Army offered him a golden opportunity when they bombed the Grand Empire Hotel, killing members of the ruling Conservative Party, maiming others and causing terrible damage to property. News broke that Herbert Williams, the mastermind, had escaped to Africa. Many believed he was hiding in Uganda because Amin was flirting with the IRA, Black September and other nationalist organizations. The intelligence officer who had sent him to Rhodesia came to his aid; he was looking for somebody of his age suicidal enough to want to go to Uganda and check out the Williams rumours. Ashes signed immediately; soon he was part of a bogus British business delegation.

It was love at first sight between him and Marshal Amin. A month before, Dr. Ali had read omens from the livers of ten white bulls and promised the Marshal a saviour from abroad. The moment the delegation arrived, Marshal Amin knew that Dr. Ali had been right as usual. It turned out to be a meeting of kindred spirits. Marshal Amin needed support as his friends became fewer and his paranoia swelled to the size of a cathedral. Robert Ashes got the Anti-Smuggling Unit draft because of his knowledge of boats, and he advised the Marshal to build a navy. They discussed weapons, whisky, music. In due time he honed the Marshal's paranoia and told him which general to demote, or send abroad as ambassador or place at the head of a phantom coup plot. He married a black woman and settled.

VICTORIA WAITED TWO MONTHS before breaking the news: the miracle had happened; she was pregnant. They were at the lake walking side by side on a Sunday afternoon. The sun was shining brightly, and apart from the noise of the birds in the trees the place was quiet. She held Bat's hand, turned her head to look him in the eye and broke the news. He looked like somebody woken from a dream-laden sleep, the eyes slightly unfocused, the mouth a bit ajar, the brow creased pensively. His face wore a puzzled look, then relaxed into a neutral expression, neither happy nor sad, as if saying, What do you expect me to say?

"Pregnant." The word seemed to stay in the air for a long time.

"Yes, I am two months pregnant,"she said cautiously, valiantly trying to dam her ecstasy.

"Why did you wait this long to tell me?"

"I wanted to make sure."

"What do you want to do with it?"

"To keep it, of course."

"Abort." His voice seemed to come from afar, slightly tremulous, as if calling back his university days, when he had given such an order and it had been obeyed. His heart was pumping hard and he felt slightly out of breath.

"I want to keep the child." Victoria's voice was high, plaintive, her face troubled.

"The situation is too hot. People are getting killed every day. Can you guarantee the safety of the child?"

"You talk like a mathematician. There are no guarantees in life."

"I want to limit the risks. I don't want to be at the office and at the same time wondering if my child is safe."

"I want to have the baby."

"It would be best for you to return to your home. I will give you financial support." Bat's heart was beating even harder; not only was he facing rebellion from the person closest to him; he did not know what would come of all this.

"I want to stay with you. I have no family," Victoria said, infusing her voice with genuine desperation.

"You have friends. You can always hire help."

"It is not the same thing. I want to be with you, cook for you."

"I already have a cook. All I need is space to concentrate on my work. If you insist on staying, well, it is a big house. You will get bored to death. If you decide to leave, inform me."

It was not terribly romantic, but she wanted a foot in the door. Some dreams needed a little pushing along the way. "It is fine with me. I want to stay and share God's blessing with you."

A WEEK LATER Bat received news that the Professor's brother had been found dead near his home. He drove to the Professor's home located on one side of Makerere University Hill. The journey brought back memories, his university days, the post-independence political situation, especially the bombardment of the king's palace in 1966 by Colonel Amin on the orders of President Obote. It was the longest and most frightful gun battle he had ever heard. At one time he thought the whole city had been bombed to the ground.

He parked outside the Professor's house, took a long breath and got out of the car. His friend came out to meet him, his teary eyes red. As he hugged him, he felt the Professor's arms shaking. They sat down on the veranda and looked into the distance.

"If things continue this way, I will seriously consider emigrating. What sort of country is this where people get killed for no reason? State Research Bureau boys found him walking home, accused him of supporting dissidents, took his money and watch, and when he resisted, they killed him. In broad daylight!" the Professor said, hardly able to contain his rage.

Bat found it hard to mount a response. "I am sorry about this. I wish there was something I could do. I would really not blame you if you decided to go abroad. The country has become a snakepit. It is a shame we have not yet found a way to get rid of the vipers."

"I have lost the most precious thing: pleasure in work," the Professor lamented, shaking his head vigorously, like a drenched zebra. "I often think that many of my students are members of the Bureau, ready to twist my words and get me killed."

"Maybe you should leave the country," Bat suggested again, wondering how his friend would fare abroad. Settling in, getting a job, balancing a new identity with the old one.

"I have thought about lecturing in Kenya or Zambia. I have colleagues there. If it hadn't been for you and the Kalandas, I would have left already. But somehow I don't want to go. I keep thinking it will get better."

"Unfortunately, I can't help you make up your mind," Bat admitted, "but whatever decision you take, I will be behind you."

"I will think about it after the funeral."

Bat took the afternoon off to attend the funeral. He perused the day's newspaper in the car. It read like Amin's diary. The day before, Amin had met the new Libyan ambassador, visited a hospital, distributed sweets to limbless children and also made a speech at a graduation parade for police cadets. The rest of the paper was full of advertisements by astrologers promising miracle cures for anything from poverty to psychosis to psoriasis. The advertisements were never edited, resulting in the most deplorable spelling mistakes he had ever seen: "pavaty" for "poverty," "cyclesis" for "psychosis," "sorryasis" for "psoriasis" and the like. It was so bad he started chuckling. He threw the paper in the back of the car and hoped the cook would use it to light the Primus stove or to wipe his ass. He remembered the Learjet at the airport and wondered who Dr. Ali really was. He had attended many government functions, but he had never met the man. As he got onto Jinja Road, it struck him that Dr. Ali was a very clever man; he was milking the regime without showing his face, the kind of man who could walk down the street unrecognized. One thousand dollars per consultation was not bad. No wonder his followers called him God. It occurred to Bat that if there was anybody who could kill Amin and rid the country of the scourge, it was this mysterious man.

At the entrance to the Mabira Forest, chills went down Bat's spine. The density of it, the height of the trees, the possibilities for robbery and carjacking. Rumours had it that soldiers dumped bodies somewhere in its depths. He put his foot on the gas, adrenaline pumping. Many kilometres later, the sky cleared and he gave a sigh of relief.

The deceased had been a builder, and his house was a stout red-roofed brick structure. The place was crawling with mourners dressed in every colour under the sun. Burials always put Bat on edge. Caught between the corpse and the raw grief of the bereaved, some of whom seemed out of their minds, he felt redundant, an intruder. Words of consolation felt so weightless, so hackneyed. Each time, one was confronted with the fact that people never got used to violent death: it still shocked, the lamentations pierced with genuine sorrow. His feelings were now complicated by the fact that he was expecting a child. It made the insinuation of death in his life more poignant. Before, it had been him against the world; death on the job had seemed heroic, even glorious. But now he felt responsible for the baby; he had to protect it, provide for it. It was the impossibility of protecting anybody with any degree of certainty these days that bothered him most.

Among the mourners were some saying that the killing had a business motive behind it. They claimed that a competitor had hired the killers to get rid of his rival and take over his business. There were cries of "eye for an eye." The Professor wisely kept out of the commotion.

The deceased was lying in the sitting-room, his jaw tied with a white cloth, his nostrils plugged with cotton wool. The sight of his orphaned children made Bat wonder what words of wisdom a parent could offer a child nowadays. Turn the other cheek? Do good when evil men were having their way? Be sensible when sense was being rewarded with punishment? The legacy to be left for the next generation struck him as one of the hardest things his own generation had to drum up. He had the impression that everyone had been touched by an evil wind, whose chill would grind on into the next generation. Maybe even beyond. How would a generation of passive parents and confused children affect the future?

The burial ceremony ground along for an hour. Bat's attention was beginning to wander when he saw a young woman he had noticed earlier on. When he first saw her, she looked as if she was waiting for somebody. Maybe him. Why he thought that, he could not tell. She was wearing a skirt and a blouse and flat shoes. She had a good shape, soft features and an open face. She seemed the exact opposite of him, but he felt something when he looked at her. He called a boy who was passing by and told him to fetch her. Why did she look surprised? She looked stiffly in his direction as if peeking at something forbidden, but she finally came.

He was leaning against his car, arms on his chest. He liked the warmth of her voice, her rapt attention. She listened carefully, as if looking for faults, lies, inconsistencies in a sworn testimony. It soon started to rain. He took shelter in his car and watched as she got soaked, making up her mind whether to follow him in or seek shelter elsewhere. She sat in the back and he watched her in the driving mirror. Her name was Babit and she had two brothers and three sisters, she said, cracking her knuckles with nerves.

As he listened to her voice, he dreamed of taking her with him. Did he want to listen to that same voice year in and year out? Probably. See the same face, lie next to that same body? Probably. How long would it last? Probably very long. Who would give in first? Probably him. Would the good memories outweigh the bad ones in the end? How would he remember her? As a shadow, a feeble sensory perception? A lovable entity? A voice? Or simply as Victoria's successor? How would she remember him?

VICTORIA HAD SEVERED her bonds with General Bazooka and no longer reported to him, partly because there was nothing to report, partly because she knew that if he was serious he had to have other spies shadowing Bat. She was too wrapped up in the world of pregnancy, motherhood, the future, to take much notice of what Bat or anybody else did officially. She loved the feeling of freedom she had. She woke up in the morning with the day to herself and engaged in fantasies. This was the best time of her life. By answering her prayers, God seemed to have forgiven her. By the time the baby arrived, she felt rejuvenated, purged, in sync with the living.

The birth of his daughter thrilled Bat in ways he had not expected. He had wanted a boy, but the sight of his daughter lying there, bunching her fat fingers, ignited something in him. A girl would definitely mean more work for Victoria, role-modeling and all. He was surprised to be confronted with this embodiment of innocence. She looked so helpless, so much at the mercy of forces around her. Here she was, an oasis of purity in a desert of madness, a demarcation of what had gone wrong and what could have been. He then felt sad. How was he going to protect her interests? He felt exposed: his character, his limitations. He felt inadequate in relation to the rampant gun-wielding madmen. He was now participant in the eternal rite of passing on the torch. But here he was, devoid of knowledge and wisdom to impart. He had fallen from his lofty sense of inde-

pendence and superior aloofness. He was now like the very
countrymen he had tried to flee, dependent on uncontrollable
forces, making stupid mistakes, hurting others out of the weakness of failing to say no to superiors, to temptation, to the possibility of upward mobility, to the susurrations from deep inside
the snakepit. Did I return partly to seek common ground, however indirect, with the people, the country? he asked himself. He
felt the tender emotions most parents felt, but what would he do
with them? He held the baby in his arms and smelled its scalp. It
struggled against him, then gradually calmed down; his blessing,
his curse. In its searching eyes was something calming, the
ability to charm and soothe him. It was his antidepressant.

Whenever Victoria saw Bat holding the baby, her love for
him multiplied, surged and kicked in her breast. He seemed so
unaware of what he had done for her, the drought he had ended,
the suffering he had eased. At such moments she wanted to put
herself at his mercy, come clean, confess the sordid past, explain
everything. But it was too great a risk to take. She might disgust
him. He might never want to see her again. The weight of her
secrets compromised her joy at such a time and injected doubt in
the proceedings.

She felt blessed because Bat's parents rejoiced when they saw
the baby. His father was especially supportive. His mother, however, wanted to meet somebody from her family. Bat's brother
showed little enthusiasm. She did not know why she was afraid
of him. Was he too silent? He looked like a man sitting on a barrel of secrets. In his silence, he seemed to know everything about
everybody, including her, and in his superior knowledge everybody bored him. At the baby's baptismal ceremony he gave the
baby a pair of white shoes and then handed Victoria a red Bible.
She was shaken: What did he mean? Was it a warning? State
Research Bureau identity cards were red; was he telling her that
he knew her secret? She remarked to Bat that his brother was
mysterious.

"He loves cars too much," Bat replied.

"But you also do."

"He is obsessed with them. I am not, but I can sympathize. Machines are docile as long as you treat them nicely."

"Is that the reason why he is unreachable?"

"Maybe, maybe not," Bat said, turning to look at Victoria for a moment. "But then again, look at the state this country is in. What has a young person got to hold on to, to obsess about? Family? When people get killed and soldiers can force a father to fornicate with his daughter for all to watch? Religion? When God is passive and astrology is the only growing faith? Education? When educated people are the enemy? I can understand what he is going through."

"Yes," Victoria said noncommittally.

"Did you like his fireworks?"

"How did he get a licence?"

"Possibly through the good offices of a friendly general. Soldiers love spectacles and the boy is a genius."

"He is good," Victoria said worriedly. Her guess was that he was a member of the Public Safety Unit. She had looked for his file at Bureau headquarters, in vain. It could of course mean a few things: Maybe he was known by other names. Maybe his file had been misplaced in the sewers of the Bureau's inventory. She hoped that he wasn't with the Public Safety Unit, the arch-enemy of the Bureau, which would make killing him easier if he blew her cover. She hoped he wouldn't do anything foolish, as she had no wish to impede her rehabilitation.

In due course, Victoria got word that Bat was in love with another woman. She asked two colleagues in the Bureau to get her a picture of this person. A search of Babit's parents' house was made: sofas were cut open, carpets ripped from floors, bedding shredded, coffee sacks emptied. Babit's modest photo collection was found and taken. The damage would have been worse, but Victoria had instructed the men not to take anything else or to harm anyone. To make sure that they followed her orders, she had paid them up front. It had cost her, but she had felt that it was the right thing to do for someone seeking salvation, for someone pursuing a dream.

The pictures, when they arrived, disappointed. Babit did not measure up to her, looks-wise. She was younger but lacked the height, the poise. It was a mystery to her how a dynamic, rich man like Bat could feel attracted to that stolid person in the pictures. How can this person take my man away from me? she cried aloud. How can she dare to? A plethora of nasty ideas flooded her mind: she wanted to hurt Bat; she wanted to hurt the woman; she wanted to hurt herself. She became afraid that her recovery had not been all that thorough. The old ways beckoned, tempting her with their effectiveness.

She went to the nursery and picked up the child; it was sleeping, oblivious to the storm. She felt a maternal love wash over her. But the child's helplessness only made her fiercer. She had sworn never to fall back into the snakepit after the birth of her child, but now she was not so sure. She felt disappointed with herself, and with the world. She seemed to be pushed back into the same life she wanted to flee. Bat had said that he was not in love. Does that deny me the right to be deeply in love with him? Had I not loved the General despite his being married and continuing to pick up other girls? Maybe I had only been in love with the General's power of life and death. Bat does not have that power and so I am the one with the finger on the trigger. I can very easily destroy him, and this woman and both their families.

When Bat returned home at eleven o'clock that evening, her anger exploded. "Where have you been?" she asked even before greeting him. Her body was rigid, her hands bunched into fists held at her sides.

"Work," he said looking at her, surprised that she had the nerve to shout like that.

"Where did you go after work?"

"None of your business. If I need somebody to track me, I will move in with the Bureau and the Public Safety Unit." He wondered why he was bothering to explain himself. Was this not his house?

Maybe you did move in with those organizations, Victoria

said under her breath before saying, "It is my business. I am your wife. I have your baby. I am in love with you."

"I don't remember ever getting married. If I did, maybe I should seek a divorce. Anyway, in this country divorce is unnecessary. One can simply ask the wife to leave. I love my daughter, but I am not about to take orders from her mother."

"You are not going to get away with this," she said heatedly. It looked as if she was about to spring and choke him.

"With what?" he said disdainfully.

"Whoring."

"I don't remember visiting a single whore in my whole life," he said as if to himself.

It occurred to him to lead a trade delegation to Saudi Arabia and get away from the stress. General Bazooka was bogged down with suppressing a revolt in the army. The Lugbaras, Amin's former favourites, had rebelled since being dropped in favour of the Nubians and Kakwas. They had made a coup attempt, storming the presidential palace with guns and bombs. Now the Hammer, as they called the General, was taking them apart, with the help of the Eunuchs. Bat decided to go to Saudi Arabia.

"Answer me. I am talking to you," Victoria said, rising from the sofa. In the blink of an eye, she was standing over him, her index finger aimed at his eyeball. It amused him and he almost laughed. The last woman to beat him was his biology teacher during his secondary-school days. He slapped the finger away and ordered her to sit down. She refused. He remembered that he knew nothing about her and had resisted the urge to run a check on her. He had assumed that his status as a high-ranking civil service official would protect him from government conspiracies. After all, was he not the saviour of the Ministry of Power and Communications? Where would General Bazooka be without him? he thought to himself, as if to vindicate his course of action, his complacency. He stood up, pushed her away, and ordered her never to raise her voice at him again.

Blind with rage, she slapped him on the temple. It did not hurt very much, his eyes did not water, and neither did his head rock or his knees buckle. But Bat saw it as a revelation of Victoria's true colours. A wave of fear coursed through his chest. What did I get myself into? he thought, remembering the toast he made to risk, to adventure, the evening they met. He pushed her away and ordered her to leave his house.

Victoria wondered if she had gone too far. But what was going too far when the General had put him at her disposal? Surely a slap was in order. It was better than a hammer, a panga slash, a gun blast. Why did he not make a fight of it and slap back? Maybe we would have rolled on the floor and finally ended up in each other's arms. What Victoria forgot was that Bat was not seeing her as a Bureau agent, bearer of life-and-death powers, but as a helpless woman living in his house, under his generosity.

"I am not going anywhere," she said defiantly, fists balled, breathing hard from internal exertion.

"If you can do what you have just done, it means you are capable of a lot more things I don't know about. These are troubled times, Vicki. Anyone is capable of anything. To avoid trouble in the future, I want us to part when we can still bear to look at each other."

"You are my first love. You performed a miracle and I bore a child. You can't escape your destiny, the role God cut out for you."

At the mention of God, Bat became suspicious. Which God did she mean: the Christian one or Dr. Ali? Had she consulted the famous astrologer or one of his assistants? Where had she gotten the money? When? He dismissed the idea. She probably meant the Christian God.

"I want you to leave in the morning. You deserve a better life."

Victoria burst into tears. She asked for forgiveness. When she tried to use the child as a shield and a weapon, Bat had a sudden attack of doubt. He could take the child away from Victoria and give it to his mother to raise, assisted by hired help or another relative. But it would scar her; she was still too young. It was best to let her stay with Victoria, but what kind of world was he sending his daughter into? What kind of men and women were going to influence her? He experienced a sense of failure. Had he not failed by not pressing for an abortion? Abortion in a land where heads were cracked with hammers, bodies dumped? Was he among the good, the sane people? Or was he as bad as the gun-wielders?

It was a very tense night, the silence in the house charged like a ton of dynamite. He thought about leaving and sleeping elsewhere, but he was determined not to run away. It was his house. At two o'clock, he went to his daughter's room. He sat in the darkness watching her sleep. She wheezed a little from a nostril clogged by an approaching cold. He listened as the air squeezed out, the sound magnified by the darkness. This was his last chance. From now on, visiting her was going to be a great effort. He felt like a creator whose creations had spun out of control.

After a very long time, he felt a change in the air, a scent, a stealthy breath. Victoria was standing in the doorway, her nightie clinging to her, her long body etched in shadow. She looked as seductive as he had ever seen her, and he could feel the beginning of an erection. It was only a matter of reaching out and she would be his again. He remembered their first meeting. A general's wife? Maybe. He pushed all erotic ideas from his mind, and she looked like a painting on the wall: beautiful, passionless. The silence deepened as each failed to find words to say to break the deadlock, making the night oppressive in its grip on the house. Not a single night crawler, bird or animal cleaved the night with its cries, howls or calls. It seemed as if Bat and Victoria were holding their breath like divers attempting to break a record. She felt her love poisoned by rejection and experienced a massive sense of despair. She had all the violence of guns at her disposal but did not have the heart to touch him. One day I will return in triumph. It is just a matter of time, she said to herself. She stole away from the room. The spell broken, Bat gave a large sigh of relief and left the room, the whiff of baby powder in his nose.

DR. AHMED MOHAMMED MAHRANI ALI'S LEARJET circled
Entebbe Airport. He hated night flights, partly because he could
not enjoy the view outside, partly because he could hardly sleep
on his plane. He hated this particular flight because it disrupted
his schedule. He had not planned to return to Uganda for two
months, but Marshal Amin had begged him to cancel his stay in
Zaïre and come to his aid. Two big coup attempts in three weeks
was enough trouble to unsettle even the toughest mind. At the
beginning of their relationship he had made it clear to the Marshal that he did not baby-sit presidents. His role was to study the
omens, offer sacrifice, but not to get bogged down in the politics
of any country. But over time the nature of the relationship had
changed and the two men had become friends. Gradually, the
Marshal had asked for his advice here and there. And he had to
admit that he had begun to like it. He found himself using information garnered from Emperor Bokassa, President Mobutu and
other leaders to try and solve the Marshal's problems. They
would spend long hours discussing the personality problems of
different dictators, from those who wore high-heeled shoes to
appear taller, to those who pulled in their bellies at photo shoots
to scale down the vastness of their stomachs, to those addicted to
cocaine, heroin or pot. They would laugh at other dictators'
miseries, especially those deposed in palace coups in the middle
of the night. Nixon's plight was a favourite subject, especially
because the Marshal had done his best to counsel him. They
would laugh at the devilry of a system which made such a powerful man eat humble pie.

Dr. Ali did not want to claim credit for what happened in
Uganda, but aside from foretelling a few events, including the
imminence of the current revolt, he had been the person who
had advised the Marshal to turn the Eunuchs into a specialized
personal army, loyal only to him and nobody else. It gave Dr. Ali
an adrenaline rush to know that he was among the most power-

ful men in the country. Why did that excite him? Because he had grown to love the country. It was so beautiful, yet so troubled. It was like a mad girl of uncommon beauty men felt tempted to rescue. He liked to think that he had played his part well. Take the spread of astrology. He had singlehandedly imported the practice. In his wake the Zanzibaris had taken over the business. It was amazing and amusing to see how quickly the revolution had taken root. The nicknames he had collected in the process amused him: God, Jesus, Satan, the Unholy Spirit, the Dream, the Giant, the Government Spokesman. He could understand why they called him the Dream. He had been the one who had advised the Marshal to hone his mystique by claiming that God talked to him in dreams. He had also advised him to proclaim unpopular laws, measures and announce embarrassing news through the Government Spokesman.

The plane landed safely. He was whisked from the airport in a dark-windowed Boomerang. He always insisted on travelling incognito. In a dictatorship, anonymity was priceless. He liked the fact that very few Ugandans, let alone generals, knew his identity. During séances, he used masks and big robes and sat on a throne, which made him look taller than he was. During meetings with Marshal Amin, he insisted on there being very few people. During his stays his assistants did most of the work, and he always walked amidst a phalanx of bodyguards.

The Boomerang parked in front of the State House at Entebbe and ten men surrounded Dr. Ali and walked him inside the building. There was commotion, soldiers everywhere. He was here to comfort his friend, encourage him, reassure him that his time had not yet come. He knew how most people overlooked the pressure leaders were under. Pressure was the main reason why from time immemorial many leaders went mad.

Marshal Amin sprang from his chair when the astrologer walked into the room. The two men embraced. Robert Ashes and two generals looked on, ready to shake hands with the diminutive astrologer and to get down to business with him. To their surprise, Amin asked them for privacy and remained

behind with his guest. He sometimes thought about imprison-
ing the little man; he meant so much to him. In the past a king
would have crippled him and put him under permanent guard.
Things were different now. However much Amin hated it, he
had to let the man leave and had to wait patiently for his return.
There was also the fact that he feared the astrologer's ire: a man
this gifted could curse you, mess up your omens and hasten your
downfall. The only weapon available was to keep him happy and
to beg him to come whenever things ran out of hand. Amin felt
relieved that the man had agreed at all to come at such short
notice.

"Ten white bulls are ready," Amin said as the two men sat
down.

"Do you want the omens read right now? It is three o'clock in
the morning. The world is asleep," the astrologer joked.

"I work twenty-four hours a day," his host said irately, pining
for his next dose of cocaine. He needed it, no, he deserved it. He
could celebrate; his peace of mind had returned. He now believed
that the rebellion would be crushed. Soon after, he would reor-
ganize his personal army and make it ten times stronger, and
give the men everything they wanted.

"Let us proceed then. Afterwards we can lie down for some
sleep," the astrologer said, yawning.

"You must be very jet-lagged, my friend."

"Never mind. Anything for you, friend."

Under moonlight, the ten bulls were slaughtered, Marshal
Amin cutting the throats according to procedure. Dr. Ali examined each liver carefully, turning over the shiny, silky lobes. He
examined the stars for a long time. The omens were favourable.
Now everybody could get some sleep. In the morning he would
study the sun and communicate its omens.

Astrology had been in Dr. Ali's family for three hundred
years. He was born on the small island of Pemba in the Indian
Ocean to a Muslim family. He was a small dark-skinned man
of mixed parentage. His ancestors had come from Arabia in
AD 1001 and settled on the East African coast. They intermar-

ried with Africans, creating the Swahili heritage. At the age of six, Dr. Ali was struck by lightning as he played outside. His parents found him an hour later, stone cold, eye whites showing. They took him to the doctor, prayed over him and waited for his death. But he survived, hovering near death for a year, hardly moving a muscle, talking in a small voice. He told his mother that he was having dreams, seeing the sun, the stars, spirits. In a family of astrologers this would have been nothing new; here, when he insisted, they thought he might have lost his head or was telling them what he had heard adults say.

After convalescing he returned to school. He surprised teachers and pupils by telling them things about themselves, a relative who fell sick, or got married, or visited. He could also tell when somebody was lying.

"It is the lightning. The electricity fried your brain. You are mad if you think you are special," they said.

In a way, they were right. There were astrologers and soothsayers everywhere. Every other week somebody claimed to be a prophet or healer or messiah. Those who couldn't prosper left for Zanzibar, Tanzania or the Arab states.

In the end, he decided to keep his counsel, never telling what he saw or knew about other people. After school he read books on astrology and Arabic. He was determined to go to Iran and study ancient religions. At twenty-five he got his university degree in religious studies. By then people had acknowledged his gift. People came from far and near to have their omens read. He got a job offer as head astrologer in Saudi Arabia, working exclusively for the royal family, but turned it down. He wanted freedom. He returned to the coast and settled in Zanzibar, where his fame grew even more.

By the time he made his first visit to Uganda, he was the most expensive astrologer on the continent. He was already on a retainer with President Mobutu of Zaïre, Emperor Bokassa of the Central African Republic, and General Gowon of Nigeria. He also had famous customers in Saudi Arabia and Europe. During their first meeting he told Amin that he would die an old man. He also described forthcoming assassination attempts to him, one of which occurred a week later, in almost exact detail. Amin became a follower. He foretold the deaths of two of Amin's wives, also in detail. Amin had shivered. His mother had been a witch-doctor and he had his own clutch of astrologers and witches, but he had never met someone like Dr. Ali. Dr. Ali became the only man Amin truly feared. To keep him away from his generals, he raised the astrologer's fees to one thousand dollars per consultation and ten thousand per séance. To weaken organized religions, he promoted the spread of astrology. Dr. Ali's writings were spread everywhere, thus the nickname God. Astrology became a department at the university.

Now, three years later, the two men had become very good friends. The Marshal loved the fact that Dr. Ali hated the limelight. The air of mystique served both parties well. He also had few vices, apart from a streak of exorbitance. Every night he consumed a thousand-dollar bottle of red wine, a habit picked up from President Mobutu, whose cellar boasted the most expensive wines in the world.

"A thousand dollars worth of piss!" Amin would exclaim.

"I have drunk wines costing fifty thousand dollars per bottle," the astrologer would counter, raising his eyebrows, turning his head slightly and smiling faintly. "I last drank that at Mobutu's birthday."

"Thank God whisky is not so expensive. Give me Johnnie Walker any day. And a bag of cocaine," Amin said, laughing out loud.

"We are talking about the fine things in life, Marshal," the astrologer said, laughing.

"Fuck them in the arse," his host said, roaring with more laughter. He rang a bell and a soldier appeared. "Bring my friend his thousand-dollar piss. Don't break the bottle. We are going to drink a toast."

The phone rang. Good news. General Bazooka had crushed the core of the rebellion. He was now busy wrapping up the operation.

BY THE TIME BAT LEFT for Saudi Arabia, the rebellion in the army had been quelled. He headed a delegation charged with the business of negotiating with the Saudi government for a supply of construction equipment. Offers had been tendered by two companies, both owned by Saudi princes. It was up to Bat to decide which company should receive the contract and to close the deal. General Bazooka and a few other generals would get a cut of the commission, delivered in cash. What Bat did not realize was just how fierce the competition was between the two princes. It almost soured an otherwise fine journey.

Bat had arrived in a good mood. Victoria had moved out, and it was now up to Babit to move in, although her parents opposed the idea, preferring to see her married first. As he contemplated while treading on the ubiquitous sand, he hoped that Babit's parents would relent. He even wished that Babit had come along to see this sand and the cities placed in its midst. He wished she could see the palace where the delegation did business under ceilings high as a pylon, in rooms uncluttered as an empty warehouse.

It was here that Bat began to feel that he had been wasting time, that he should already have made his fortune. The prince who seemed more eager to get his tender accepted invited him to his home. They went by helicopter, a white capsule with luxurious fittings. It brought back memories of General Bazooka's Avenger. It felt like he was standing on a very high hill, looking down at a gargantuan city wrapped in sand, with vertigo pulling him down to the bottom at a dizzying pace. Do I want to take the offer? Do I have a choice? Is this how it goes down: an offer is presented to you, and you take it and wait for the men with guns who come or do not come? Is there any way out of this? Before this I did not know how I would make my money, at least not the details. But this is blackmail, an insult, not the clean deal I dreamed of where everybody would be happy with the results.

Bat's host was a large bearded man with big eyes, a hooked nose, a serious face. Wrapped in brown flowing robes billowing like a full sail, he resembled an Old Testament prophet burning with zeal as he talked about his business empire: shares in American corporations, houses in New York, Montego Bay, Buckingham, the Spanish coast.

"I plan to carve for myself a chunk of Africa and South America," he declared. "They are the continents of the future where everything goes."

And I am the grease that is supposed to facilitate the process, Bat thought morosely, no better than General Bazooka or the other goondas, sliding down the slimy walls of the snakepit without a hand- or foothold. And if I refuse, I will face the threat of death or disappearance.

The helicopter landed somewhere in the desert. It looked as if they had not moved at all: it was still sand, curvaceous and glossy like something made out of burnished glass or sanded wood.

"With a foothold in Uganda I will be able to buy one hundred islands in Uganda, Kenya and Tanzania and develop tourism. Ultimately, I intend to build a string of hotels on the Kenyan coast and compete with the Italian mafia. At the moment, they are having it all their way. It is simply not fair. Arabs came to the coast first. Mombasa, Malindi and Lamu are Arab towns. I want to claim them from the Kenyan government. If all my plans go well, I will become the most influential businessman in East Africa and leave the wranglings over the Saudi throne to my brothers."

Bat did not know whether to believe his ears or not. He knew that the first Arabs on the East African coast had come from Arabia fleeing persecution. It just seemed strange that somebody wanted to claim their heritage fourteen hundred years later. Did this man want to take over East Africa? With the petrol dollars gushing from the Middle East, eagerly lent to dictators and anybody the European and American banks thought could guarantee payment and a healthy interest rate, maybe the man was not deluded.

"I have never failed to close a deal. I win, no matter what it takes. I want us to be friends because we will be seeing a lot of each other. My generosity has never been spurned. My brother knows this. Everybody else does. I have already made a decision. The usual rate is ten percent commission, which comes to five million dollars. I have arranged for my men to give you brief-cases with the said amount in cash for the generals. For you personally I have opened a numbered account and deposited the equivalent of five percent commission. It is not enough to buy a decent house in any livable place today, but I hope you will accept it. It is just a beginning, a sign that I treasure your friend-ship. You and I know well that you are the government, not those generals who can hardly tell left from right, and it is you I need more than anything else. Members of the elite need each other, because we all speak the same language. We are brothers."

Bat felt insulted and humiliated by the veiled threats, the tying of his hands so that he could not defend himself, and could only crawl like a legless, armless creature, which in his host's eyes he was. He did not buy that "we are brothers" stuff at all because one does not threaten to take a brother's life, least of all in these reckless, terrorist- and assassination-filled years, where the value of an individual human life was almost nothing. In Uganda the kind of money he was talking about could buy assassins to kill a hundred presidents. Out of a sense of self-preservation he had no choice but to take the bribe. His fantasies of making his fortune in a more sophisticated fashion were now gone. Still, there was the matter of the other prince. Bat started sweating as the anxiety in him grew, as the sense of his own importance dwindled, as he realized that he was being hired and treated like a labourer.

"Is anything the matter? Should I turn the air-conditioning up?" his host asked politely. He knew what was happening and he enjoyed it very much. The moment when an opponent or a business associate capitulated was one of the things he enjoyed most in life; there was nothing better than witnessing the other man's fantasies of morality, self-importance, power, self-esteem haemorrhage at one's feet. However many times he saw it, he never got tired of it. It was like a pugilist throwing a killer punch and watching his opponent's eyes pop out of their sockets, his knees buckle, the gum shield fly out of the ring, his head banging the canvas. He wished there was a way of videotaping it or preserving it in another form, but, like the moment of orgasm, it is best preserved in memory.

"I am fine," Bat murmured, gulping a glass of ice water and not feeling much better.

"You told me earlier that you love cars. Why don't you and I take a spin? I have a few old tins in the garage," the prince said, smiling at his own sense of humour.

"I would be delighted," Bat said, hoping that, ensconced in a car, he would be able to relax, to regain his equilibrium.

In the hangar which housed the garage were a Cadillac, a Rolls and a customized Porsche 999, which, at first sight, looked too small to hold his host's bulk, but had, in fact, been provided with a wider chassis to accommodate his barge-like girth. Seeing that Bat was taken by the Porsche, he touched it and said, "I love it very much. I didn't change it much. I just provided it with a solid-gold gear lever and exhaust pipe."

Bat whistled pensively. Such luxury, such obscenity. The 999 felt totally different from his XJ10, even though the only differences were that the seats were lower on the ground and everything was so compact. He liked the way it roared as he drove into the yard. He felt life flowing slowly back into him. Speed always did it. He liked the sensation of running, outracing ghouls, floating on a wave of air. For the moment he could forget the nasty decision he had to make, or which had already been made for him by the owner of this car, and the consequences. It was just a shame that there were no cars to overtake on this stretch of road, and however far away he went, he would have to return and face the man who had threatened his life if he turned down his offer.

Bat got out of the car fizzing with energy, his legs trembling. There was little else to do and he felt he had seen enough of his host's ostentatious home. He wanted to get away and enjoy some solitude. There was a state dinner in the evening, a prospect he did not look forward to with any sense of joy.

"How will the other prince take the loss?" he asked resignedly.

"Don't worry about him," his host said, smiling smugly. "I will straighten him out myself. It has always been like that. It would be good though to hire a bodyguard back home."

"I intend to hire ten," Bat said to hide his unease.

"I would not worry if I were you. Everything is under control."

Bat decided to make no further inquiries. What was the use? The deed had already been done. It was better to accept and if possible enjoy it. Suddenly, he was aware of a beautiful floating sensation, as if he were sitting on a very fast motorcycle. He also experienced the transparency of guilt, as if his secret were ringing bells. More than ever he became aware that great fortunes were made and lost in Africa. It was the biblical land where riches got eaten by locusts. The present did not last, the future got rancid before you touched it, blighted by the looming past: the stultification of slavery, the humiliation of colonialism, the debilitation of neo-colonialism, the raging war between capitalism and communism. The colonials, the Asians, the royals, the dictators, had all tasted the bitter truth. Amin and his cohorts knew it; they had their luggage ready. What will be my fate? Bat wondered.

After his return Bat met General Bazooka and handed him the briefcases stuffed with dollars and briefed him about the details of the deal. Separated by the vastness of a mahogany bureau on which stood the Ugandan flag, a battery of golden Parker pens, three telephones and in whose drawers were guns and bullet clips, Bat looked like a junior teacher reporting to the headmaster. There were enough guns in the General's office to arm a hundred soldiers, and Bat felt that they were trained on him, ready to go off. The General nodded up and down with his handsome face, like a blue gecko sunning itself on a rock, appreciating the windfall, happy that his stash of dollars was going to increase spectacularly. There was a growing dearth of foreign exchange in the country, and anybody with dollars in cash was in a very privileged position. Now and then, the corners of the

General's mouth pointed downwards and, in harmony with the continuous up-and-down nodding motion, created an expression of supreme smugness of the school of "I am the king of this hill and there is nothing anybody can do about it." The General, who had only recently put down a rebellion in the army, needed this cash reward to augment his sense of self-importance as a counter-measure to the humiliation he had suffered at the hands of Robert Ashes. As long as the General kept nodding with satisfaction, Bat knew that the rival prince had not sought his revenge by informing the General about his brother's tactics and Bat's role in the drama. The General was not very interested in the technical details, and Bat could see that whenever he started in that direction his boss stopped nodding. After half an hour of explanations Bat stood up to go, leaving behind the briefcases.

Bat's anxiety expressed itself in his increased intake of alcohol. He also tried to steady his nerves by thinking about Babit who, when he really came to think of it, would not be able to help him if things came to a head. But the knowledge that she would be there for him calmed him. In the end, his conscience would not leave him alone. It fertilized his imagination with all kinds of threats: abduction, imprisonment, torture, blackmail. If he walked to his car and heard somebody coming behind him, he would stop, turn around and see who it was. If a car followed him on the road and he could not shake it off, he started to worry. If a car was parked at his neighbour's house with people inside, he wondered if they were after him. If at night a twig fell on the roof or a bat knocked on a window-pane, he would panic, afraid that they had come for him. He asked the police department not to change the guard whom he was used to, but even then he wondered if the man had not been given instructions by the General to let killers in while he slept.

Bat had bought Babit costly jewellery, things which were no longer available in the country, most of the items in yellow gold, the most popular colour. He enjoyed the genuine appreciation Babit exhibited as she tried on the necklaces, the bangles, the rings, the watches. Spread out in heaps in the Saudi shops, they had been useless objects, baubles; sliding or fitting snugly on Babit's neck or wrist, they were transformed into special objects, an enhancement of her beauty, a sign of the love between the two hearts. Her parents had welcomed him back with a feast, and the Kalandas and the Professor had come along to celebrate with him. Surrounded by his friends, who knew nothing about the deal, he felt safe. Even if something happened to him, they would not go under with him. It was the way one protected friends these days. On that day, Babit's parents allowed her to move in with him, with the understanding that within a year they would get married. He was glad to have her around to share the big house.

After three months of living together Bat decided to organize a party for Babit. He watched as she moved among the guests. She seemed too aware of herself, afraid to make mistakes, like an apologetic caretaker explaining herself to the residents. The Professor's wife had made a rare public appearance and looked well, if only a bit too skinny. The Professor kept her at his side all the time, as if afraid that she might develop a renewed attack of the disease at any moment. The Kalandas mingled with everybody, and Mrs. Kalanda looked very seductive in her expensive clothes, which two of her sisters sent from Kenya and Britain. Bat followed her with his eyes on a few occasions, remarking on how she resembled Victoria. Her athletic body triggered langourous fantasies in his mind, especially when he thought about how infrequently she and her husband made love. She was aware of his attraction to her, but it never bothered her. She enjoyed admiration from the right corners.

Sister had come the day before, belly swollen, feet burdened by the new pressure of pregnancy, her face beaming with the approaching joy of motherhood. Her husband looked even fatter. He had given up planning towns doomed never to leave the drawing board and flower into real houses with walls and roofs and had gone into the cattle trade. He travelled a lot, and Bat wondered if he was faithful to Sister, who looked very much in love, following her husband's wide body around with adoring eyes, speaking of him as if he were a prince on a royal visit.

Bat's younger brother had put in an appearance and Bat was glad to see him, although he was worried about his excessive drinking.

"Why do you drink so much at your age?"

"It is an act of resistance. I am resisting the violence of a regime drunk on blood and chaos."

Bat did not know whether to take him seriously or not.

"How long are you going to continue exploding fireworks?"

"If you mean that I should take a job, forget it, brother. I earn enough repairing cars. If I need more, I know where to get it."

"Do you still want to drive in the East African Safari Rally?"

"I am not fast or steady enough to drive. In fact, there are many better drivers. All I can do is navigate, but I hate map-reading under such pressure. I decided to wait. I am happy with what I have," he said nonchalantly, as if he were talking about somebody whose prospects did not interest him a jot.

At the party he exploded some spectacular fireworks which climbed the sky in a noisy rush, unfurled and dominated the air in short piercing intervals. Bat couldn't get enough of the sight, even if Babit was worried about drawing attention.

Amidst the explosions, a Euphoria 707 full of Bureau agents parked one house away from them. The men got out and spied on the proceedings. They anticipated action, the turning of tables, emptying of wallets, maybe even the abduction of a woman. Unfortunately for them, they had to stop their salivating; it was one of those untouchable houses, with untouchable guests. They swore and cursed. One of the most frustrating aspects of Bureau work was having to show restraint, and being careful not to get into shoot-outs with the Public Safety Unit or the notorious Eunuchs, even if you were in the mood. With gallons of adrenaline and testosterone to jettison, the men drove away looking for some fool to fall into their itching hands.

At one interval Bat was called away to the phone. He swore under his breath, thinking that it was General Bazooka, who had the habit of calling him at awkward times, sometimes on Saturday or Sunday, sometimes deep in the night, on ministry business, but really to test him.

"Why didn't you invite me?"

"What happens in this house is none of your business," he said firmly.

"It is my business. You are the father of my child, my first love."

"I don't remember seeing any virginal first blood that night."

"You don't understand. Maybe you don't know how to love."

"I have no intentions of taking lessons. Stop calling my house for no reason."

"Your daughter wants to see you."

"I will come round. Now get off the phone. My guests are waiting."

"One day you will beg me to return. I am the rightful lady of the house."

"Keep on dreaming. Good night," he said, replacing the receiver.

Half an hour later the phone rang again.

"Is that the housegirl speaking?"

"It is the lady of the house speaking," Babit replied curtly.

"I am the lady of the house, child."

"I am not your child, woman. Stop bothering us. Get yourself a man."

"Bat is my man. You are the intruder. Before you brought your fat face into the house everything was fine. You are responsible for my child's suffering, my suffering, everybody else's suffering. Why don't you just leave?"

"Bat made his choice. Live with it. He will never take you back."

"Wait and see. You are barren as a stone. You will not last. Save yourself the humiliation and leave with some dignity. Leave before something happens to you."

"Nothing is going to happen to me. You are going to remain where you are. I am staying here, with or without a child," she said, and replaced the receiver. The phone rang immediately after. She picked it up and replaced it. It rang again and again. She unplugged it.

When most of the guests had left and the two of them were sitting on the sofa before going to bed, Babit told Bat about the phone calls.

"She called me earlier. Why should she have bothered you?"

"I don't know."

"I told her to stop calling. I will have a firm word with her."

"She said that you don't like barren women."

"Who said you were barren?"

"I have not yet conceived, have I? How many months is it since . . . ?"

"I am not thinking about children, dear," he said, squeezing her and pulling her into his chest.

"It would be nice to give you a son."

"What has brought this on? Are you in the mood to compete?"

"A man needs an heir though," she said pensively.

"To need an heir you have to be dead first, and I am alive. I am going nowhere," he said, holding her hand and stroking her palm suggestively.

"It was a very nice party. It made me feel special."

"One day I will take you to England. I want you to see Cambridge and meet my friend Damon Villeneuve. We will stay in luxury hotels and enjoy the best of everything."

"It all sounds fantastic, but how will you pay for it?"

"There you are, worrying again."

"I am sorry."

"A good woman checks the nuts and bolts."

Bat kept thinking that everything he wanted was in his house that night. It felt as complete as a fortress, a moated castle. Outside, the guard kept an eye on the night. In one room, his sister and her husband slept. In another, his brother and his exploding dreams. In the master bedroom, he lay next to Babit, feeling her hot skin as she slept. The room itself was cool, the smell of wildflowers stealing in with the wind. Two colonial administrators had slept here. Two white kings; top members of the elite, as the Saudi prince would have put it; two brothers, in other words. The brotherhood of veiled threats, blackmail, brutal arm-twisting, humiliation and guilt? Or something more subtle? He himself felt like royalty of sorts. Kingship had become democratized by money and power. Soldiers and the elite were the new royalty, with new rituals and hierarchies. Mimicking the princes of old by stabbing, poisoning, and burning each other in a quest for a little more power and money and prestige. The lucky losers went into exile, the unlucky ones died. I have no intention of going into exile. I want to die right here in this country but in due course. I want dictators to come and go, leaving me behind to run new ministries. My friend Villeneuve has only recently had his own coronation. He is now a Member of Parliament in the House of Commons. I am happy for him. The Conservative MP he replaced was found dead in his flat with a garbage bag over his head, his stiff bluish dick in his hand, a pornographic movie in the video deck, pornographic magazines strewn around his feet like autumn leaves. Royalty, eh?

THE SAUDIS WERE as good as their word. They started delivering construction equipment, large aggressive machines which tore up the earth to make room for military barracks and installations. By now Bat knew that the Ministry of Power had been used to divert resources from other ministries for military purposes. The leeway the Saudis enjoyed was immense. Was this the beginning of the prince's island-buying spree? Were the islands going to be used for military purposes? Nobody seemed to have the answers. The situation was made hazier by rumours that Amin had given the green light for the demolition of the king's palace, which would be replaced by the biggest military barracks in the country, with mosques, playgrounds, swimming pools and gigantic hangars to house MiG 200 fighter-bombers.

It was said that he wanted the grand project finished in time to mark ten years since his defeat of the king's forces in 1966. There were rumours of impending civil unrest among southerners if he dared go through with the plans. There were threats to poison food and water used by the military and to flood their barracks with dysentery and diarrhoea. The country was awash with fictions and fabrications, with both opponents and proponents chopping up scanty fact and liberally mingling it with fantasy.

The feverish rivalry between the Saudi princes was bound to surface and bear consequences locally. Trouble took an indirect route. One day at a state banquet Robert Ashes called General Bazooka aside and confronted him with the fact that money had changed hands before the elder prince had been awarded the contract. The news hit the General like a scalding gust of foul wind. The fact that it was his arch-enemy who broke the news to him made him mad. Is there no limit to the power this bastard wields?

Since taking over the Anti-Smuggling Unit, Robert Ashes' power had multiplied tenfold: he now also investigated corruption, whatever that was. What if he told the Marshal about all the money? Was the man trying to blackmail or threaten him? Or was he just flaunting his powers, rubbing it in? More troubling was the fact that he had failed to plant spies in this snake's camp. How long would this imbalance of power remain unaddressed? Why weren't other disgruntled generals taking action against this reptile?

Within a very short time Robert Ashes had become the Marshal's darling confidant. General Bazooka had hoped that the relationship would cool down after a year or so, but it was just gaining momentum. Ashes had added the role of court jester to his repertoire. He cracked jokes and played pranks nobody would get away with. He made generals unwittingly sit on balloons which made prolonged farting noises at big functions or meetings of the Defence Council, which he dared call the Farting Council. The Marshal loved it.

One day he drove to a state banquet in a dirty lorry which carried four Englishmen dressed as eighteenth-century nobles, complete with white wigs, powdered faces and knickerbockers. The Marshal laughed loud and long as the clowns held a beer-drinking and beef-eating competition. When it was discovered that the clowns had eaten pork instead of halal meat, the Muslim generals were scandalized and wanted to use the case to get rid of Ashes. But the cocaine-snorting, whisky-swilling Marshal only made Ashes apologize, and the matter was forgotten.

Another time Ashes brought three white nuns dressed as Kakwa traditional dancers. They wore flamboyant headgear, skin loincloths, beads and amulets, and carried spears and bull-horns. They leaped and swayed clumsily while the scandalized audience clapped and whispered. A large bathtub was brought and they held a mud-wrestling contest. Afterwards the Marshal found out that the women were not nuns but the wives of Copper Motors officials. He loved Ashes' creativity and improvisation.

On another occasion Ashes came wearing a gorilla suit with axe teeth and red lips. The audience froze, expecting Amin to take grave offence. The gorilla hopped about snatching hats from the heads of appalled generals. Amin clapped loudest. Some generals suspected that the Marshal had ordered the hat-snatching just to humiliate and unsettle them. Maybe they were the gorillas. In a world of shifting loyalties and acute uncertainty, Robert Ashes seemed to be the only person above it all, if you disregarded Dr. Ali, who alternated as God or Satan and came and went as he pleased. He could do no wrong. He was a loaded gun which could go off in anybody's face. To cap it all, the Marshal had promoted Robert Ashes to the rank of colonel in the Uganda army, as a reward for his tireless efforts to stamp out the cancer of coffee-smuggling. This, General Bazooka thought bitterly, at a time when the cancer was grinding to its climax. And why was he not promoted for putting down the most recent rebellion in the army?

Up to this moment General Bazooka had feared only one man: the Marshal. Now he discovered that he also feared Colonel

Robert Ashes. How long would it take before this reptile got promoted to general? And how much more dangerous would he become?

"General, I am thinking about investigating this affair properly," Ashes said, grinning, savouring the fact that he had made the word "general" sound like it meant "pus." He lit his Cuban cigar and pulled a large volume of smoke into his lungs. "Uganda cannot afford to be in the bad books of the Saudi royal family. Those people can topple this government in the blink of an eye."

General Bazooka overlooked the insult and started panicking. He really did not know what to do. He thought about begging Ashes for time, for mercy, for any scrap of benevolence out of desperation. "Take it easy, Colonel. It is nothing serious," he said, mustering up his courage.

"Marshal Amin will decide what is serious and what is not, General."

By now General Bazooka was sure that there was a spy in his ministry, just like he planted spies in other ministries. He was determined to take swift action. With the spy, or spies, gone, he knew that Ashes would be stalled.

"Enjoy the party, General," Robert Ashes said enigmatically, and walked away.

General Bazooka became so angry that he almost had a fit. His lower lip quivered and his hands shook. He was losing touch. What had become of the Victoria woman? Nothing. He had sent her on a mission and instead of doing her job she had become pregnant. He could have set things right, but he had just ignored it. He had become soft and lost sight of his priorities. Perhaps that was why he had lost his beautiful islands and crocodiles and the command of the prestigious Anti-Smuggling Unit. Perhaps the Marshal saw that he was no longer as sharp as before and had decided to teach him a lesson and send him a big warning. This had to end. Now. He had to nip it in the bud. He had to show that he was still the best commander, or one of the best commanders, in the country.

AT A FEW MINUTES PAST FOUR that afternoon, Bat got a
phone call summoning him to the Nile Perch Hotel. It was not
unusual to be in the middle of something important and then be
called away. On his cynical days Bat said that he was nothing
more than a messenger boy for the General. It always put him in
a temper to be torn away from something, but he was learning to
live with it. He set everything aside, slid on his coat, straight-
ened his tie, and walked out. Cursing, he got into his car and
drove off. It was a fine day: clear, hot, windy, not a trace of
humidity in the air. The Parliament Building looked majestic, a
monument to power carved out of ivory. The soldiers at the gate
were statuesque, the smoke coming from their cigarettes adding
a grotesque touch to their figures. A string of Boomerangs swept
past, horns blaring, tailed by Stinger jeeps with swaying aerials.

Within minutes he was at his destination. He parked, locked,
and walked away from his car. He briefly thought about the
prince's Porsche 999. He could feel the vibrations that monster
engine had given him in the desert. He walked quickly, hardly
noticing the soldiers lying about in the grass, weapons held idly,
now benign as sticks. Did this sort of boredom breed the killer
instinct and fire up the explosions? The soldiers looked at him
with supreme indifference. He was just another suit, another
boss to many people in a certain office or factory brown-nosing
with a general or colonel or somebody else of real importance. Nothing showed on the faces of the soldiers, which
looked dead, buried in the depths where no man, except their
commanders, could reach them. They seemed untouched by
love, hate, passion, moved only by the order to act.

He entered the hotel lobby, which was empty and airy,
making it look like any other hotel during the off-season. He
relaxed, remembering the wonderful hotel he had slept in in
Saudi Arabia, with its air-conditioner, Jacuzzi, huge rooms,
obsequious room attendants and twenty-four-hour room ser-

vice. As he was beginning to wonder where the hotel staff were, in an instant four soldiers in combat uniform, wearing helmets covered with jungle webbing, surrounded him. They twisted his arms behind his back, forced his head down, and frog-marched him toward the guest rooms. He was in such shock that he did not say a word. If he had seen such frightening faces before, it had been in his dreams. The time between his last moments of freedom and his present state had lasted barely over a minute. He was thrown in a very dark room. They tore the clothes off his back like hyenas ripping a kill's coat. They left him in his underwear. Bad sign. Stabbed, shot, strangled in his underwear was common news. They marched out of the room without saying a word.

He stretched out his hands and felt his way around the empty room. An alarmingly musty smell was coming from somewhere. The windows had been blackened out with layers of cloth held up by tight wire mesh. The room was not soundproof, and he could hear army boots hammering the floor, army vehicles being parked outside, and army men barking orders in chilling harsh voices. He sat down on the floor, back against the wall, and tried not to think. His own pain he could deal with well: the athletic spirit was still in him. It was the pain his condition was going to cause others—Babit, his family, her family, his friends—that sat on his chest like a sack of rotting potatoes. What was Babit going to do? Wait and wait, become desperate? In a land where anything was possible, imagining the worst scenario was the best antidote against optimism and the unnecessary pain it brought. Who was going to inform whom? Had somebody seen him? Of course. Would he or she risk talking? That was the question. Was this going to be passed off as just another disappearance? What would his staff do? He realized how little he personally knew them. He heard very loud steps. They reverberated in his chest, kicked off a cold sweat as they hammered past the door. Where was General Bazooka? When was he going to show his face?

Late in the evening the door was flung open. Bat was shaken

by a scalding rush of fear. Soldiers entered, lifted him off the
floor, blindfolded him and, twisting his arms behind his back,
led him out. He felt his stomach fall to below his knees. Outside,
the cold wind smacked his skin. He imagined the city around
him eating, drinking, cowering in self-preserving indifference. A
cold shiver of futility went down his back. They threw him in a
Stinger and drove off. He could feel the vehicle going round and
round, charging up hills and rushing down valleys. The city had
long since become a catacomb, swallowing its people while
keeping a straight face. Nakasero and Naguru hills housed notorious detention centres. Police stations had also become infected
with the killers' bug. People were kept there incommunicado
while relatives went crazy searching the more well-known detention centres.

At last, the circuitous journey ended. They drove through a
gate: he could hear the guards barking, growling, and the gate
banging to a close. The vehicle then dipped and braked. They
pulled him out and marched him up a flight of stairs, then down
some corridors. They dumped him in an underground storage
space, freed his hands, ripped the cloth off his face, and switched
on the light. It was a large room with a single spring bed, a finger-
thin mattress, a torn blanket and a basin. The window was shoe-
box small and looked out onto the yard. He could see lights
winking, beckoning from far away. So they were not going to kill
him tonight. He sighed. He sat on the bed and tried to think.
Was this about work? Did the General want him to leave, now
that the ministry had been cleaned up? Maybe the Saudi prince
had struck as he had threatened. Uganda was a runaway, slave to
neither the slide-rule nor the crystal ball. Patience worked better than empty speculation.

Up till now there had been a thrill to living, each day a mystery, a package full of anticipation. The sting of guilt had intensified the thrill. Now that they had caught up with him, he felt
calm and the calm decapitated his temper. Uganda was a land of
guilt, where sons were sometimes held accountable for the sins
of their fathers and grandfathers. Guilt was not altogether nega-

tive. Admitting it could help you work out a plan of survival. Right now innocence was the foe. It tempted you down the slippery road of sentimentality and self-pity, a lethal combination at the best of times. By thinking that he was paying for his sins, Bat found the strength to go on. After all, his punishers were not in any moral position to judge him. By taking his punishment like the guilty man he was, he was giving pain its proper place in the scheme of things, and with his burden lightened, his inner strength increased or remaining level. He felt abandoned, like many other Ugandans, left to fight for his life all alone. He wasn't the first; neither would he be the last. He had no personal regrets. He did not wish to flee the country. He only wanted to get out of detention with as little damage as possible.

Contrary to expectation, he slept. In the morning a soldier opened the door and ordered him to take up his basin. Was he going to be forced to breakfast on his faeces? On the turd that now swam in his urine? He could of course empty the basin on the soldier, get kicked and rifle-butted to a pulp, and dangle on the lip of his own grave. But he marched out of the room, his evidence of mortality carried out in front of him like some holy sacrifice.

On the way he saw other prisoners, some dressed, some in different stages of undress. Some looked fat, some skinny, bones glaring. Some were injured, limping, swollen, bruised; some looked scratch-free like presidential Boomerangs. They were all joined together by the sounds of silence, water splashing, the wheezing, the sneezing, the coughing.

After disposing of the faeces in the latrines and washing up in the common bathrooms, he was led back to his room. He looked out the window and could see part of a compound, a concrete wall and leaves of a leafy tree. Beyond was part of a lane, chalky buildings, movement. The familiarity of it struck him. It dawned on him that he was in the basement of the Parliament Building, a mere hundred metres from his office! Is this a joke? he asked himself.

The building had a long history of detention and misuse.

Amin's predecessor, Obote, had his offices here, security agencies on floors above and below him. Political detainees were held here, and he could listen in as his boys worked over his favourite prisoners. On the steps of this building, somebody shot him in the jaw, but the grenade thrown to finish him off did not explode. In the turbulent sixties, four cabinet ministers were held here. The main difference between then and now was that prisoners were more likely now to receive a speedy death. Amin did not like wasting the taxpayers' money on feeding people destined to die.

For detention purposes the building was perfect: it was big, impregnable, communications-friendly. Prisoners could look out, catch glimpses of what they were missing, till they gave in or went nuts. It occurred to Bat that the Parliament was never free of the dirty hand of corruption, right from the time of empire till now when it ostensibly served as the clearing-house of inequity and injustice. Its workings had deepened Bat's cynicism and his conviction to stay out of politics. Now he was imprisoned in its very bowels.

At the end of the day he received a prison uniform: a coarse white cotton shirt and shorts. Also, a pair of sapatu, thin bathroom sandals. Routine set in: Thin porridge for breakfast. Posho and beans on an aluminium plate for lunch and supper. Time started to sit on him, crushing him, like the ass of a hippo, he thought.

THE NEWS of Bat's disappearance did not break; it just seeped drop by drop into the consciousness of those concerned. Babit felt it as the sundering of a now familiar routine. They used to wake up each morning at six. She was usually the first. She would greet him, remove his hands from her body and go to the bathroom. He would roll off the bed, draw the curtains, stand at the window to see what kind of morning it was. He hated rainy mornings because of the mud. He didn't want his XJ10 bespattered. He would stand there yawning while she prepared his bath. She insisted on scrubbing his back, launching him into a new day with firm fingers. While he completed his bath, she would go see to breakfast. She wanted to make sure that the cook had boiled four green bananas in salt water, with a tomato, to the right softness. She would see to the tea, the boiled egg, the greens. By the time she was ready, she would hear him calling her to check if he looked good, if the tie was straight, if it matched the shirt and the shoes. She would give her approval and announce breakfast. The bananas would arrive on a plate swimming in meat soup. She would sit opposite him and watch him eat, drinking a cup of tea to warm her stomach.

On his feet again, he would thank her, fuss her hair as he left the table and head for the bedroom. He would take his briefcase to the garage and park the XJ10 in front of the house. She would stand in the doorway, dressing gown wrapped round her, hair fanning out, and see him off. The flamboyance of the car worried her sometimes. Didn't it draw too much attention, too much envy?

The rest of the day was hers to do with as she liked, freed like a parish priest after the bishop's visit. She would bathe, do her hair, and prepare herself for the day. She would breakfast, note things to buy, clothes to be washed, surfaces to be cleaned and polished. In the afternoons she sometimes went to town, visited friends, had a siesta or did some reading in preparation for a teaching course she wanted to take some time in the future.

They had recently agreed that on a day or two each week he would drive home for lunch. On that particular day everything was prepared early so that by midday the food was ready. She would put on her best clothes, jewellery, shoes, and wait for him, like a bride expecting her groom. The car's distinctive sound would fetch her to the door. She would see him rush in, tie loosened, the first two shirt buttons open. A quarter of an hour later they would sit down at table and eat. He would tell her jokes, stories about people who had showed up at work, how they spoke or behaved. If she had stories to tell, he would listen. If not, he would dominate the conversation, teasing, entertaining. Time often cut him short. She would see him off, exhaust heat from the car leaving a hot spot on her leg where it puffed at her, burning fuel lingering in her nose.

The afternoons were slow. There was so much time before he returned. They usually ate supper at ten. If by then he was not yet back, she would eat alone. This time when he did not show up, she expected to see him in the morning. She assumed that he got caught up, what with meetings with ministers and so many things to do. By midday the following day she was restless, wondering whether this was going to be the first of many strange and unfamiliar hours. She called his office again; he was not there. She called Mrs. Kalanda. Mrs. Kalanda contacted Bat's office and was told he was not there. She reported the case at the Central Police Station in Kampala. Babit contacted local police in Entebbe.

Nobody expected much from police nowadays. Corruption and impotence were rampant. Arrestees could be freed through army intervention. The justice system was groaning under gross interference from government. Judges had been killed, intimidated, pushed out of the system or the country, and others were afraid to pass sentence against elements of the security organizations. The missing people's desk had lists choked with names, all that was left of people nobody expected to see again. The officer in charge wrote down Bat's name and promised action.

Babit travelled to Kampala to join the Kalandas with little idea of what was happening. She needed the comfort of movement to reassure her that something was being done. In the city, she changed vehicles. She was dropped near her destination, among houses surrounded by wire fences and swallowed by thick walls of cypress. She walked right past the house, realized her mistake, doubled back, collected her thoughts, and knocked on the door.

Mrs. Kalanda did her best to be positive, hiding her confusion with heartfelt optimism. Babit had already started blaming herself for everything, echoing Victoria's accusations. She seemed to think that she had brought bad luck with her. Otherwise, how could he disappear so quickly after their union? Mrs. Kalanda told her to pull herself together, to get ready to fight and not fall apart so early in the game. This was a national catastrophe striking families everywhere, she said. But Babit wouldn't see it as anything but a curse: first a glimpse of heaven in the life she wanted; then this hell. Mrs. Kalanda let Babit exhaust herself. It would take much longer for sense to show itself in the young woman's troubled mind.

Mr. Kalanda found the two women struggling with what to do about the situation. He hardly knew what to say. They talked about informing Sister, then Bat's parents. They started listing everybody they knew who might know somebody in the security agencies. It had become clear that running round the city in a daze would not do. It was better to set the bloodhounds on the scent. Insiders were more likely to solve the problem. Few names, however, fell into the hat. And when contacted they cautioned against too much optimism; a familiar refrain to an old song.

Efforts to contact Sister failed. She had no phone. Babit volunteered to inform her in person. She was relieved to be on the road again, feeling the world whirl about her. Kabasanda was a small town, reminiscent of an outpost town, situated in a wedge of land between two big tarmac roads. It was a link in a chain of towns which fed the city with supplies.

As soon as she saw Babit, Sister knew that something was wrong. To make matters worse, Mafuta was away on business. She questioned Babit in detail, going over everything. The car had not been found, a worrying sign. Dealing with disappearances was like working in the dark. Sometimes details meant something, sometimes nothing. Why hadn't anybody at the office called, volunteered anonymous information?

As the gravity of the situation sank in deeper, Sister feared for her brother's life. It felt strange that she was privy to secrets Babit didn't know. She weighed what to reveal and what to keep to herself. The fact that she and her brother didn't see each other much made the gravity of the trust more poignant. She knew that she held the keys, some of the keys, to his freedom. The weight of this knowledge had a searing effect on her nerves.

On the day Bat told her about the deal money, she trembled, and it made her look at her husband in another light for some time. It happened at a time when things were going badly for her Mafuta, the former planner of fantasy towns. She could not help comparing, feeling somehow let down. But she had also soon realized that her brother was operating on another level, in a different hemisphere, in a world of absolute power. She had almost told Mafuta. Now she stood on the brink again, wanting to share the burden with Babit. It hurt almost physically to maintain the load of trust in such a dire situation. It seemed as if Babit should know, but what if it backfired? She would lose her brother's trust and incur Babit's displeasure. She decided to grit her teeth a little bit longer, drawing strength from remembering her confusion when she heard that her brother was coming back after his stay at Cambridge. Why was he coming back at a time when many intellectuals were leaving? she asked herself at the time. She had been of the opinion that it was better for him to get a job in Britain. But within two weeks of his return he had landed a terrific job. She remembered how surprised and elated she became. It helped her to hold on to his trust.

That night, however, Sister got a severe attack of cramps; it was as if the baby were forcing its way out. Her world seemed to be collapsing on the ruins of her brother's life. It was a harrowing night spent between states of mind, but the storm eventually passed.

In the morning Babit returned to the city. She hoped to find new developments. Unfortunately, there was no change in the situation. All leads were dead, oozing pessimism or euphemisms to cover inaction, failure. She fled to Entebbe, hoping to find solace in familiar surroundings.

The house felt strange. It lacked warmth, the casual reassurance of days gone by. The house staff seemed to be locked in a muddy inertia, as if awaiting their missing boss. They eyed her suspiciously, as though it was she who was keeping them in the dark. The lake was bereft of its consoling powers, the tireless waves a torment. She sat down on a rock, feet in the water, thoughts all over the sky. It was the wrong thing to do; she kept hallucinating about being swept away. She returned to the house. The cook had informed her that Victoria had called more than a dozen times in the past few days. She decided to pack quickly and flee. She paid the staff, just to make sure that they would stick around, and made ready to leave. Then the phone rang. It kicked off a gong in her chest. She snapped up the receiver.

"You are responsible for this. You are going to burn in hell for it," Victoria shouted at the other end.

"For what?" Babit shouted back.

"You have destroyed this house. It is your *kisirani*; disaster follows you around like a bad smell."

"I have the feeling that you engineered this just to punish him for throwing you out."

"I would never do that. He is the father of my baby, remember? I love him. It is you who needs to be put down."

"You will go first."

"It is barren women like you who deserve that. What have you got to show for yourselves?"

Babit suddenly felt weary; she was consumed by pain. She was no good at this. She had never learned to fight mean and dirty, and she always took the bait. The fact that two of her aunts were barren made her feel tremors of uncertainty, fear.

"Have you suffered a heart attack? Why do you not speak?" Victoria taunted.

"You are a sick, demented woman. I have no time to waste on you."

"Poor you. All my time is devoted to you. You are my project. I designed you, I implemented you. I am going to monitor and evaluate you to the end. If he stays away for a month, I am going to call for a month. If it is a year, I will be on your case for a year.

If he never returns, it will be you and me for the rest of your life. If I were you, I would leave for good."

"You will have to lie with your father before I go."

"He is dead," Victoria said in defeated tones.

Babit kept thinking that she was no good at this: "What do you expect from me? Flowers?"

"I will let you know in due time," a sober Victoria said.

Babit slammed the phone down and saw the cook looking at her. She was old enough to be her mother, and it looked as if she wanted to overstep the boundaries and proffer advice. They locked looks for one long moment, then Babit walked away feeling confused.

The trouble with living in posh areas was the lack of public transport. The nearest bus stop was two kilometres away. Babit reluctantly called a taxi. How long would the money stretch? She had been the one who refused a joint account, for fear that he might be testing her to see if she was after his money. He had offered to open an account for her, but she had stopped him. He will be back, she said to herself as the taxi drove away. Deep blue skies, green leaves, red flowers gripped her imagination.

Babit's arrival at her parents' home was an ordeal. The beaming faces, the glinting eyes that came to welcome her were to be slashed to ribbons with the news. She had fortified herself with the words of the Bible, but in the end she gave in and cried. Her father looked on, mouth open, perplexed. It struck him that if Bat had married his daughter she would be a potential widow. The family sat down and went over the details. The uncertainty seemed to temper all emotions, cautioning against extreme reactions, outbursts. They remembered the first day he came to visit, exuding the kind of class every parent wished on his or her children. They remembered the recent feast, the gifts from Arabia. They remembered the time he appeared on national television, seeing a dignitary off at the airport. Babit's father had talked it over with his friends. Television was only for those with status, power, and knowledge, something to say or show. He had felt a bit afraid, as if his future son-in-law had become too visible.

Two
In the Morgue

General Bazooka's favourite method of breaking the tension knotted inside him by paranoia, too much work, and the unending pressure of power and responsibility, was hosting orgies. This was the time when he indulged himself and did whatever came into his head. The house, a huge bungalow lighted like a burning ship, would be full of his friends, who would drink, smoke pot, gamble, fornicate and swear deep into the night. His favourite trick was to shoot beer bottles placed next to his friends, and, to perfect the skill, he practised assiduously every week. In the migratory season he often challenged them to shoot birds flying over his house for five hundred dollars per bird. He won most of the time because even if he was drunk, his aim was steady and his friends became reluctant to accept the challenges.

"Come on, Major," he would say playfully, knowing that nobody could refuse, at least not on two separate occasions, "what will you tell your grandchildren? This is the only occasion we get to spend money meaningfully, I can assure you."

"All right, General, we shoot two birds and only two and then resume our drinking," the victim would say to all-round approval and raucous laughter.

As always, they would get carried away as soon as they handled the gun, miss a lot and eventually a heap of dollar bills would pile up at the General's feet.

"I told you," General Bazooka would say, "the best man wins, I can assure you."

In the middle of the night, with every guest drunk or stoned, with nothing to aim at except the trees, the whole group would go outside and start shooting at the stars. There were often Russian roulette competitions, beer-drinking contests and duels fought out in bulletproof vests. The General loved holding beer in his cheeks and spraying his guests, especially his dates or pick-ups. At other times, they all pissed in the bathtub all night long, rolled the dice at the end of the party, and the loser would be made to strip and bathe in the piss. During those moments of wildness, with guns blazing, beer frothing, drugs smouldering, he would imagine somebody, a rival general, an officer from the Military Police, stepping in to interrupt the meeting. He always wondered how the encounter would end. Most probably in a fatal shoot-out.

"I am a prince," he always said when he became drunk. "I can do whatever I want, I can assure you. If I want somebody's eye, I pluck it. If I want somebody's arm, I harvest it, ha-ha-ha. It is what the princes of old used to do, ha-ha-ha." And the whole group would join in and cheer.

"This is what we fought for," a general or colonel would say.

"That was before that reptile came," a brigadier cut in one evening, shutting up every guest, all of them afraid that General Bazooka was going to erupt or reach for his gun.

"Forget about the reptile, Brigadier. When we are here, it does not exist, I can assure you."

"Long live Marshal Amin Dada."

There were times when General Bazooka drank and pissed and shat his pants. He would command his date to disrobe him and clean the mess. He would watch as the woman struggled not to show outward disgust, now and then firing his pistol and swearing. His bodyguards enjoyed the fuss and could be heard laughing in adjacent rooms.

For the orgies, the General had two houses in the suburbs. For decent parties, when he entertained normal guests, he went to his first wife's home. He had given her a mansion at Kasubi, a place famous for the tombs of the banned kings. Driving past the tombs in his fleet of Boomerangs, headed and tailed by Stingers with soldiers hanging precariously on the sides like fruit bats, gave him untold satisfaction. At such moments he felt linked to the old kings, whose centuries of absolute rule he had played a part in ending, first with the attack on the palace, then when Marshal Amin refused to reinstate the kingdoms. As he rolled by, he would think back to 1942 when the last king was crowned. This man with titles such as the Professor of Almighty Knowledge, the Father of All Twins, the Cook with All the Fire-wood, the Power of the Sun, the Conqueror, had fled when he, Colonel Bazooka, had attacked his palace. The Conqueror had been in exile when Marshal Amin, King of Africa, created the new line of kings and princes now in power. It felt sublime to be the man of the moment.

When the body of the Conqueror was brought back to Uganda for burial in 1973, he had been the officer in charge of security at the airport, at Namirembe Cathedral, at the burial site. It was as if the Marshal wanted the people who had begun the demolition of this institution to hammer the last nail in its coffin. He liked to think that his father would have enjoyed see-ing his son wielding so much power. Sleep well, old man, he would think, I hope there is a lot of booze where you are.

The only thing the General envied the old kings was the loy-alty of their subjects. However grotesquely they misused their power, however many people they killed, people still loved and obeyed them, ready to give their lives for them. He remembered the lines of mourners filing past the coffin, orderly tear-sodden kilometres peopled by men and women who would have braved the hottest sun or the heaviest rain just to have the chance to peek at their king for the last time. As a non-monarchist, the sight made him sick. More so, because now he knew that not many southerners would mourn the passing of Marshal Amin's regime; but then again, no one came to power in order to court a grand funeral procession. Power was there for more basic things, like a fleet of Boomerangs, money, the ability to hammer your word into law.

Through the tinted window of his car he saw civilians walking, cycling, hurrying to their destinations before the curfew set in. It was good not to be afraid of violating curfew laws as these men and women were. It seemed their world never changed: the old kings might as well have been lording it over these very same people; the new kings and princes were now having their turn. At one time he had been like them, caught in a static world devoid of power, shat on up to the eyeballs. Now he was doing the dumping on, and it felt good. At one time he was a victim, swaying to the whims and will of other men; now he was the one whom victims begged for mercy, the man they respected or feared, the man who had the option of treating them with utter contempt and getting away with it.

In the same vein, he had no respect for intellectuals; he had no respect for people paid to split hairs. That Bat was still alive was a miracle to him. How many times had he wanted to kill him? But each time his advisor, who believed that Bat was special, restrained him. Special, when he was a rabid dog? Talking to Robert Ashes? Rabid Dog had to be put down, if only to save the herd. As for the ministry, there was bound to be somebody else to run it. Rabid Dog had to go, Bazooka decided. He has made too much money too quickly, whereas it took me ages to get some decent cash in my pocket. I fought for this government; he didn't. Where would this government be without me? Down in the sewers. It is not fair. Why does the government still need men like him?

The cars started climbing to the crest of the hill. He could see the top of his wife's house beckoning, bragging, resisting the encroaching veils of the night because it stood at the very top.

From the front, one could see the city sprawled out at one's feet in a huge semicircle. From the back, distance-flattened forest and marshland took over up to the horizon. The hill was decked out in tall trees, fields, and grassy compounds. The owners of the houses along the way had been bought out or forced to move. These houses were now occupied by his bodyguards or very trusted friends. This was the place he loved most in the city. He loved hills in general. He never forgot that he had been born in a swamp and that Rabid Dog had been born in the embrace of a hill.

He emerged from the limo and swept the compound with his eyes. He loved the massive structure of the house, the huge windows, the large roof. He loved the brick-red walls and the brown tiles. The gigantic trees filled him with a vision of power greater than his. A thousand years old, they made him feel young, at the beginning of his life. At first, he had wanted to cut all the trees and use them for firewood, but his wife had told him that they were gods, visions of eternity. Now he loved them like extensions of himself.

Guests, faces upturned, teeth flashing, pressed forward to welcome him. It was as if they expected him to dish out miracles and turn drums of water into casks of gold. Among them he saw people who expected bigger things from him. These held back, waiting for his eye of recognition, his benediction. He shook hands, slapped backs, shared jokes. He walked among the dozens, feeling his robe touched, his body caressed, his spirit enlarging to embrace them all. Music was in the air. There was a drifting scent of beer and roast goat which made him feel rapaciously hungry. For the first time that week he felt happy, in his element.

His wife, tall, dark, erect, met him at the door. They exchanged greetings as if they had spent the whole week together. This meant that things were going well. She did not like his soldiers but had learned to put up with them, and they were extra-careful when she was in the vicinity. She had grown up around soldiers and her opinion of them was not high. For the same reason, she had refused a chauffeur-cum-bodyguard. She kept out of the limelight and only accompanied him to very special functions. She did her level best to keep family away from the madness of power. They had reached a mature understanding never to stand in each other's way. They said goodbye as if for the last time and welcomed each other back as if they had not been apart. She never pried into his business, preferring not to know what he got up to with his friends. From early on she had made it clear that she would not tolerate drunken excess. Her house was a home, not a bar. He had felt disappointed because he had wanted to enjoy some of the wildness with her, as a way of showing how high they had climbed; but she would have none of it. He had begged, cajoled, commanded. In vain. Being his first wife, the one who had seen him through poverty, the one he could talk to, the one he fully trusted, the mother of his favourite children, he let her have her way.

He had given her a big shop in Kampala where she sold clothes to rich officers' wives. Sometimes she dealt in foreign currency, selling dollars from a gunnysack with a girth like a rhino, hidden in the house.

She led him into the bedroom. He sat on the bed bouncing, suddenly playful. She sat on a chair leaning forward. They held hands in greeting, and he felt erotic pangs, because their love-making always began with holding hands. He sat back looking at her, admiring her, listening to her talk. For a moment he drifted back to the day he met her. In her plain dress, her bathroom sandals, her gap-toothed smile. The children interrupted the moment.

His eldest son, ten, tall, lean, brought him a glass of his favourite liquor. He drank the glass and accepted the boy's manly greetings. His daughter, twelve, fat, brownish, brought him a glass of millet beer, giggles and greetings. He always wondered where the gene that made her fat and light-skinned had come from. His wife's side obviously. Somebody, a grand-father probably, must have fooled around with southerners. He accepted both offerings calmly. His second son, eight, tall, dark, brought him a set of mud soldiers he had made and baked. He laughed and patted the boy on the back. He was in such a good mood that he looked at his wife and children tenderly. They were his world, he felt, what would remain after the madness of power had passed. He took out his wallet and gave each of his children a hundred-dollar bill, remembering that it was a fortune when he was growing up.

"Sweets, buy yourselves sweets," he said proudly, spreading his arms like somebody shooing away chickens.

"Spoil them, go on and spoil them."

"Yes, I will, because they are mine. And then finally I will recruit them into the army. You too, woman, I can assure you," he said, smiling at his wife.

"That will be the day, that will be the day," she said, bursting into laughter at the idea of wearing a uniform.

General Bazooka finally went outside to join the guests. There were groups sitting around pots of beer with sucking pipes in their mouths, and others drinking liquor from bottles. He visited each group, tasted the drinks, munched the roast goat and talked. He picked up a woman, went to the dance floor and opened the dance. Disco music was playing, heavy beats conducive to bumping and grinding. He jumped about and wiggled, preparing to go and hold court.

At the back of the house, under the shadow of a mighty oak, a table and two chairs had been set out. A bottle of liquor and two glasses stood on the table near a notepad and a battery of golden Parker pens, which were never used, as the General kept every agreement in his head. Two soldiers stood on guard out of earshot.

The General installed himself on his throne, listened to the thumping of the music on the other side of the house, smelled the night air and rubbed his hands together. He always looked forward to these sessions because they enabled him to stretch his imagination and play various roles and present different images to different people.

The first person he called was an old schoolmate. They had

been friends many years ago. They had washed cars, mowed grass, stolen mangoes and picked pockets together. The General used to envy the boy his stable home. He was one of the southerners he liked. The man was now a veterinary officer in the mountains of eastern Uganda. His son had got caught smuggling coffee across the lake. Robert Ashes' men had shot four of his comrades and beaten him badly on the way to custody. It was not the most pleasant set of circumstances for a reunion.

"How are you?" the General said neutrally.

"I am all right, sah," the man said timidly.

"Where have you been hiding all these years?" the General inquired, feeling curiosity welling up inside him.

"In the east, working hard, tending to cows and pigs, sah."

The General laughed and said, "Tending to cows and forgetting all about us."

"I knew that you were extremely busy and I could not pluck up the courage to disturb you, sah."

"A man needs his friends. It is a cold, mean world out there," he said complacently, almost amusedly, knowing that he could take care of himself in said world.

"You are right, sah."

The General looked at the man's clothes: a bad-fitting suit, a cheap shirt, cheap shoes. The man was developing a bald patch despite being so young. He lacked the gleam of well-being on his forehead; in fact, he looked as if he had not been paid for years. The large scuffed hands that used to steal mangoes, the sunken eyes, the clothes hanging sadly on his frame, made the General wonder what the man's wife looked like. Another sad-eyed case left behind by the revolution, he thought. He wanted to ask him where his parents were, but he decided to wait. He wanted to remind him of some of the escapades of their youth, but he did not want to bring him too close too quickly, at least not before knowing what he wanted from him.

"What can I do for you?"

"I have a very big problem, General. My son got himself in

big trouble. He joined a group of bad people and they tried to ferry coffee to Kenya," the man said, looking fixedly at the table.

"Smugglers! Smugglers!"

"I failed in my parental responsibility. I was too busy trying to make ends meet to keep track of what the boy was doing. Now he is in police custody. Who knows what the Anti-Smuggling Unit people will do to him? They might burn him as they have done others."

"Those people are sick, I can assure you," the General said, thinking about his days as king of the lake. He remembered seeing all those beautiful little islands from his helicopter and feeling that he owned each and every one of them. He remembered thinking that he owned all the fishes, the crocodiles, the tadpoles swimming in the lake. He remembered thinking that he owned the air everybody on the lake breathed. Now it was all gone. Stripped from him in front of his mother. He kept quiet for such a long time that the man thought he had fallen asleep. He coughed a few times in a bid to remind him of his presence.

"You are my last hope, General."

"What do you expect me to do?" he asked, looking at the stars. The Southern Cross constellation always reminded him of his favourite islands. The water used to look that icy at times.

"I am sure that if you ordered a soldier to move, he would move without question, sah, General."

The General kept quiet for a long time. He took a swig from his glass. Why should he help this man? Was his son the only one with the threat of death hanging over his head? "Do you realize what you are asking me to do? Do you want me to break the law? And interfere in the affairs of another ministry?"

"Sah, if my cow fell in a pit, I would call friends with ropes and try to pull it out. I would lower myself in and do what I could. In this case I just can't."

"Well said, cowboy," laughed the General. Here was his chance to fuck Ashes. This he would do for fun. It was high time his men did something dramatic. It would wake them up; maybe even whet their appetite for something stiffer. "I don't condone smuggling. It is treason. It is punishable by death. However, I make an exception. I will free the boy. Warn him never to sin again. Next time, it will be the bullet. A bazooka shell. There would be nothing left to bury, I can assure you."

"I am in your debt, General," the man said, kneeling down and placing his palms on the table, face upturned as if for a slap or a string of spittle. Peasants always greeted the king prostrate; kneeling was not a bad substitute for a prince.

"Get up and go and enjoy the party. You owe me nothing. I don't have time to collect debts."

"I will send you a bull, General. You deserve a bull, a very big bull, sah."

Trembling with relief, the man almost fell over as he tried to rise and walk away.

The second man to be called was a tribesman. The mothers of the two men had been friends. Twice before, the General had helped this man. The problem was that he had too many troubles, too many debts. He had helped him to get a business, which had run aground. He had bought him cows on credit, but the money never got repaid, and he had to force the bank to cancel the loan at gunpoint.

"I am not worthy to be in your presence, General. Tolerating me is a sign of your magnanimity."

"You are right. Twice I used my good offices to help you, all in vain. What do you want now?" he roared, and banged the table.

"I need help," the man said, trembling.

"You need locking up and learning some discipline. Do you know how much a common soldier makes a month? No, you don't. Very little. My father was a soldier. He got nothing from the service except a drinking habit. I had to organize his funeral and pay off his debts. Such a humiliation after decades of selfless service. Do you expect me to pay your drinking debts for you? The best thing I can do is to organize your funeral, I assure you."

"I am sorry, General. I just need another chance."

"You don't have any sense. Now go. I don't want to see you again."

Next the colonel in charge of his security, his chief advisor, came. They had known each other for a long time, and he was the man behind the colonel's promotion. The General saw more of this man than he did his own family. He liked the colonel's advice because it was always sound, even if it was repugnant at times. He was a university graduate, the only learned man close to him. He was the one who handled the most sensitive assignments.

"What a fetid asshole!" the General complained lightheartedly as his last visitor disappeared.

"Some people are not worth anybody's time, General," the colonel said, smiling. He knew that the General was in a good mood. It was a good omen.

"Are you having a good time yourself?"

"Of course. There is a lot of booze, meat and music. What more does a man want?"

"Getting down to business, Colonel. I still want to kill Bat. The quicker the better," the General said, looking very businesslike.

"We still don't know the whole story, General."

"Since when does one need to know the whole fucking story in order to act? You see a traitor, you hit him. That is our way."

"Rabid Dog knows a lot about the ministry. We need him. He is our tool. We can punish him, but killing him would be a waste. Ashes is bluffing. If we kill this man, that reptile wins. Remember he tried to threaten you with investigation. Why didn't he do it if he knew so much? He is winding you up. Don't fall into his cheap traps."

"Rabid Dog is a thief. I don't even know why we hired him in the first place, I can assure you."

"It was because he is brilliant."

"On whose side are you, Colonel?"

"Ours, of course."

"Rabid Dog is the worst example of a southerner. He got everything for nothing. Nothing. He just walked in from Britain and got this wonderful job. What hardship has he ever undergone? Wiping his ass, I guess," he said morosely, maliciously. He signalled a soldier to bring him a joint. His wife would complain about it, but he could live with that. He needed the topper.

"Give him some more time while we watch the developments, General," the colonel said, aware that his boss would relent. It was a personal matter, after all, not treason, not smuggling, not plotting a coup. General Bazooka was not the only one; many others had grudges like this one to settle, and some settled them at the cost of national interest. After all, the Marshal was the biggest grudge-settler of them all. The colonel was at times surprised by how petty some of these top leaders were, how insecure they felt because of their lack of education. Many suspected that their underlings despised them and it hurt, because they were the rulers, exposing their inefficiency day by day. He intervened whenever he could; sometimes it worked; sometimes it didn't. This time he had hope. He felt very good whenever he could get somebody off because he had studied law, although he was involved more in breaking it than upholding it.

"I won't give him forever, I can assure you, Colonel," the General said aggressively, the strain of holding back visible in his dilated eyes and exaggerated gestures.

"Reptile is the real trouble-causer as far as I am concerned."

"I am auctioning him tonight. Do you hear me, Colonel? Any man who brings me his dick gets ten thousand dollars. American. Cash. Day or night. Rain or shine. Do you hear me? Ten thousand. Plus promotion. I want him that badly, I can assure you."

"You can rely on me, General," the colonel said stiffly, wondering where the escalation of hostilities would lead. He had told his boss time and again to ignore Reptile most of the time, not to feel unnecessarily provoked, to accept that he was part and parcel of the power structure, without much success.

"Bomb his house. Ambush him. Cut out his tongue, anything.

I want to shake the hand of the man who will rid me of this scourge and give me back my peace of mind. Everywhere I look I see that snake, crawling, slithering, smearing everything with slime. Bring me its head and I will make you a cabinet minister, man of the books. This snake wants to investigate me! Who is investigating it? What does it want from me? Tell me, what does that snake want from me?"

"He is bluffing."

"Well, he won't bluff when he is dead. I can assure you."

"True." The colonel wondered how many times he got to hear the words "I can assure you" in a day. If only each assurance delivered!

"Now tell me, who do you think poses the biggest threat after Ashes?"

"The Vice President."

"How high do you rate his chances?"

"If he mobilises from other tribes, the non-Muslims, malcontents, he can stage a coup. He is that popular, that close to the soldiers, that anti-you and anti–Marshal Amin."

The General pulled hard on his joint. "The Marshal seems to think so too."

"Is he on the red list already?"

"He is nowhere. He is nothing. One grenade; one car crash is enough, I can assure you," said the General contemptuously.

"This government is expert at traffic control," the colonel joked. He liked this kind of talk, reading intelligence reports, knowing who was on the way up and who was speedily descending.

The General burst out laughing and said: "One more small business. A little rescue operation to warm your hands for the big task. Get the boy out before Reptile's men burn him."

"You mean the smuggler?"

"A greedy, brainless bastard who thought he could make easy money."

"No problem. We will get him out."

"Now let us go and get drunk. I am a happy man. Reptile stands on the auction block. What a prospect!"

A very costly one, thought the colonel, biting his lower lip. He liked action and enjoyed to the full being the General's brain, planning, advising, organizing, delegating authority to the men on the ground who carried out the General's will. He knew that Amin and his regime would not last; unlike most henchmen, he had his certificates; he could go anywhere and begin anew.

The General never discussed details with the colonel. He had discovered that the more leeway you gave a man, the harder he worked trying to please you. The system had worked remarkably well. General Bazooka had in fact copied it from the Marshal.

General Bazooka was in the mood for his gun pranks, but at the same time he did not want to quarrel with his wife in front of his men. He would have wanted his eldest son to shoot a few glasses, but the boy's mother would raise so much hell that it would not be worth the bother. Those things the boy would have to learn later in the company of men. What does she teach the children? What do they learn at school? It is definitely not to shoot a piece of chalk out of a teacher's hand or a pen from behind his ear or a cigarette from his mouth. It struck him that his children might have a different future, a more sedate life. His wife and mother seemed to prefer that to the rigours of army life. But he did not want a teacher for a son, a nurse for a daughter. Except if they were army teachers and nurses. I will look into that, he thought.

He looked forward to a long hot night. A groany, sweaty, satisfactory affair. He liked tilling familiar ground after weeks away. The waiting created a change, a razor edge. It made the familiar sex sounds rendered in his mother tongue, laced with his earliest memories of the act, all the more fulfilling. They would bounce, roll, turn and milk each other like donkeys. Then he would lie in her arms, a delicacy uneroded by the years, watch the light going out of her eyes like receding stars, and feel reconnected to the past in sleep.

At daybreak he would rise, the past night an oasis in an encroaching desert, a lingering of fatigue in his veins, a bunch of memories in his pulsating head, a trace of sweet pain on his sex skin. He would rise out of it tentatively, a plant shooting out of a swamp, and climb into the new day, rejuvenated, invigorated. Ready for business as usual.

COLONEL ROBERT ASHES OFTEN THOUGHT of himself as an airborne bird, an eagle cruising, surveying its domains. His meteoric rise felt like a huge thermal thrust keeping him in the air with minimum effort. He had settled into the fast life. He enjoyed the banquets, the fleet of Boomerangs, the cameras, the sabre-rattling, the marriage, the wealth amidst poverty, the envy he generated and wore like an eagle's monstrous wings. Only in Africa, he continually said to himself, can a man be reborn this fully, this gloriously.

When he set out for Uganda on the trail of the elusive Irish bomber Williams, he knew that everything was on the line. It was the watershed in his frantic effort to enter Uganda, and at the same time it was like a death sentence. The cover of the delegation could get blown; somebody could cave in under pressure; they could be shot by trigger-happy soldiers; Amin could fail to take the bait. He remembered arriving in Kenya and thinking fleetingly that he had made a mistake and should have remained in Britain or gone back to South Africa. He remembered the sleepless nights in a Kenyan hotel while they waited for a plane. In those days he subsisted on whisky, cigars and biscuits, the food too unpalatable to swallow. He remembered stepping on the plane with the words of his handler ringing in his ears: "You are on your own. If caught, we will deny any knowledge of you. Your head will probably end up in Amin's fridge, your balls on his breakfast fork."

He remembered the flight, the glorious scenes outside the window, the rolling mountains, the snaking rivers, the blinding greens of forests. He kept thinking about paradise. He also remembered Williams' Bombing of the Century, as the Irish

Republic Army called the mainland campaign. He remembered hearing the news of the arrest of the bombers, and stories about men thrown from speeding cars, men with teeth pulled during interrogations. Then rumours that Williams was in Uganda and the massive thudding of his heart. It was like being struck by electricity, the muscles burning and tearing with excitement. He remembered the hours of waiting before getting to hear whether he would be sent to Uganda or not. He never believed for once that a man as important as Williams could risk hiding in Uganda; but what did he care? It was the break he needed. In those days there was fear that the IRA would export the campaign and start bombing British embassies abroad, but he did not believe it. The IRA knew what they wanted and how to get it. What did he care?

When he stepped on Ugandan soil, he had the feeling that he had done it before in some hazy past. He was not at all intimidated by the soldiers. He found the statues of Amin ridiculous and ugly. One of the things he remembered most clearly was the vicious urge to supplant Copper Motors officials as the top business force and its head as the top white man in the country.

A year later he heard that the famous astrologer had prophesied his coming messiah-style. The news was unbelievable to him because he did not believe in astrology. He believed in hard work and a lucky break or two, but not in omens read from the sky or from the livers of bulls. He had come across witchcraft in the past in southern and northern Africa, but he never paid it much attention. He was not going to begin now. He just made it a point to avoid the astrologer, which was easy since he was so reclusive; and he neither liked nor hated him.

According to Ashes, Amin welcomed him with open arms because, like many tyrants, he was lonely amidst a crowd of worshippers, sycophants, wives. He needed a confidant, somebody of his level, a mirror to make the enchanted nebulous world he inhabited real, a thorn to prick him with the occasional pang of inadequacy he needed to spur him on. His knowledge of the

West and his ability to analyse it was just a bonus. In fact, it wasn't as if there was a shortage of learned men who could feed Amin the information he needed. It was just that they could not get away from their high-couched language, the intricacies of their trade. They ended up confusing the Marshal, making him change plans he had approved, thus losing face. Ashes special-ized in chewing cud for the Marshal; and he was ready to fulfil his role as cattle prod, keeping the generals on tenterhooks.

Robert Ashes was given the job of turning Amin's bodyguard, the Eunuchs, into a specialized unit. The fact that they were all Kakwas and Nubians lessened the internal divisions. They knew that their life depended on Amin's staying alive. Ashes found many of them dull, violent, predictable, but those were the qualities needed. All he did was drill them harder, teach them the necessary tactics, and let them loose.

Amin put them under the command of Major Ozi, increased their salary, improved their food and told them they were above all army officers and security agents. Both Amin and Ashes knew about the atrocities committed by them—robbery, kidnapping—but they turned a blind eye. They felt that a bit of leeway would only make them more loyal to their president. Ashes enjoyed stories of conflicts between the State Research Bureau and the Eunuchs. The Eunuchs liked to provoke the Bureau by driving them out of bars and night-clubs and taking their women. Ashes felt that divisions between the security agencies were always good. No conspiracy possible. Everybody on their toes.

Ashes was wearing it well. He loved to tease the generals and their men. They could hate him all they wanted but could not kill him, not without killing Amin first. He had the odd night-mare of waking up amidst a successful coup and finding Amin swinging from a tree by his balls. It always ended with a gun in his mouth. But he loved danger; he thrived on it. He had his own personal army now, and he liked to flaunt his status as a warlord. He had this thing with General Fart, as he called Bazooka in private. He knew that the man was insecure about his position, his future. He was cocksure that the man was infected with the vertigo of those who rose to prominence too early in life. He enjoyed teasing him, making him feel as if Amin was about to skewer his balls and make him eat them for breakfast. He could have made him beg over that Saudi deal; the rival prince had given him all the details. General Fart's head could have rolled. But he had not liked the Saudi prince, a shapeless, unpleasant mass of a man. Nobody talked to him as if he were a messenger boy and got what he wanted.

Luckily for General Fart, at the time, Ashes had been busy putting the finishing moves on the deal which would have earned him millions. He had made a deal with Alan Witherthrush, known as the Big Bossman to everybody, who was the head of Copper Motors, to import spares for military helicopters, Stinger jeeps, Leyland buses and lorries. He was bound to cream off a clean ten million dollars through inflation of prices and commissions. Amin had approved the deal, and the spares were already on the way. According to plan, his millions should already have been paid into his account. When he confronted Bossman about it, he was told to wait. He waited because he wanted to handle the affair carefully, without the Marshal knowing about it. But when nothing changed, he realized that Big Bossman had cheated him.

The head of Copper Motors deeply resented Robert Ashes' interference in the affairs of his company because Ashes did not have any sense of history, any respect for what Witherthrush had been through to keep it going. Copper Motors had begun as a branch of a multinational company that mined copper and cobalt in Kilembe, in the South-western Region, and was further involved in small-scale manufacturing. The copper plant and the manufacturing divisions had folded soon after Amin came to power. The foreign employees had cleared out. Big Bossman had found himself in a precarious situation: he could leave and work in Kenya or South Africa, or take a gamble and rebuild the flagging motor division. He decided to stay; he reorganized; he hired and fired; he blackmailed and curried favour. With great success. By 1973 he was the sole importer of spare parts for the whole country. Competitors came and went, leaving him stronger. Barclays Bank remained his faithful banker, switching money, transferring bribes, offering loans, maintaining the mechanism which kept the company solvent.

The first meeting between Bossman and Ashes had been acrimonious.

"I want a cut of the action," Ashes dourly demanded. "It is protection money. I want shares, a partnership."

"You are joking," Big Bossman said, laughing.

"We will see," Ashes said in parting.

Ashes swallowed the insult, went home and decided to contact the Bossman's deputy. He threatened to link him with guerrillas if he did not comply. The man refused. Ashes hanged him, making it look like a suicide. The next time he held talks with the Bossman, the latter obliged. Ashes was made a partner. His contribution to the mega-deal had been to make Amin approve and finance the importation of the biggest haul of spares in years.

At that time, Bossman realized that Ashes wanted to take over everything. It was clear that his dream was ending. He and his wife decided to exit with a big bang. Friends at Barclays Uganda and Barclays Britain transferred Ashes' cut not to his account, but to a secret numbered account in the Cayman Islands. At about the same time, the Bossmans sent their only son abroad and made him sole beneficiary of their fortune. Just in case. Mrs. Bossman was supposed to follow a fortnight later. Her husband would leave last. They had planned to travel separately so as not to arouse suspicion.

But Ashes knew very well that the only way to make Bossman tell him the truth was to go for the softest target: his wife. It was also insurance in case Bossman managed to get away or decided to tell Amin what was going on. Ashes sent his men to abduct the woman. They arrived in Euphoria 707s, surrounded the compound, cut the phone, stormed the house, gagged her, threw her in the boot and drove off. At their rendezvous they transferred her into a Shark helicopter which took her to Ashes' island, the base of the Anti-Smuggling Unit.

The island was five kilometres long and three kilometres wide at its widest. It was full of chunky, imposing rocks, extremely tall grey-trunked trees filled with the song of yellow-legged parrots and other birds. From the distance, it looked like a green, grey-stemmed blur, dovetailed by rocks. There were houses, gun emplacements, speedboats, and a massive bunker Ashes used as his headquarters. The island sat by itself in the water, battered by moody waves, combed by sharp-toothed winds. It conjured up images of enchantment, freedom, glorious isolation, especially when viewed from a distance on a bright sun-drenched day.

Kate Witherthrush was a sun-burned, long-haired woman in her early forties. She had a seductive figure and a pleasant face which often belied her inner strength. She had spent the last ten years in Uganda, staying when others gave up and left, hell-bent on accumulating a big fortune. Her family had at one time had money, but had lost it in the Second World War. She had met her husband in London, where he was holidaying. She had been waiting all her life for such a man, an adventurer, a charmer, a man ready to risk all and gain all. The last decade had been the happiest period in the couple's life.

She remembered the years as action-packed, often giddy, often calm, often unpredictable. There was always something happening, nights loaded with shooting, days calm as a sleeping baby, and vice versa. She had witnessed the fall of one government and the rise of another. She had witnessed lynchings, shoot-outs, beatings, burials, flamboyant weddings, wild Christmas celebrations lasting days, pleasure and pain see-sawing on an invisible, ever-changing pivot. She had been robbed five times, two at gunpoint. All by soldiers. Amidst all this they had their son, the icing on their cake of success which seemed to grow bigger and bigger. They had enjoyed so much success that at times they felt invincible, like gods walking among the uniformed scum and the people yearning for salvation from tyranny. They were in the unique position of trading with a tyrant, knowing that as they helped they did both good and bad. His capacity to oppress increased but at the same time the spares for the buses and lorries used by the populace were indispensable.

She was glad that her son was out of Ashes' reach, safe in an exclusive boarding school. She still appreciated the wit, the danger, the revenge, the intoxication involved in the deal. They had decided to fuck Ashes back after he had fucked them, undercut their position, endangered their lives, and killed their colleague. The fake suicide note had been an insult both to his memory and to them. They would not be around when Ashes appointed stooges to run Copper Motors. They would take the spirit of the company with them to the Caribbean where they had just bought a mansion, a yacht, and a piece of paradise.

Mrs. Bossman sat opposite Robert Ashes, hardly able to hide her loathing for him. It seemed to seep through her pores and spread like a gas. After the way they had treated her, transporting her like a sack of onions, she knew that lines were already drawn. She had to stand firm. Any show of weakness would be the ruin of everything. She knew by now that her life, and that of her husband, and the career of Ashes, were all in the balance. She just prayed and hoped that her husband would also stand firm and not cave in to the violence of this gangster.

From the dignified way she conducted herself, Robert Ashes knew that he would get absolutely nothing from her. The fact that her son was already secured and out of his reach said it all. He regretted that he had let the boy escape the country. Why had he been fooled by Big Bossman and waited? He realized that his pride, his feeling of infallibility, had cost him a great fortune. If he had been more paranoid, the boy would be here, and Mrs. Bossman would be singing.

He stood up, a Havana in his hand, walked about and asked the woman where his money was. When he introduced the ways he intended to treat her son on capture, she did not flinch. She saw through his lies and that infuriated him. He looked at her coldly, and at that moment both of them knew that one would have to kill the other in order to walk away. Ashes could not risk releasing her for the fear that she might talk. He kept thinking about Mau Mau women caught with guns under their robes. Two decades later, he could still see them, their immobile faces giving away nothing even after rigorous torture, dying with their secrets and ruining a perfect day, a week or month's campaign. His nightmare had caught up with him. He was after secrets, probably the most important in his whole life, which the witch didn't want to divulge.

"You don't know where my money is?" he said with his gloomy face looking odious.

"No, I don't."

"What can I say?" he said coldly, suppressing his ire, shrugging his massive shoulders. "Ten years of eating and fucking with the bugger and you don't know anything about the most important deal in his career!"

"No, I don't."

"I am not going to waste your time," he said looking outside, the effort of keeping calm almost causing him tears. "Guard, lock her up."

Ashes walked out and left the guards to lock the woman in the room they used for the detention and interrogation of smugglers. He wished she would shout, call him back, and confess.

In the meantime, Big Bossman became frantic. He reported the abduction of his wife to the State Research Bureau, who did nothing when they found out that it was the boss of the Anti-Smuggling Unit who had her. The same morning, Ashes visited Bossman at his offices on Kampala Road and asked him where his money was. Big Bossman sat behind a huge gleaming bureau with a black telephone and open paper files covering half of it. His large head was as red as ripe coffee berries and his hands were trembling. He was dressed in a grey suit with a blue tie, which he thought gave the impression that he was still in control. The fact that another Englishman, not a Ugandan general, was standing in his office, threatening to crush his dreams to a pulp, troubled him deeply although he did his best to appear calm.

"Be patient, will you? The papers are coming today or tomorrow. As soon as they are here, I will inform you immediately and you will know that I have been telling the truth all along."

"Your time is up, Alan, or Bossman or whatever they call you," Ashes declared, standing in front of him and fixing his morose bulldog eyes on him.

"I want my wife back," his adversary said, his voice almost breaking with emotion.

"She is an accessory to murder and fraud. I have information to show that you and your wife murdered your deputy and made it look like a suicide. There is also information linking you to guerrilla activity. Now, tell me where my money is, and I let both of you get out of the country never to return," Ashes said softly, menacingly.

"Give me time, but please don't hurt her," Bossman pleaded as he realized that things had slipped out of his control.

"I have not touched a hair on her head or groin," Ashes replied with distaste.

"Give me two days and your money will be here."

"Deal," Ashes said coldly, knowing that Bossman was lying to him.

As soon as Ashes left, Bossman contacted General MiG 300, another passionate hater of the man.

"Relax and leave everything to me. This is the easiest assignment you have ever given me," the man replied.

Bossman gave him one hundred thousand dollars in cash and promised him a big bonus after the mission.

"I am going to do whatever it takes, friend. You know me, when I say everything, I mean including sending a MiG 200 bomber. The plane is just one phone call away. It will strafe the island and a helicopter gunship will then land and fly her away. I have the dollars to bribe everybody concerned twice over."

Bossman was reassured. How desperately he wanted to hear

somebody call him a friend. MiG 300 never issued idle threats or bouncing promises. He had asked for two days. Bossman knew that Ashes would wait because time was all he had. He could not jeopardize his position by doing anything foolish. Two days and his wife would be out of the country.

Ashes, however, acted very swiftly and contrary to Bossman's expectations. Within hours of leaving Bossman's office, he accused him of colluding with Tanzania-based dissidents. Using fabricated evidence, he arrested him. By now Ashes could hardly control his rage. Ten million! Added to the fortune in Switzerland, he would have been thirty million to the good. He could not believe that Bossman had expected to get away with the swindle. In Amin's Uganda! People died for a pancake, a kilo of sugar, for nothing. But ten million dollars!

Big Bossman, still in his grey suit and blue tie and black Clarks, was flown to the island. It was not an enchanted view that greeted his arrival. The air felt too chilly, too loaded with pollen and the noise of parrots. The sight of his wife in a cage pumped him with confusion, impatience for rescue. He could see that she had given nothing away. He felt a massive jolt of relief. Soon MiG 300 would be here, tearing roofs off houses, cutting trees in half, sending the bastards packing. Within hours of rescue, they would be over the border; within days, they would be on a tropical island sipping rum punch.

Bossman had met his wife at a time when a man begins to doubt whether he will ever meet a soul mate. No white woman wanted to accompany him to Uganda. Many thought he was mad even to suggest it. They quaked when they heard of the killings. And Kate came and everything changed. He always prayed that they die would together, and be buried side by side. He could not see himself continuing without her, getting used to another person or spending his last days alone. Ashes might shake them but would not destroy them. The soldiers had put them in the same room, behind the same bars, and left. The Bossmans held, kissed, talked, cried and encouraged each other as the hours ticked away and birds sang, monkeys howled and other animals called. He forced her to eat, in case they had to run or walk long distances after the rescue. They now felt an intimacy only danger and hysteria can generate. Their lives lay scoured to the core. The night together fortified them; they sucked energy from each gesture, loading their souls for the rough ride to freedom.

Ashes appeared early the next morning. He entered the room, sat on a chair, a Havana in his mouth, a whisky in his hand. He looked tired, dishevelled, manic.

"Where is my money? I have given you a whole night to remember the details and put together a credible story."

Nothing was forthcoming from Mr. and Mrs. Bossman, as the Witherthrushes liked to be called in their days of power, except stubborn silence.

Ashes called the Pounder. The giant man came feeling with his free hand the weight of a metre-long pestle, smooth as an egg. The woman was held down and the man started to work on her feet. Two blows and they were gone. She fainted, frothed, and oozed all over the place. The exercise lasted barely four seconds; it was so fast that Bossman could hardly believe it had occurred. He hardly had time to swallow, cough and speak up. At that moment he knew that his world lay in ruins. Ashes wanted their lives and the money, if possible. He would get one, not both. In another four seconds the woman's arms were gone. Bossman soiled himself and let out a long tortured wail that would have chilled the blood of less hardened mortals. Ashes barely took notice.

By this time Bossman was kneeling on the ground, hitting his palms on the floor with uncontrolled grief. The speed of his descent from cocky British businessman to dejected, pathetic old man was blinding. He felt angry with himself for having underestimated his fellow Englishman. He had been too confident of the protection of the local British Embassy, who were among his customers; contacts in the British government in London; friendly generals in the Uganda army; his connections in the murky world of business; his reputation as a tough guy who not only faced down dictators but made lesser men cringe and do his will. It was all gone, reduced to straw in the wind by this odious man with the cigar and the large nose.

Ashes looked at his former conspirator reduced to a miserable wretch and drew no satisfaction from the sight. In future I will be more careful, less trusting, he thought angrily. Whoever I do business with, be it a Britisher, American or Greenlander, will have to earn my trust. I will follow them like a shadow. Nobody will have any benefit of the doubt. It struck Ashes that maybe the two had been counting on a rescue. It almost made him laugh. By whom? And how? Short of Amin, who was out of the country, intervening, he saw nobody with the balls to tackle him at all, least of all on home turf. At the end of it all, he realized that he did not care any more what his captives had or had not been planning or expecting.

He stood up, spat at Bossman, and left the room. At the door he turned round and said, "Maybe she will tell you where my money is."

Bossman was left in the cage with his wife, or what remained of her. He knew what was in store for him unless MiG 300 acted quickly. Where was he? Today was the day of the rescue. Where were the plane and the helicopter? Where had they been when these animals were killing his wife? He felt he owed it to her to survive and raise their son and avenge her death. As the hours seeped away and the place started to be oppressed by the stink of death and the roar of flies, he realized that they had made a serious miscalculation. They had assumed that Ashes would drop the case for fear that Amin would get wind of it. As boss of the sanctimonious Anti-Smuggling Unit, he could not afford to be implicated in swindling the government he was chosen to defend from corruption. It turned out that he was a man not afraid to take his chances. It was too late to regret chances of escape not taken. Suddenly, he knew that General MiG 300 was not coming. Nobody in his right senses could dare challenge Ashes' might in so frontal a manner. He let out a very loud cry of despair.

IN THE MEANTIME, Ashes sent his men to Bossman's home to check every leaf of paper and spread and split every piece of property where information might have been concealed. They went to his office and gave it the same treatment. They checked his list of friends and turned their homes upside down. They came away empty-handed, covered in dust and mites. Ashes wanted to arrest the directors of Barclays Bank, but even he realized that the move would stir more trouble than he could handle. In self-defence, the bankers might release some very compromising information. He parked his car in front of the bank and violent thoughts ran through his mind. How he would have loved to shoot those banker bastards and bomb the building to the ground! But he knew better. He watched the traffic speeding up and down Kampala Road, cars full of soldiers and soldiers' wives and relatives, agents of security organizations, expatriates working for embassies, civilians going about their business, and cursed them all for being unable to help him to recover his lost millions. He hawked deep in his throat and sent a huge yellow-green gob flying out of the window. It landed on a man walking past who, when he saw who had spat on him, just kept walking. Ashes threw his arms in the air in utter despair and headed for the island.

That night he stormed the cage and released Mr. Bossman who, weighed down by grief and ulcers, looked ancient and less imposing than his bulk normally permitted. He led him to the woods and made him collect small logs in a field. All around them insects chirped, sawed, harked. Now and then an animal cried as it warned others or celebrated catching its supper. Bossman was oblivious to it all, moving like an automaton, mechanically, jerkily. When quite a heap had been collected, Ashes led him back into the cage and made him carry his wife to the field.

"Say goodbye and a few prayers for her soul. It is a privilege I give you, old friend," Ashes sneered.

Helped by the Pounder, whose face betrayed no emotion and whose movements were cat-like in their speed and coordination, Bossman piled logs on his wife, tears flowing down his face. A guard brought a jerrycan of petrol, poured it on the wood, made sure he was on the right side of the wind, and struck a match. The flames leaped and roared.

Ashes was delighted for the first time that day. He started whistling, "He has the whole world in his hands . . ."

As the flames weakened and the fire started to die down, the Pounder knocked Bossman down, tied him with a rope, and threw him into the fire. The man's screams and grunts mixed with the renewed roaring of the flames fed by fresh fuel. Ashes smiled and continued whistling monotonously. He stayed behind till the fire died down.

General MiG 300 never turned up. Everybody was still afraid of Colonel Robert Ashes.

A FEW DAYS LATER, smugglers awaiting interrogation in police custody near Jinja were freed in a spectacular attack. Armed men swooped onto the police station, disarmed and tied up the guards, released all in custody and told the police chief to send their greetings to Mr. Ashes. Ashes treated it like a joke. He knew that it was most probably General Fart who was responsible. After all, he had never expected him to take the loss of the powerful Anti-Smuggling Unit lying down.

A MONTH LATER, Ashes' wife's home was attacked. She lived in Mengo, very near the city centre. The attackers came armed with incendiary grenades and machine guns. They bombed the house till it caught fire. Luckily for the couple, they had gone to the island. Three guards and two servants were killed. Ashes was privately shaken but remained openly defiant. He went about his job as if nothing had happened. He appeared with his wife in public, determined to lead his life to the full. Two losses are not going to knock me out. It comes with the territory, he said to himself. I know who is behind these cowardly acts and I will deal with him in due time.

The government ascribed the attack to guerrillas aiming to destabilize the peace-loving government of Uganda.

In the meantime, Ashes had to deal with the British Embassy, explaining the disappearance of the Bossmans on behalf of the government. He maintained that the Bossmans had absconded with government money and could as yet not be located. He turned the question round and asked the embassy to trace the fugitives and help bring them to justice. Tempers flared, with Ashes outdoing the embassy suits, who had to show diplomatic restraint. He knew well that time was on his side, since like all macabre affairs in a macabre time, the significance of the Bossmans' case would pale and die quickly in the incessant heat and rain, replaced by more momentous issues, till it fell off the tree of topical issues. Forgotten.

In those days, Ashes spent much time scouring the lake in his speedboat for pleasure or in pursuit of smugglers. He loved the hypnotizing sound of the engine, the soothing winds, the colourful scenery. He often went out fishing. He would bring large fishes ashore, watch the shiny silver bodies flop and flap in final death throes, and help his men build a fire. The smell of the lake, the magic of the trees, the flavour of the fish, would evoke paradise. Wine would be uncorked, liquor would flow, and the impromptu party would branch out in music and dance. Hidden out there, secured by a ton of ammunition, protected by water on all sides, they were like modern-day pirates, dangerous, transient.

On weekends he would fly his wife to the island, take her on boat rides or escort her deep in the forest to look for yellow-legged parrots. They would take skilled men, borrowed from other islands, and watch as they shinned their way up incredibly high trees in search of eggs and young birds.

His wife came from a well-to-do Ugandan family which had gone down when the kingdoms were banned. He had met some of her people, but, with his reputation, it hadn't been the most successful of encounters. It suited him just fine; after all, he was not looking for an extended family. As long as she loved him— meaning if she stayed devoted, loyal, subservient—he did not care. His major worry was that she did not want to leave the country. She believed that she could always hide in the villages after the fall of the government. Where did that leave him? She had studied in America in the sixties; she had been to Britain for holidays on a number of occasions; she said she had had enough.

"I am too old to live in a foreign land," she would say firmly.

"But you are only forty, my dear. How can you say that?"

"I am not a nomad by nature, Bob."

"We can go to Rhodesia."

"And live among those racist farmers?"

"Or to South Africa. You have never seen such a beautiful country."

"The blacks will kill you."

"South America is perfect. Beautiful weather, wine, luxury."

"Next you are going to suggest the Caribbeans."

"Yes, nobody gives a damn over there. Nobody will bother you."

"We will see, Bob," she would say in a conciliatory tone that did not mean she had changed her mind, "but don't tell Amin of your travel plans."

"Are you crazy, woman?"

Ashes had a cageful of parrots. He and his wife enjoyed hearing them curse, sing, whistle. His favourite, a green one with red spots, he had christened General Fart. To entertain his wife, he would dress in a pirate outfit imported from Britain—eyepatch, scarf and all—and play with General Fart.

Sometimes he would look at the lake and momentarily visualize his escape route. He planned to slip away as noiselessly as he had arrived. Did Dr. Ali also prophesy my escape? he would think amusedly.

SISTER FINALLY MANAGED to get away. She cleaned the uten-
sils, scrubbed the floor and closed the house, leaving a message
behind for Mafuta. It was with a heavy heart that she began the
journey. She felt the burden of leadership slipping onto her
shoulders, heavy like lead, hot like a disc saw in action. She was
going to have to keep everybody hopeful. As the car took her
away from the place she had come to love, it felt as if she would
not return. Harder than leaving was keeping the load of secrets
gnawing away inside her.

Her brother's money made her think of Saudi Arabia, a fabled
land spouting oil and oozing with billions of dollars. That some
of it had found its way into her brother's pocket could only be
good news. She herself would never touch anybody's money,
but she had nothing against people fighting their way out of
poverty, as long as they did not take from defenceless people. It
struck her again that maybe he was dead. If so, her life would
change very quickly; Mafuta's too. She did not know if she could
handle it.

She now realized how wise she had been to resist expensive
gifts from him.

"Sister, I have never given you anything of value, something
to reflect what you mean to me."

"I have you. If you are alive, I am rich," she had replied.

"I know, but unexpressed love and appreciation go mouldy."

"Not if there is sincerity. Take care of your wife; Mafuta will
take care of me. If anything happens to him, I can always turn to
you. You are my insurance and that is enough for me."

"The offer still stands."

"I appreciate it."

Bat had looked disappointed.

She arrived safely. People had gathered at her parents' home.
Relatives, friends, strangers. Her brother Tayari had broken the
news to them the day before and had forestalled everybody by

bringing an astrologer from the city and a bull. He had killed the bull and the astrologer had read the omens, which had been favourable. There was the smell of roasting and cooking meat in the compound as the people regaled themselves on the meat. Some staunch Catholics and Protestants were still offended that an astrologer, an agent of the Devil, had been called in instead of priests. They refused to touch the meat, saying that it was unholy.

Sister was surprised by Tayari's action; she felt outsmarted. Her friends had suggested consulting an astrologer, but she had not made up her mind. She took her brother aside and asked him what had happened.

"You say that the omens were good."

"Yes, they were," Tayari said pensively.

"Did he say what is going to happen next?"

"Nobody can, except God, I mean Dr. Ali. I decided to do it just to get it out of the way. I knew that many people were thinking about it but were afraid to take action."

"What did Father say?"

"Under the circumstances he would kiss the man's feet if he said that Bat was returning home tomorrow."

"Where did you get the money?"

"From the fireworks displays. I also have other sources."

"I am very proud of you."

"Thank you, Sister."

Sister did not have to do much; Tayari had taken over the show. She returned home the next morning. Mafuta had arrived the night before and was in a bad mood. They almost had a row. He wanted her to listen to his story first before burdening him with her worries. She maintained that her brother's life was in mortal danger. He agreed but said that he had missed her and needed some attention. He had had a difficult fortnight. He had bought cattle, sold it, but the buyer had tried to cheat him. He had spent the week trying to get his money.

She knew that he was being difficult because he did not like

Bat. He had gotten the news the previous night and gone out to drink. He had felt happy that his enemy had bitten the dust. Maybe now he had learned what it felt like not to be accepted. Maybe he would learn some humility, some manners, some respect, some consideration. It was only at the end of the evening, replete with beer and meat, that he had admitted that it could have happened to anybody.

It surprised him that a day later he still could not resist showing resentment to his wife. He had thought about it, planned to be nice, but when he saw her lumbering home, he felt angry. Angry that she had not been home to receive him.

"It is terrible news," he finally conceded. "What do you want me to do?"

"Accompany me to Kampala."

"All right," he said grudgingly, thinking about the cost. Spending so much on a person he did not like. He did not say it out loud, but she sensed it in his tone of voice, in the way he brooded. If she hadn't been pregnant, he would have prolonged the fight.

The atmosphere in the house and on the bus could have done with some cheer. It looked and felt grey. Everything was so different from what they were used to, for they usually enjoyed each other's company. Maybe he missed the big meals she cooked him, the little things she slid his way. He definitely did not like competition, and was already worried that the baby might come between them and usurp his position. The little bastard might get some of Bat's characteristics and that would be a disaster. Then he would have to doubly assert his authority.

Mafuta was irritated by having to meet Bat's rich and more educated friends. He resented them and the way they made him feel. There was the Professor: he would be preaching and paying attention to Sister. These people did not seem to see him or did not know how to talk to him, the intruder who took their friend's sister away from the circles she should have joined as a permanent member, by marriage to one of their colleagues. The

Kalandas had the ways of the newly rich. They had subtle means of flaunting their class, little references to artists, painters, foreign places, as if saying, If you don't know so-and-so, or this or that place, you are a peasant with grime under your nails. Such subtlety annoyed him. Mrs. Kalanda had her sisters in Kenya and in Britain and the things they sent her. He had heard it all before at his wedding; he knew he was going to hear it again, swaddled in new words or shamelessly displayed in the old ones. These days it seemed that the quickest way to rise in status or class was to go abroad; the interesting thing was that those left behind, family or friends, all rose with you. "I have a brother in America, a sister in Australia, they are leading such a wonderful life," some fool would chirp boastfully at you, as if he had won the lottery or been made a minister.

Mafuta had put on his best clothes, well ironed by his wife; he had put on his best black shoes, polished to a shine with his very own hands. But Bat's friends were probably going to be talking about Italian shoes, English clothes, as if Drapers were still on Kampala Road, as if in the bygone days everyone had access to chic shops and the goods they sold. Now he felt happy that Amin had chased the Indian and British merchants away. It has not made everybody equal, but it has removed the alluring, unattainable goods from the public's eye, and whoever wants them has to take the trouble to go to London, which most people can't afford to do, Mafuta thought with some satisfaction. The soldiers are in power, flaunting their wealth, but it is transient and they lack style, which makes few jealous of them.

Mafuta had grown up with no materialistic instincts, and he still did not care very much, but when in good company he did not want to feel locked out. It made his bulk feel cumbersome, like a heap of stones, with his heart palpitating inside like a fisted frog. It seemed he had been too optimistic in going into old-fashioned town-planning in the fifties, when it looked as if the country was going to expand its modern tentacles aggressively. But then again, he hadn't had the grades for medicine or economics. Why was he brooding over spilt milk? Because some Cambridge-educated bastard had refused to accept him? Because he did not fit in with the bastard's friends? Because he sold cattle?

Brooding at such a time seemed ridiculous. He felt a little bit guilty. He wondered why it never bothered his wife that she did not know some of the things the Kalandas went on about. They had accepted her because of her brother. They even felt protective of her.

"We are going first to the Kalandas . . ." his wife was saying.

"I know," he said rather loudly, with a touch of unfriendliness.

The city looked hospitable when he had money to milk from it, cows to offload at a profit. Now it looked desolate, as if half its occupants had died, as if the remnants were combatting ghoulish fevers. Soldiers were joyriding down the streets in open Stinger jeeps, guns and bums sticking out. State Research Bureau boys were prominently displaying bell-bottom trousers wide as tents, platform shoes high as ladders, silver sunglasses shiny as chrome and walkie-talkies bulky as phone booths. Looking at them, spectral as scorched trees and menacing as bee-stung bulldogs, one might get the impression that an arrest was taking place every minute, the country locked in a spastic daze. They made this look like another city, compared with the earlier Kampala— accursed, dirty, haunted.

In the villages where he had just been, these boys were absent. Cattle farmers went about their business seemingly oblivious to the crisis in the city. Stepping from the horizon-kissed grasslands into urban filth, violence, uncertainty, was to step into a broken, alien world. But they were two thinly joined worlds, flying the same flag, using the same inflated currency, ruled by the same scum. To most villagers Marshal Amin was a spectre floating on rumour, occasionally projecting from a feeble radio speaker, never seen, never touched. Mafuta started feeling that he had made the right decision. Living in this atmosphere was not conducive to one's health, sanity, equilibrium. How he now itched to go back to the cattle trail, where a heap of dung meant that cows were in the vicinity. Here they were in the city, chasing a trail of human dung, but without the certainty that there was a human being, living or dead, at the end of it.

The stay at the Kalandas' was as agonizing as he had imagined. The two women went off to another room and talked for ages. He studied the pictures on the wall, the furniture, the trees outside, till he gave up. Meanwhile, Mr. Kalanda arrived and they struck up a conversation. There were no new developments. Contacts had been made far and wide, but nobody seemed to have seen Bat on the fateful day or afterwards. There was a conspiracy of silence at the ministry, which nobody had managed to crack. The car had been sighted at the Nile Perch Hotel, but the police were holding it as evidence.

At long last Sister emerged and announced that she had been trying to call Bat's friend in London. A politician with an unpronounceable name.

"What is he going to do? He is in London, and we are here trapped in the mire," Mafuta said irritably, getting more and more wound up and drawing looks of disapproval from the formidable Mrs. Kalanda. He had heard of the fellow, another Cambridge product. Amin has little respect for such foreigners and rightly so, Mafuta thought with some relief. He had jerked them around like dolls on a string on many occasions. This one too seemed destined for the same treatment, if he had the time to invest in the venture.

"Every possible avenue has to be explored," Mr. Kalanda said diplomatically. He knew that the two in-laws did not get along; he did not want to make things worse.

"Right," Mafuta said grudgingly, redundancy biting at him.

It was agreed that if there were no new developments in the next few days, they would have to start searching dumping sites.

"Are we going to wade in the ooze and turn the remains over ourselves?" Mafuta said, feeling sick and beginning to enjoy his position as outsider, asking the hard questions or at least making his hosts think, or explain things which did not need much explanation.

"There are people paid to do that. They know all the places. They are called surgeons," Mrs. Kalanda explained, using a superior tone, as if talking to a wayward child.

"Let us hire one and get going," Mafuta said, using the same tone and noticing that Mrs. Kalanda was more worked up about the disappearance than even his wife.

"We have to wait for Tayari and Babit to join us," Sister explained to no one in particular, tears appearing in her eyes and voice.

Mafuta's opinion of the city was not improved by the nightly shooting sprees. They would begin with single shots, as if somebody were alerting his comrades to get ready to party, and deteriorate into rapid volleys coming from all directions. The hours after midnight were the worst; it felt like a fire was raging over the city, and houses and people were exploding. The mind wandered to war, past and future. It stumbled onto the armed robbers who had terrorized the city at the end of the sixties, before the army put them down. It stumbled on all kinds of real and imaginary situations in which the gun was used to victimize unarmed people.

The strange thing was that in the morning nothing was heard of the shooting. Nobody talked about it. They talked about the weather, the fluctuating prices, inflation, but never about guns. It felt like a conspiracy. It was as if the shooting took place inside his head and was only heard by his drugged ears. His wife wasn't too bothered by it. It was as if she expected drunken or frustrated soldiers to behave that way. The arrival of Bat's brother did not alleviate Mafuta's tension. The young man spoke only when spoken to, preferring to maintain silence or go for long walks by himself.

Mafuta's burden lightened when he accompanied his wife to see Victoria and her child to get any information she might have. He was struck by the woman's beauty, but he felt there was something hard and dangerous about her. She expressed much grief, but there was something superficial, overdone about it. Is it simply that she has too much energy or is there something wrong with her? Mafuta asked himself as he watched her, irked by the fact that it was rich or powerful men like his in-law who played around with such women. He had expected a spurned woman to be cool, restrained, dignified in her loss. Victoria, on the other hand, looked like a house on fire, barely holding back its zeal to consume itself. Maybe the bastard has a way of bringing hardness, insanity, out of people, Mafuta thought. Victoria's child kept walking about, pulling things, going off to play, and coming back to interrupt conversation. He wondered what his child would look like.

"I have done my best," Victoria reported, wiping tears from her eyes. "Friends in high places refused to talk."

"What friends?" Sister asked eagerly.

"I know some people in high office, you know," she said almost casually.

"Ministers?" Mafuta said suddenly, attempting to escape neglect.

"A minister, yes. And people who know people. They all don't know where he is." Wiping tears clumsily, she cut a scatter-brained figure, quite different from her usual collected self.

"I have been to three different astrologers. They all say different things. I don't know what to think and what to believe."

"Do you have enough money to live on?" Sister asked with concern.

"I have a job. I can look after myself. It is love I am without. I love him so much. I miss him," she said tearfully.

Mafuta was not impressed. A swinger like her had to know better than to get trapped in love. He had seen many of her kind, hard-drinking, night-clubbing types Amin had put out of miniskirts and business. They were good for a night, but a nightmare to live with. Victoria's house could do with more cleaning. A peek in her inner rooms had revealed chaos: clothes all over the bed, the child's playthings all over the floor. Could the bastard have let her go because of her carelessness? Or did she make too many sexual demands? Mafuta remembered his princess, how she used to ride him, and how he had felt good about it in the beginning. Wouldn't be a bad idea if this woman had ridden the bastard like a donkey, he thought, and almost broke out laughing.

"I don't know much about this woman, but I believe she was a mistake in my brother's life," Sister said as they drove away, Victoria waving from the courtyard.

"Why do you say that?" Mafuta said in an almost playful voice, again enjoying being in opposition.

"She calls Babit and threatens her. She openly confesses to seeing astrologers. She claims to be still deeply in love with a man who threw her out long ago."

"Everybody is using the good offices of astrologers, but because of hypocrisy nobody owns up to it. Your family slaughtered a bull for omens to be read, didn't they? Such a beautiful woman would hate being replaced. Maybe it made her go over."

"Somebody has to investigate her."

"Your brother should have done that before investigating her nakedness," Mafuta observed, hardly able to hide his glee.

"I am serious."

"She didn't make him disappear, did she? Surely not even she could do that."

"I am not saying that. I used to like her. But women who threaten other women are dangerous. They either believe in evil magic, or physical violence. And those tears . . ."

"Rarely do women admit defeat at the hands of rivals, except for my princess, who cleaned out my house in retaliation before going off and allowing you in. Most women would rather destroy their rivals. Gone are the days when polygamy was a respected institution and rivals had to be tolerated. Nowadays, it is every woman for herself and the Devil for them all."

"Don't remind me of your princess."

"Don't worry. Let us concentrate on finding your brother. He will sort out his mess afterwards."

"Yes, you are talking sense."

VICTORIA HAD BEEN on the trail sounding out people on Bat's disappearance, but to no avail. General Bazooka had warned everybody not to talk to the "widow," as he called her, and at best to stop her at the gate. Thus doors kept getting slammed in her face. Former colleagues looked the other way when they saw her. She had been to the headquarters of different security agencies and received the same disheartening treatment. In her desperation she had tried the astrologers. Two omens had been bad, one good. They had robbed her of much of her hope. Her life had started to look futile. If it hadn't been for her daughter, she would have gone out of her mind.

She woke in the morning with fear in the pit of her stomach, and dressed to go to work with doubt plaguing her mind. She arrived at her office feeling nervous, as if she expected a bullet in the back, and she started sorting papers, useless files. Hers was a dead department, hollowed by the fact that rural roads had not been repaired in ages. She sat in her office waiting, she did not know for what, drinking tea, staring out the window at passersby, the trees, at nothing. Her hopes seemed to grow dimmer by the day. She was now afraid that the General would take his revenge and strike back at her. In what way? She didn't know. She kept thinking about her disappeared father and her failure to find him. She thought about her family and the fact that the General had run them off. She saw him cocking guns, asking her to shoot him. She would gladly shoot him now, for she believed that he had made Bat disappear. And robbed her of her hope. Her escape route. I have to get Bat back, she said out aloud. I have to get Bat back, I have to get Bat back, I have to . . .

Things had changed at the Bureau. It had fallen into the hands of Amin's tribesmen. She felt that if it hadn't been for

General Bazooka they would have killed her. She wanted to get out. She prayed for a miracle to find Bat and take him away from that other woman. Then I will walk safely into a secure future, she thought. It was still a dream. When frustration got the better of her, she picked up the phone and called Babit. Hearing her hold her breath or begging to be left alone empowered her, made her want to smash the receiver in her face, and erase her from Bat's life. Calling her barren had at first been a slip of the tongue, but it was now a major weapon. A bazooka. She loved its soul-crushing potency. But why didn't it drive her out of the house? When she got tired of harassing her, she would leave the dead office and roam the city looking for clues, flimsy leads to turn her into Bat's saviour. A whore had been the first person to witness Jesus' resurrection. Wouldn't it be fantastic if I resurrected Bat out of the morgue?

THE SEARCH for Bat's body began at midday on a rainy day with Sister, Babit, Tayari, Mafuta, the Professor, and Mr. and Mrs. Kalanda dressed in gumboots and raincoats and looking sombre as stormy weather. Afternoons were most convenient because one was sure that all dumpers had retired for their siesta. Now and then, bodies were dumped during the day, but then by the roadside, not deep in the forest where the group was headed. The "surgeon" the group had hired lived on the blind side of Mabira Forest, where most settlements were. The taxi van which brought the group stopped three kilometres from their final destination. They walked the muddy paths deeper into the forest, the trees above wetting their heads at a monotonous tempo.

The man lived in a small settlement of iron-roofed mud houses where children were playing inside, now and then one or two of them venturing into the rain and the red mud before dashing back indoors. The women were busy making the best of the soggy, muddy situation: cooking, cleaning, making sure their children did not stay out in the rain and catch fever. The man had been doing the job for a number of years and oozed with the confidence of an expert. These were in fact the boom years. He had begun by going to strip corpses of watches, rings, necklaces, clothes, any valuables the soldiers overlooked in their haste. Business had been good then because the victims of purges were mostly well-to-do people. Nowadays the soldiers had become wiser, hungrier. There were no more pickings, but the "surgeoning" was booming because of the dramatic rise in disappearances.

He was in his thirties, in the prime of his life, dressed in gumboots, jeans and a khaki shirt. He was a very average-looking fellow who could have passed for a teacher, a carpenter, or a driver if you found him walking on the street in his Sunday best, because of the air of calm and control he had about him. He had worked in a hospital morgue but had resigned over bad pay and decided to become self-employed. Hands sheathed in surgical gloves, a cigarette smouldering in his mouth, a flash-light dangling at his hip, he led the group into the forest.

"We are the only remaining true foresters. We care more about the forest than those trained to name the trees. We know where the animals are, where the people live. The name 'sur-geon' does us an injustice," he said at the beginning of the jour-ney. But nobody had been in the mood to appreciate his sense of humour.

Light gradually dimmed, little insects started screeching, the forest floor felt thicker, softer, with dead leaves. The silence of the people seemed to make the ambience grimmer. When they had walked for a long time, a change in smell warned them of what lay ahead. As they drew nearer, the intensity rose, attaining a well-nigh physical pressure. The "forester" just marched on, a man in his element, a vulture surveying his domains. Suddenly, they were there. He turned around to face the group, as if asking them if they had the nerve to get down to business.

They were lying on their backs, on their sides, on their faces, some in coils like pricked millipedes. They were lying on top of each other, arms and heads over their neighbours, as if for fun or in ritual. They were lying singly, in twos, or in bigger bunches. They were dressed, naked, half-naked, sheathed only in coats of blood. There were those who seemed to have dozed off midway in prayer, rapture, boredom, disgust, dirtied as if they had failed to find the time or patience to wash. There were the faceless, the half-faced, the ones daring you to blow their cover. There were the fresh ones, with heat seeping out, and the stone-cold, with collapsed skin coats betraying bones. He guided them through them, past them, over them. With his gloved hand he pulled, exposed, unveiled, rearranged. He went on and on, a conductor musically twitching; a surgeon rubbing, probing; a history teacher selling faces, fictions. At the end of the exercise, with his bloodied glove and impassive face, he spread his hands like a priest at mass beckoning the congregation to embrace the Lord and told them that he could do no more for them. He wished them well, studying their faces, as if checking as to who had vomited most, who mourned most, who couldn't wait to get away. He brought his hands down by his sides, shrugged his shoulders like a doctor who has failed in his duties, and one by one the group turned around ready to get out of the forest and go to meet another appointment, another fisher of men.

The final search occurred on a riverbank turning to marsh. In the razor-sharp bulrushes, as if looking for floating baskets with babies, water up to their shins, they surveyed bodies surfeited with sun and cordite. Most faces were upturned in supplication, mortification, abortion. Weeds and flowers bent in the wind and touched the faces, as though to wipe snot from runny noses, or pus from sick eyes. Here and there was a trouser-ripping erection, obscenely captured in death in all its glory. Tortured by hope and despair, they retired to spend the night listening to exploding bullets and grinding out new plans, better ways to handle the present and confront the unknown.

In the morning Mafuta, Sister and Babit went to Entebbe to attack the phone in search of the elusive British politician. Sister wanted to give him the news. She dialled away, working through

a cacophony of honking faulty connections, snorting discon-
nections, and a ringing, echoing maze of failure sounds. It was
towards late evening when she got somebody on the line. Emergency. A British emergency in Uganda? She tried to explain that
it was about her brother. The woman at the other end wanted to
cut her off. Too many weird callers these days, some threatening
violence to her boss, some saying obscene things to her or anybody else answering the phone. Sister held her ground. She
insisted; she demanded; she informed. She came away with the
promise that the politician would call her back. She spent a bad
night loaded with doubt, hope, fear.

Much to her surprise the man did return her call, and
expressed deep regret. He chatted. Bat had called him to congratulate him on becoming MP. He had sent Bat greetings on a
few occasions. He promised to study the case.

THE FIRST TWO WEEKS in detention slipped by steeped in
suspense, boredom, fear. His spirit felt compressed, cut off,
strangled by the weight of isolation. A candle starved of oxygen
slowly going out. His own company depressed him. His mind
tried to roam outside, a bird without a song or a worm. He kept
thinking that man was a strange animal: in a group he often
sought isolation; isolated, he did his best to fit into the group.
How many hours did he spend thinking about people he normally fled or whose company he found mediocre? How many
hours did he spend re-creating banal conversations, images he
had found boring at the time? He tried to concentrate on clinical things, reasoning his way out of the maze.

The knowledge that government was doing business just a
few floors above him brought with it a crushing sense of redundancy, insignificance. The thugs could do their demolition job
without his forlorn efforts to keep some things running. The
Ministry of Power hadn't collapsed: delegations were being sent
abroad, deals were being cut, the machinery grinding on, just a

few blocks away, in his own office. As he wasted away, he tried to imagine what he would do if suddenly released. It had happened to others. Would he go abroad and seek asylum in Britain or America? Did he want to leave the country? No. He wanted to stay.

He wasted hours going over calculus, various mathematical theorems, geometry. He remembered that when he was young he used to believe that it was the British who had discovered mathematics and was later surprised to learn that it had started in Arabia. And that writing began in Baghdad. He remembered the sand of the Arabian Peninsula as he constructed tunnels, calculating the depth, the width, the time it would take to dig so much each day. He devised the most efficient means of waste disposal. He planned escape attempts using a climber's gear, helicopter rescue, smoke grenades, massive shoot-outs in which he would have to depend on the expertise of other people, as other people depended on his own expertise at the office.

He felt no bitterness towards the General; it cost too much precious energy. He just excised him from his mind, his life. He liked to think of his tormentors as a group in order to avoid hating them too much, seeing their faces in his sleep. From the flimsy residues of his Catholicism, he dredged enough stoicism, saintly resignation, to accept his punishment. Good people got punished; so did bad ones. That was the beauty of it. He now and then went over his life, the class wall he had built to protect him and his interests, and tried not to lose hope. He tried to look for those moments which would fortify him, keep his spirits up. They kept shifting, changing position according to mood.

He thought a lot about justice; it did not make much sense. He was living outside the bounds of book justice; most Ugandans, most people groaning under dictatorships of all sorts, did. In many places it was the criminals handling the apparatus of justice, meting out their version of book justice. I am also compromised. By accepting the Saudi prince's money I participated in corruption, albeit involuntarily. Now I am being punished by criminals, killers with dripping hands. It did not make much sense. Salvation lay in the passivity and patience of a crocodile. Maybe something will happen and I will be free to go and do my work.

In the fourth month, when he had quit thinking about Babit, his family, his former life, because it disturbed his equilibrium, a soldier entered his room deep in the night. He switched on the light and barked at him to wake up.

"Job. Exercise. Good for body."

He marched out of the room. He felt weak in the knees with fear. At the end of the corridor were five other men. He knew them by sight. They stood under the light looking at the soldiers.

"Move."

They were herded together towards the garage and then outside into the yard. The air was cold, fresh, the sky a marvellous deep blue dipped in twinkling icy stars dominated by a fat moon. It was a very quiet night, with no shooting, no shouting. Bat felt momentarily free. Fantasies and memories rushed to the surface. His body tingled with excitement. He was then pushed inside a Stinger, which cruised past his office and entered the gates of the Nile Perch Hotel. He saw the spot where he had left his XJ10 and tried not to think who owned it now.

They were herded inside the hotel. He found himself in a room with two other men. The sight at his feet made his legs buckle. There were six bodies on the floor. He realized that he was standing in blood, pools of it.

"What are you looking at? Roll them in blankets and take them outside. Quick," a soldier with a very nasty voice barked, gesticulating fiercely with his hands.

Bat did not know how he brought himself to do the sordid job. It was an out-of-body experience, something the brain washed clean and locked away in order to preserve its sanity. It was heavy lifting, with sandals squeaking, slipping on the marble floor. Outside, a lorry was parked, tail-gate open. They hoisted the bundles, coming away sodden, panting. He stood at the side and looked out. The dome of the mosque on Kibuli Hill looked imposing, like a huge egg. They were ordered to climb in the back together with four armed soldiers. The lorry drove away towards Jinja Road. The cold air whipped in through the slats and over the tail-gate. Everybody shivered, teeth clattering. The soldiers smoked to keep the demons at bay, to generate heat in their bodies and to fight the stink.

He had been on this road before, going to visit Babit's parents. He remembered the last time, the reception, the joy, the going home with Babit. Now he was going to pass right by those people. He thought about jumping off, an impossibility. But he had convinced himself that he did not care if he got shot or not. Had he not seen it all? What did he have to look forward to? More money? More power? More love? Would the rest of his life not be just nostalgia, the re-created taste of familiar stuff?

The vehicle entered Mabira Forest with a squeal of abused gears. The driver went faster. The massive forest looked even more formidable, more ominous, more pregnant with secrets of life and death. The overpowering darkness was opposed only by the headlights and the groan of the engine.

They swerved off the main road. Tree limbs whacked the side of the lorry and the top slats. They stopped. For a moment nobody moved or talked. A rifle clattered against the tail-gate, sending chills down spines. Then two soldiers barked orders at once. Grabbing a head, Bat led the way, stumbling, hurting his legs on sharp sticks. The human cargo was dumped, naked, the blankets taken back for further use. The soldiers smoked, puffing away, doing their best not to look. Everybody seemed eager to get away.

The next stop was at a river on the edge of the forest.

More orders: Wash blanket. Wash lorry. Wash self.

They washed the blankets, glad that they were thin. They scrubbed the lorry floor, the sides, the tail-gate, while fighting the mosquitoes and other biting and stinging insects of the night. They finally got into the lukewarm water to bathe off the filth which they could no longer smell. It took them an hour of endeavour to get everything ready. They shivered all the way back to the hotel. There they had to wash the rooms, the corridors, the entrance.

"Cleaning woman's job. You still long way off, you pussies," one soldier said.

They were given new clothes and sandals before being taken back to Parliament.

It became a fortnightly event. Each time he was sent out with different prisoners. What happened to the others? Was there no end to the number of people held here?

On the fifth trip the soldiers had a surprise for them. At the hotel there were no bodies awaiting disposal. Instead, men were lined up, hands tied in front of them. Every prisoner was given somebody to dispose of. Bat tried not to look. He hesitated, waiting to see what others would do. He was viciously prodded with a rifle barrel. He lifted the hammer, said a prayer of absolution, and smashed. A clinical exercise robbed of either the thrill of anger or the satisfaction of malice. He remembered beheading, gutting and roasting chickens for the family when he was young. The jump from chicken to man, without progression between, seemed ridiculous. He had always wondered what butchers felt when they slit the throats of huge bulls. If they felt as empty as he did now, he pitied them.

At the river he thought of drowning himself and what a waste that would be. The soldiers would return to the hotel without him; his people wouldn't know where his bones lay. He had almost stopped washing the blanket. At that moment the nastiest soldier with a face like the night rushed towards him.

"Hurry, hurry, hurry. You think you still big man, eh? You think because some white snake go making noise you are special? Tell me," he barked, collaring and bringing him close to his face. He could see envy all over it.

At that moment Bat knew that he wasn't abandoned. It struck him like an electric shock, short and sharp. Now he could handle this man. "No, sir. I am not a big man."

"That is right. You nothing. You hear that? Nothing. You going nowhere."

"Yes, sir," he said, feeling so excited that he wanted to dance. A white man! Damon Villeneuve, MP? Had he stepped on a few corns? The moments of exuberance tasted delicious. The fact that a soldier knew about it meant that something was really happening. It was possible that this man had got wind of the affair a few weeks back and had been smouldering with resentment ever since. They had made him do these grisly things hoping that he would refuse and they would get a chance to injure him badly or to kill him. They were mistaken; he was going to play their game. The chance would come for him to hurt them later.

"First kill make you no special, you pussies. Be very careful. I catch you little mistake, I kill you."

"Yes, sir."

"Wash, wash, wash," he ordered, pushing him away.

DAMON VILLENEUVE, MP, met with reluctance and indifference from the very start. The members of the English Parliament he usually cut deals with were busy with more momentous international issues. They had had enough of Idi Amin's capers. It was quite entertaining to hear or read about them but dreary business to try and unravel them. Politicians were interested in the aftermath of the Vietnam War, the oil crisis, the Watergate scandal, terrorist attacks, hijackers, unemployment and riots in Britain, the nuclear threat from the East, the ramifications of the Cold War for the West. The disappearance of a small civil servant in an obscure country was far from top priority. There was no political percentage in it, domestic or foreign. Dictators like Amin had been largely left alone as long as they did not fall into the Cold War territory and the fight against Communism. They could do whatever they wanted as long as it was not to key British subjects. Nobody expected Britain to play world policeman. The empire was gone. When there had been incidents of British involvement, the outcome had been very mixed indeed. There

was that Bossmans affair, Villeneuve was reminded more than
once by colleagues who were knowledgeable about Uganda.
Trouble in Uganda was not worth anybody's attention. In consolation, a few colleagues promised to sign a letter if he wanted
to write to the British and the Ugandan Embassies, maybe
Idi Amin too. Villeneuve consulted Ugandan exiles and British
expatriates, who advised him to play it low-key, but he started
making phone calls, writing letters.

The news slowly seeped into Uganda. The British Embassy
was reluctant to take up the case. There were heaps of similar
cases involving more distinguished Ugandans lying unsolved.
What was so special about this one? Villeneuve was insistent. A
Member of Parliament usually got his way; the news finally
reached the right ears. Amin asked Colonel Robert Ashes to
look into the affair.

At the time Ashes was busy putting together another megadeal
with Copper Motors. Big Bossman had been replaced by a more
sensible fellow, and big bucks were in the making. The last thing
Ashes wanted was interference from back home. He felt he had
suffered enough over the Bossmans affair, explaining himself
to embassy people he despised, people who had threatened to
bring in Scotland Yard to investigate the disappearances and
claims of fraud. Nothing came of the threats, but now he wanted
nothing to do with the embassy. Besides, people were disappearing every day. Over trivial things like offending the wrong
person, land disputes, women, grudges, politics, business. Why
should he get involved in this case?

When Ashes discovered that the missing man used to hold a
key post in the Ministry of Power, a jolt of excitement cut
through him. Here was a golden chance to deal General Fart a
blow. He had threatened to investigate the bastard but had let
him off the hook. Not this time.

Colonel Robert Ashes called and promised to look into the
matter with immediate effect. His first course of action was to
send his men, the Acolytes, to the headquarters of the Ministry
of Power and arrest everyone in Bat's department. In the early

afternoon, without a warning, Stingers swooped onto the place. Men jumped out, guns drawn, dashed into the offices and came out with eight people, including Bureaucrat One.

By the time General Bazooka received the news, two hours later, the damage had already been done. It was unclear who had captured his men. Word was his office had been attacked by armed men in Military Police uniforms. Efforts to find who they were had so far failed. He dispatched emissaries, made frantic phone calls to all security agencies, to no avail. His first guess was that he had fallen out of favour with Marshal Amin. He had not seen the Marshal lately, and he wondered if somebody had betrayed him. Had some envious back-biting general accused him of treason? Plotting a coup? Corruption? Had some astrologer seen him in his dreams and accused him of political ambition? Where was the Unholy Spirit? Was he in the country or abroad? What he said nowadays the Marshal swallowed. General Bazooka's hands started shaking. He lit a joint and puffed on it nervously.

In this unruly time, favours were gained and lost in the blink of an eye. At the start it had been exciting to find his way through the confusion; nowadays the game had become lethal as a mine field. General Bazooka felt his chest tightening. His wife could become a widow, his children orphans. In a fit of panic he called friendly officials hoping that at least one would tell him the truth before it was too late for damage control. Nobody seemed to have seen or heard anything. Are they lying to me just to keep their distance, or have I become too paranoid? But you cannot become paranoid enough these days; you cannot trust anybody for more than two minutes, he said to himself. Then one colleague suggested Ashes might be behind the mess.

"That dog again!" he swore, relief spreading in his body. It all smelled like Ashes. "I want to tear out his entrails with my bare hands."

In his helicopter he flew to the desecrated office. Phones were ringing, unfinished work was strewn on desks, employees were moving about with no idea what to do next. He berated the

guards and every person he came across. In a rage, he called
Ashes' office, but he was out and nobody knew when he would
return. He called the Office of the President, now run by the
Eunuchs, and heard that Ashes had been authorized to find the
missing man.

"I want to beat that goat-fucker to a pulp," he told his advisor.

"Not yet, General," the colonel said. "A man acting on behalf
of the Marshal cannot be taken lightly. Especially not when he
is the boss of the Anti-Smuggling Unit. He can easily ruin us
completely."

"What am I supposed to do? Sit here and wait like some dog's
dick trapped inside a bitch's pussy?"

"Ah . . ."

"I auctioned that man some time ago, Colonel. I offered you
ten thousand dollars in cash for his worthless balls. Why is he
still alive? Are there no men hungry enough to take him on?
Why do I still have this cross to bear?"

"You saw what we did to his house, General. I have got
another trap nicely laid out for him. At the lake. I will nail that
shit-eater this time," said the colonel, thinking that ten thousand dollars was too miserly a price on the head of a man like
Robert Ashes, and that if the General wanted a symbolic gesture
to show his disregard, he should have auctioned him for a dollar.
Now that would be something.

"How long do I have to wait inside this bitch's pussy? How
long? My Bureaucrat One is gone. What greater humiliation is
there for a minister than to have his biggest official carted off
like a bucket of shit?" He hit his chest, flailed his arms and
finally rested them on his hips. "I participated in the coup that
launched this royal family. I have defended the government
against all its enemies. And now I have to grovel at the feet of
this stinking turd?"

"Things change, General," the colonel began tentatively,
thinking that it should be the General, such a powerful man,
saying these words, not him. "You can never tell what Marshal
Amin in his deep wisdom is thinking. Otherwise, why didn't

he inform you of that reptile's order? How long has it been since he invited you to his home to play hide-and-seek with his children?"

"You are right. There must be something going on, somebody poisoning the Marshal's mind. What do you think I should do?"

"Caution while we work out the next move."

"Caution! Caution! Again! How long am I supposed to be cautious? When will you bring me his head on a stick?"

"Soon, pretty soon. He is aware that we are after him. He switches cars at the eleventh hour. He goes by air when everybody expects him to go by boat. It is hard to nail the dog-fucker, but it is just a matter of time, General."

"I should have killed that Cambridge turd and it is you who stopped me. He should die before Reptile gets to him. It will rob his victory of meaning. A coffin will be a good reward for his investigations." The General looked outside his office at the Parliament, rising squarely out of the ground to symbolize the power of the nation, or rather of those at the helm, and thought about the man held in its bowels. Things have indeed changed in a bizarre way, if a general can't get his way in matters like this, he thought, feeling angrier by the minute.

"It won't help, General," the colonel said, knowing that his boss was not thinking straight at all and was too caught up in his vanity and sense of power to see the big picture. "Ashes knows where he is by now. He wants to use this incident for personal profit. If you thwart him at the eleventh hour, he is going to come down hard on us. He could even tell the Marshal about it. If he doesn't, he is going to hurt us badly in some other way."

"You are right. I am going to wait," General Bazooka hissed, and stormed out. He realized that a prince was no king: he still had to take crap from his king, especially if he was a self-declared king of Africa. As a prince, he could piss on the heads of peasants, but he could not get his way all the time. Princes tended to be disposable and they often destroyed each other. Ashes was a prince too, with equal powers of destruction.

THE ACOLYTES LOCKED Bazooka's men in a villa in Nakasero. Under interrogation, they revealed what they knew. Ashes learned that Bat was called away to the Nile Perch Hotel ostensibly to meet his boss. The motive for the disappearance remained unclear, which was common among these incidents, and he could only guess. The news that the man was still alive cheered him. The mission was going to end more quickly than he had expected.

But the Acolytes arrived too late; the prisoner had been moved. General Bazooka had taken him to an unknown location. This turn of events put Ashes in a very foul mood. He hated this kind of game when he was not the one initiating play.

GENERAL BAZOOKA MADE HIMSELF as elusive as possible. He travelled in unmarked cars, singly or with two men. He stayed most of the time at Kasubi with his wife and children. The first week as a full-time husband and dad was interesting. He drank a lot and slept a lot. He kept an eye on things when he was awake; he barked at servants and looked at his children's exercise books. He was happy to learn that his favourite son did not like school and did not perform well. He talked to him about the importance of the army and the chances he stood as the son of a general. He showed him different guns, told him heroic stories and made him promise to enlist as soon as he finished primary school. Secondary school he could do in the army. The boy was very happy to hear that his father was on his side. The other children were less enthusiastic, but he believed he would get them eventually. He visited his wife's shop. He found the business of waiting for customers and drinking tea or beer tedious, to say the least. He fled to the city, driving around, dropping in on friends.

After a week small things started making him lose his temper. One morning he shot at a housegirl because she did not move quickly enough when he ordered her to bring a fresh spoon to stir his coffee. His wife intervened and reprimanded him. He took offence. It had just been a warning shot, he said, and no big deal. He felt walled in. Deflated by his helplessness in the face of Ashes. He decided to go north, by road, to see what was going on up there. He needed the inspiration and a break from all the madness. He hoped to come back renewed, combative, sharp.

The first part of the journey was very exciting. He was travelling through familiar territory. It felt very reassuring to see soldiers at roadblocks taking care of business. They reminded him of his days as a hunter of armed robbers. At one roadblock, however, he caught soldiers taking bribes. He stripped them naked, made them roll in mud and jump up and down while singing his favourite nursery rhyme: "Humpty-Dumpty." The fun part was saying the lines and hearing the miscreants repeat them after him. Afterwards he made a little speech excusing himself to the civilians, who would go away praising this big officer who came from nowhere and saved them from the rapacious soldiers at the roadblock. He left the place feeling good and eager to see what lay ahead.

But the farther he drove north, the more it dawned on him that, outside the city and the towns, government was a very thin concept. To begin with, people did not recognize him at all. He stopped several times to buy things, taking the trouble to enter the small dusty shops with old rusty roofs, but nobody called his name. The goods he wanted were almost always unavailable, except on black market, which was not for soldiers with medals dangling on their chests. He got irritated by these empty shops whose shelves were yawning except for empty cigarette cartons stuffed in for decoration. There was no cooking oil, no paraffin, no food, nothing.

"Nothing!" he yelled at the tenth shop. "Then what the Devil are you doing opening an empty shop? How long have you been here?"

"Since 1971," the man said dolorously, his eyes as sad as his clothes. "Each year the prices kept going up till we could not afford the stock any more."

"Are you blaming the government for this?"

"The government is doing a very good job. It is the factories; they closed down."

The General found himself tongue-tied, and he stormed out to save face.

At the next trading centre, with a line of flat-faced shops with porches, he could bear it no longer. As soon as he heard the same dirge, he rushed into the back of the empty shop, kicking aside jerrycans and boxes. Miraculously, he found there bags of sugar, salt, tins of cooking oil, cartons of beans . . .

"Hoarding! You are sabotaging the government by hoarding goods and keeping the prices up," he shouted at the top of his voice, as if he wanted the whole country to hear.

The man, wearing a faded blue shirt with sleeves rolled to the elbows, old-fashioned stove-pipe trousers and bathroom sandals, said nothing; neither did he look impressed.

General Bazooka wanted to call the people of the town together and cane the man in public before selling his stock at government prices. But when he asked the man who he was, he turned out to be the father of a friendly general. In fact, the shop was registered in the general's name. General Bazooka was mortified. He ordered his men to take a few kilos of whatever they wanted and marched back to his jeep. Yes, he was in the north, this huge sweeping area peopled by so many tribes lumped together under the term "northerner." He felt detached from the terminology and from the people. The connection seemed to have broken when he left for the south. The language of his dreams and ambitions did not flourish in this soil. The shallowness of his solidarity with these people shocked him. He was irritated by the stifling heat, the thinning vegetation, the luxuries of the city he had left behind.

"It is a bloody desert out here," he told his men. They shook their heads, as if to say he had been corrupted by the south, for they were glad to be back, to travel through the land of their fondest memories.

The farther he went, the more convinced he became that the journey was a mistake. I should have gone to visit my mother instead of coming here, he said to himself. He could get no coherent picture here, only fragments. The whole country seemed about to fall to pieces. To the north-east, the Karamojong were busy with their cattle-herding, raiding neighbouring tribes as far as the Kenyan border. If these guys wanted cattle, they took the war all the way down to the east, laying waste hundreds of kilometres if necessary. For many of them Kenya was just an extension of Uganda, and they crossed over the border, firing their guns and arrows till they got cattle or defeat.

Guns proliferated in the region, making cattle-rustling a lethal explosion of internecine warfare. The gun had risen to become a symbol of manhood, an integral part of the culture. Many soldiers had sold their guns for cash in this region. He felt angry that this had been allowed to happen. The result was that most parts of Karamoja were no-go areas. The people did what they wanted. Police, army, the taxman; nobody dared go there. The place was the toughest spot in the country.

The more he neared his home area, the place where he was born, the more impatient he grew. He regretted having left his helicopter behind. He had seen enough on the ground for a lifetime. This place would have looked better from the air, less challenging, flattened to blandness by the science of flight. I would not have had to see those haggard cows, he thought, at least not in detail. I came here on holiday, not on a fault-finding mission. I am not a fucking vet or the Minister of Agriculture and Animal Husbandry. Where did those little black pigs come from? They are so small they look like rabbits. The pathetic goats look no better. They seem to be blaming people for keeping them alive.

He got on the radio; he wanted his Mirage Avenger sent immediately. There was no connection. He tried to call the nearest barracks, seventy kilometres away, and also failed. He suddenly felt stranded. What the hell was going on if a general was not assured of a working radio? What if something happened to his family? It looked like a trap which might have been set by Reptile.

In the West Nile District, he felt calm again. He was among his tribesmen. He realized how little the government had done for the area despite the promises made almost every day: there was no electricity; there were few schools and hospitals; there was a dearth of drinking water. The most visible change was that young people wore bell-bottom trousers and silver sunglasses, and dreamed of going south to work for the State Research Bureau.

In the evenings, he had meetings with a number of chiefs. He promised them cattle, cars, mansions, helicopters if they encouraged young men to join the army. He wanted to have men in the army who looked up to him, men he could trust. He could employ them as his personal bodyguard, a sort of personal army within the army to fight for him. He knew that his promises were hollow, but they were the currency a leader spent in order to get certain things done.

He missed being able to indulge his rage, the blazing urge to dominate, which he felt in the south. There was no kick in it here. Spitting beer at these people would only look and feel foolish. Shitting his pants would simply be pathetic. The south did things to him the north didn't. The biggest part of him was down there; without it, he felt out of balance. It came to him that power was a very atmospheric liquor; where you drank it mattered most. Feeling lost, he decided to go and see his mother.

At Jinja his mother was very glad to see him. She had a big house among trees not far from the lake. She cooked him big meals, went with him for walks and showed him around. She liked the town, with its spacious roads, large houses, the nice weather. She really loved doing business, talking to customers, visiting local ones to see how her fish nets performed. She took him to visit her circle of friends, old ladies in their sixties and seventies. They met every week to drink tea and spend lazy afternoons talking about the past. He did not pay attention to what they said but liked the fact that they treated his mother with great respect. On the way home, she reminded him to bring the children to stay with her when the city became dangerous.

"It is so quiet here. It feels like another world. We spend weeks without hearing anybody shooting. The commanding officer of the barracks is extremely strict. Soldiers don't fool around. I wish they could transfer you here. We would spend weekends together boating, eating, talking, watching the children grow."

"It sounds so idyllic, Mother. It is all I ever wanted for you. I will send the children more often. It is not easy to get a transfer. They need me elsewhere."

"It will break my heart to leave this town."

"Nobody is going to make you leave this town. The government is in control. You don't have to worry about anything. You talk as if the government were going to fall tomorrow."

"When you grow old, you start to worry. So many memories. I see your father sometimes."

"Is he still drinking?" he said, laughing.

"He seems calmer now."

"Maybe he doesn't have the money to buy booze."

"Stop making cheap jokes about the dead."

"No offence, Mother."

GENERAL BAZOOKA LEFT feeling invigorated, spoiling for a fight. A prince back from travel had to show that he was again in residence, in total control. But his men were still being held by Ashes. So he called him and arranged a meeting to break the deadlock. He would gladly have carved him up like a grease-dripping chicken on a spit, but that would have to wait.

The two men met on the third floor of the Parliament Building, overlooking part of the city, which seemed laid down at

their feet. There was no small talk. Ashes, a Havana smouldering in his hand like a gun, laid his cards on the table. He wanted
Bat freed within twenty-four hours.

"I have started counting."

"What if I refuse?"

"Marshal Amin would not be very pleased to hear that his
orders have been disobeyed," Ashes smirked and bared his teeth
in a menacing gesture.

"Are you his messenger boy now?"

"There are things you don't understand, General. Before I
came along, this country was going down the latrine with corruption, smuggling, and all kinds of shit stinking to high heaven.
I have cleaned it up. It is the only reason why the Marshal trusts
me. If you people did your work with panache, I would not be
here, would I? And about the messenger boy part; it is what we
all are or try to be; some more capable than others." He stuck
the cigar in his mouth and took a drag.

General Bazooka took the insult like a hardened soldier,
although he would very much have liked to gouge out the man's
eyeballs and made him eat them. He hated the Marshal for
humiliating him through this man, this reptile, this scavenger
who had come when everything was running smoothly. First he
had taken his job; now he had paralyzed his ministry for weeks.

"I will release the bastard, but I want my men freed first."

"I am the one squeezing the trigger. You kidnapped the man
from this building, then you disappeared. Now you are expecting me to take your word, as if I were a whore you could fuck
any time you wanted. No way. Deliver the man to me and then,
only then, will I free your men. They have been well treated;
they only need a good bath," he said, creasing his nose in mock
disgust.

"Tomorrow."

"I don't enjoy this any more than you do, General," he rubbed
the salt in Bazooka's wound, "I am a very busy man, you know."

The General rose to go. Ashes watched him coldly, as if looking at a cockroach crawl into a shithole, satisfied that he had won

the little duel. Not a bad afternoon after all, he said to himself; first this sweet drama, then a swim in the lake.

ON THE DAY of Bat's release, they dragged him from the basement where they had dumped him. They tore the clothes off his back and hosed him down in the compound like a car, scrubbing him with a stiff brush. They scrubbed and hosed and laughed till he felt raw all over. The soap suds went into his eyes, making the soldiers laugh harder. They let him drip dry like a shirt on a hanger, gave him a pair of trousers and a shirt and no underwear, and a pair of used Bata shoes with no socks. They put him in a Stinger and started driving round. They moved from lane to lane in an unfamiliar place of trees and shadows. He had spent the last days sleeping on gunny sacks next to old tools, broken televisions, and chairs. Now it seemed his ordeal was over, but he dared not celebrate. They stopped in front of a mansion hidden behind a steel gate and a tall wall. He was ordered to get out.

It was a grey day from yesterday's rain. It felt as if he were walking into a trap. The guard at the gate opened it for him without asking questions. The compound was huge, and he walked on gravel flanked by patches of well-cut grass. A soldier opened the front door for him. Robert Ashes appeared and stood in the doorway. Bushy eyebrows, large forehead, thinning hair, close-together eyes, wide mouth. He looked mean and dangerous as always, a grenade about to go off, a pit bull terrier about to bite. He grinned at him and offered his hand. They exchanged greetings and he was invited inside. Large sofas, big carpets, hunting trophies on the walls: buffalo horns, a leopard skin, a lion's bearded head, crossed elephant tusks, a rhino's face, a stuffed eagle, and a three-metre python. He sat down and moments later his fomer colleagues walked in. They exited without saying a word. He was relieved because, in his ill-fitting clothes and shoes, with hair down to his shoulders, he did not have anything to say to them.

"You are free now. Aren't you happy?" Ashes asked effusively, which looked odd on a face so morose.

"I am very excited."

"You certainly don't look it. By the way, where do you want to go?"

"I don't know yet."

"I am going to meet Marshal Amin to give him the good news. The crisis is over."

"What crisis?"

"A British politician contacted us saying that a friend of his had disappeared. Marshal Amin gave me the task to free the man, and here you are."

"I am very grateful for your efforts."

"We can go together. The Marshal would be glad to see you. And you never know, he might promote you as a way of saying sorry."

"I appreciate the offer. But I would rather make my way home to digest this. I haven't seen my people for half a year. They must be worried sick. Thank the president for me."

"My driver will take you home."

"That is very kind of you."

Ashes shook his hand and left; he heard him drive away. He drank a cup of tea he had been served. A man in civilian clothes came and introduced himself.

"I am your driver, sah."

"Just give me a moment, please," he said, wondering where he should go. To whom should I reveal myself first? he wondered. He felt like a dead man come back to life, realigning his vision, his alliances, adjusting his expectations. Lazarus. Burial clothes unwrapped. Death stink washed off. Outlandish nails cut. Getting used to his skin, his voice, to the world he had left behind.

The driver dropped him at the brick-red YMCA building because Bat did not want to show him where the Kalandas lived. In fact, when he got out of the car, he rushed into the building. He went to the toilets and looked at himself in the mirror for the first time in months. He was shocked: he looked ghastly, cadaverous. He made a quick exit and walked the few hundred metres to his destination, keeping close to the fences. It was still early; the Kalandas were not yet back for lunch. He sat on the front steps and looked through the gate. He could see a small portion of Wandegeya and Makerere University. The Professor was there, busy lecturing, dreaming of getting away.

"Is that you? My God, Bat, it is you! I hadn't recognized you, can you imagine that! I thought it must be some madman or lost person. Christ, I am so happy to see you back," Mrs. Kalanda said, crying. They embraced: she heartily, he stiffly, too much aware of the smell of soap on him. She let him into the house and walked up and down, unable to decide what to do next. She rushed into the kitchen to prepare food but kept coming back to ask questions.

In the meantime, Bat decided to take a long bath. He put on Mr. Kalanda's clothes and shoes and slapped a generous dose of aftershave on his neck. He could hear Mrs. Kalanda on the phone spreading the good news. Mary Magdalene and the Saviour. He had saved them from further anxiety, expenditure, fruitless searches. Were they disappointed that he had no brutal scars or wounds to show for his half year away? Locked away in basements and other dark places for that long, he now found the fuss strange, hard to take. It was good that she was doing the talking; otherwise, he would not know how to break the news himself. He would end up sounding as casual as somebody announcing rain in a wet season. From Mrs. Kalanda, he heard that Babit was not at Entebbe. Where was she? he wondered. Had she changed, been dented by recent events?

Kalanda arrived in the afternoon with the Professor. The two men hugged him, squeezed his reduced form, and made fun of his appearance.

"Not all Amin's men are bad; at least they are considerate to the undertakers. You must be weighing the same as a baby gorilla," the Professor said deadpan, tapping him on the shoulders. "I have never touched sharper shoulderblades. Maybe that is why they call them that: blades they are indeed."

"When I came in, I thought my wife had taken on a starving gardener. Then I saw my clothes on the fellow. Lice, I thought, he must have lice. Then it struck me that you were not yet dead."

"For that you will have to be a little bit more patient," Bat said, grinning. He was relieved that the men made light of the situation. Nothing worse than a heavy, wet reception.

"Where are the drinks?" Kalanda shouted. "Bring the drinks and the fattest pig. My prodigal brother is back."

"We were scared boneless, man," the Professor confessed. "I said to myself, If they can squeeze his balls like that, they can push ours in our ears any time, any place with impunity."

"I was already thinking of emigrating to Australia or America," Kalanda confided. "We searched for you all over the bloody place. Nobody talked. We bribed and bribed and bribed; the dog-fuckers kept taking the money and revealing nothing."

"The language, the language, please," Mrs. Kalanda protested.

"Our brother is back from the dead. I am sure he has heard fouler language on the other side," her husband retorted.

"It wasn't that bad," Bat said awkwardly.

"Oh, please. It is always bad. They are like anacondas; just smelling their halitosis gives you ulcers. You are lucky they didn't shave your pubic hair with broken bottles," the Professor cut in.

"Boys, boys, boys," Mrs. Kalanda cried ineffectually.

"You have given us hope and happiness, you bugger. Let us drink to your return from the morgue," the Professor said, looking around as if he expected opposition to his toast.

"When did you last see a woman?" Kalanda teased. His wife looked embarrassed.

"I had my faithful chamber-pot."

"You always hear stories of prisoners bribing guards," Mrs. Kalanda mused.

"To fuck them or to bring them rutting dogs?" her husband bellowed.

"Jesus Christ, what is the matter with you?" she said rather hotly.

"We were just talking about bribery, fucking dogs, and . . ." Kalanda said, rubbing his chin as if he did not remember any more.

"I only had God to bribe, but the bastard was not at all interested. I knew that He could turn me into an insect and let me walk out, even crawl onto the boots of a soldier, but He refused. I even thought about Dr. Ali. Anything. I wanted to turn into a turd, get flushed and rejoin the living in the sewers of life, but I could not digest myself."

The men laughed, but Mrs. Kalanda feebly protested, "The children, boys, the children."

"They are living in Uganda. They had better get used to turds," her husband said with paternal licence.

Beer flowed in an effort to wash away months of anxiety, despair, bleakness. The afternoon was slowly sinking into the mellow shades of colour, which then dissolved into evening and night. Everybody agreed that it was the most beautiful afternoon they had had in half a year or longer.

"How does it feel to be back?" the Professor asked blandly, betraying growing intoxication. He had never been one to hold alcohol well.

"Feels like fuck. I don't have a job to wake up to, no home, no guards. I am a bit afraid of soldiers now. I am a bit afraid of you. I am a bit afraid of myself. It is great, isn't it?" he elaborated, smiling, and then burst into drunken laughter.

"I could do with joblessness for a while," the Professor confessed. "I need a break. If only I could afford it."

"You should have thought about that before choosing to become a teacher," Bat joked. "You should have gone into banking like the Honourable Right Reverend Mr. and Mrs. Kalanda."

"It is not what it used to be."

"Says every gangster," Bat laughed. "It might not be a bad idea to clean out your bank and take us all on a holiday."

"You don't want us to end up like the Bossmans, do you? Your liberator killed them for liberating him of millions of dollars.

Everybody in town knows it. I think the Bossmans stretched the concept of greed just a little bit too far," Kalanda said.

"Is that huge white man dead? Man, did he have a huge voice," Bat cried, remembering the many times the late Big Bossman came to the ministry to complain about power failure at his premises. "Man, could he bitch! It is hard to believe that his fellow Englishman took care of him and walked away scot-free."

"Oh, yes, he did. Ten million dollars is a lot of money," Kalanda said, shaking his head in wonder. "The surprising thing is that Ashes is still Amin's favourite. I wonder what he told his boss."

"You have to be terribly stupid to steal from a man like Ashes. Ten million!" the Professor whistled.

"But he was stealing from a thief, a killer," Mrs. Kalanda insisted.

"All the same, all the same," the Professor said, thinking what a man of modest tastes could do with so much money.

"Anyway, for cleaning out our bank you need a bunch of false passports and two T3000 tanks," Kalanda advised.

"I would drive the tanks myself," the Professor said, making driving motions with his hands.

"The children, boys, the children," Mrs. Kalanda interjected.

"What is this with the children all the time? Every time we open our mouths to talk, out come the children," Kalanda shouted, exhibiting the aggression that came when he got really drunk.

"Bat, you should have cleaned out that mother-shagging ministry," the Professor said almost dreamily.

"His head would be hanging on a spear in his boss' office," Kalanda said. Bat laughed.

"Did they can you for nothing?"

"They did not like my haircut," Bat replied evasively. "But I can't complain. I have met people. Including the killer of the Megaphone, as we called the Big Bossman at the office."

"Did he like your haircut?" Coming from Mrs. Kalanda, it sounded very funny.

"He didn't say and neither did I care. He is a man of few words."

"Maybe he had a toothache or indigestion," Kalanda volunteered.

"Any news from your former boss?" the Professor asked.

"Not that I know of. Whether that is due to toothache or indigestion, I can't say."

"Plans, any plans?" Mrs. Kalanda asked, trying to rejoin the conversation.

"A man has just escaped the claws of death and you are asking him what he wants to do? Would you know what you wanted to do if you were in his shoes?" her husband asked rather angrily.

"Yes, I would. I wouldn't want to go back, for sure. Let them not patronize you," she said, laying a hand on Bat's knee.

"We went to Mabira looking for you," the Professor announced solemnly.

"Christ! It must be unspeakable," Bat cut in, wondering whether they needed to know all the details. Was it really necessary?

"There are no words for it," the Professor said, shaking his head. "Just the thought that your friend could be there!"

"With a stiff dick," said Bat, laughing to forestall the Professor's maudlin outpourings, which alcohol always brought on. He was in his forties, but he already had grey hair. At such times he looked like a sad old man. He kept relighting his pipe, tamping, puffing. Bat knew that soon the Professor would be talking about his sickly wife, going back to the days when she was healthy, full of life. It was not the kind of story he wanted to hear now.

"Do you know the number of times we have all passed by the Parliament these last months? And the bastard was there watching us!" Mrs. Kalanda finally said.

"That sounds better. Bastard sounds perfect coming from your lips. I can see him in there," her husband said drunkenly.

"Welcome to Uganda. I will drink to Mrs. Kalanda's first bastard this evening," Bat said excitedly.

"You are all making a meal of it as if I have never used these words before," Mrs. Kalanda said defensively.

"Not often enough, dear wife. You should swear and curse a little bit more. There is so much to swear at in this country," Kalanda said, slapping her thigh.

The group kept vigil till late into the night. They ate and drank and rejoiced, and by the time they decided to go to bed, it was too late for the Professor to leave. His house was half a kilometre away, but he couldn't risk getting attacked by drunken soldiers. He and Bat shared a guest bedroom.

"It is a bloody shame I can't give you my wife to warm your bed for the night," Kalanda said as he left the room with his wife.

"Don't mind him," she cooed coyly, licking her bee-stung lips. "He has had too much to drink. Haven't we all?"

The Professor was a big snorer and filled the room with his half-choked piggy grunts. Bat was tormented by insomnia triggered by unfamiliar comfort and thoughts about how Babit was doing. He felt bad because there had been no chance of contacting her since she was not at home. He hoped she still loved him and had not suffered too much; her family too. He hoped she had managed to get some money. The comforting thought was that he was back, eager to undo much of the suffering and to pay for whatever debts she might have run up. His stomach's protestations against drastic diet changes resulted in a bout of diarrhoea, which kept him on his feet for part of the night. He would rise in the darkness, seek out his sandals with his feet, and make his way to the door. The Professor slept soundly through it all, sounding like a small herd of overfed pigs.

This was Bat's second time to sleep in this room. The first time had been soon after his return from Britain. It felt strange, for now there was nothing to show that he had been here before.

DURING HIS FIRST WEEKS of freedom, he was gripped by undue fear of soldiers. It came in flashes: the roar of a speeding

Stinger, a snatch of hammering boots or harsh, chilling voices. The sight of these creatures, with green and brown combat fatigues spotted like leopard skins, made his stomach clutch or his heart race for a while. He would feel fear rising from deep within him like bile, and he would make an effort to hold himself together. It was as if he missed the old order, where this fear had been a staple part of the day. Now it was as if they were stalking him. The fact that he still had the house at Entebbe and that his salary kept coming added to the confusion. The fear of eviction had been at the back of his mind for some time. Visions of Babit being flung from the house had tortured him. He knew that many generals would kill for a house with so much history, but the fact that they did not make a move made the picture unclear. A systematic, logical man, he expected his enemies to be methodical too.

As the car approached the house, he started to panic. How was the staff going to react? He had always kept them at a distance, and now he felt uneasy about having to deal with them. He was sure that Babit was not at home, and he planned to send her a messenger later in the day. He spent an anxious moment in the parked car, taking in the trees, the yard, the lake, the house. Where was everybody? Everything seemed frozen. It looked like a house where somebody had died weeks ago. He felt awkward in Kalanda's clothes. A refugee unsure of the reception awaiting him.

As he plucked up the courage to get out of the car, the front door flew open. Babit appeared, an anxious frown on her face. She had returned the previous evening, in between flights from Victoria's threats, disconnected the phone and gone to sleep. She stood on top of the steps waiting to see who had come to visit. She had lost weight and looked drawn. It was a positive sign: she had been waiting. He wanted to prolong the moment and see what would happen. She could not see clearly inside the car and the waiting made her nervous. She opened her mouth to ask who was in the car.

He emerged, head and neck like a tortoise's, and he saw her

eyes popping, her jaw dropping open. He had become an apparition. She started hurrying down the steps, almost tripping and falling over. She stopped at the bottom, as if seized, as if unsure how to proceed. He stood still beside the car, not knowing whether he was smiling or frowning, and then rushed towards her, arms spread wing-like, propelled by all the choked feelings of love laced with guilt, desire, relief, and enclosed her. She flopped onto his chest, tears wetting his shoulder, her sighs penetrating deep into his starving, tormented body. Her shape felt reassuringly familiar. He could feel his spirit expanding, making way for her once again, combatting the selfishness and indifference which had held his sanity intact in detention. They mounted the steps in awkward fashion. Things looked more familiar now, as if she were the guide through whose eyes he saw the house. They sat next to each other, trying to read each other. The tears in her eyes flickered like a random spread of gems, charming him with their message of steadfast love, longing, anxiety.

She waited, an open chalice, ready to absorb his story, his body, his spirit. He gave her scattered bits in the bedroom, arms fumbling, groping. Clad in borrowed clothes, he was a hungry refugee in dire need of the nourishment her replete depths promised. The curtain-filtered rays pouring into the room fell on her skin and made it glow, like a ripe fruit bursting to release its sticky juice. All the stolidity, the indifference induced in him by captivity seemed to erupt and empty into her, the receptacle which could hold it without overflowing. Charged by deprivation, he prodded her swollen womanhood, reminding himself how it had been and setting the course for the future.

Let us fuck all afternoon, his greed said somewhere.

He had missed her husky, impassioned voice, and the way coitus penetrated it and extracted the underlying childish whimpers he cherished. He had missed her heat, her tightness, the clean sheets, the trees outside, the lake, the luxury of contemplating it all while riding her, while lying beside her, freshly wiped with a smooth white cloth. Without her, the world felt remote, expendable, parched, hostile.

Drained, glowing, he could see her clearly, hear her, open himself to her, a kid after a good suck at the tit. Her trials and tribulations of the recent past, her fears, the frantic searches, the dread of finding him in the pile of oozing bodies, she told him. It sounded terrible, depressing, searing to the soul. He could imagine the anguish her family had undergone, the doubts, the pain. This was what he had all along been protecting himself against. He did not feel any immediate need to confess his sins, nor that he knew the secrets of the forest intimately. By withholding his secrets he believed he was doing penance, suffering like the others had suffered on his behalf. He knew that if he told her, she would absolve him too quickly, cry about it and leave him without a clear sense of what to do next. The secrets were his reminder, his warning. They made him protective of her, made him feel he wasn't using her to unload his problems.

"It wasn't your fault, dear. Don't think about it . . . Anybody would have done the same . . ." she would have said to reassure him.

His detention secrets and money secrets made him feel in control. They made him feel responsible for those nearest and dearest to him.

News of Victoria's evil campaign saddened him. It took him back to the threatening letter he had written the boy so many years ago. It was like an old wound opening. He didn't know exactly what to do, apart from talking to her, and demanding that she stop harassing Babit. Was Victoria capable of carrying out her threats? He had brought her into his house; he had chased her out, but keeping her spirit out was going to be that much more difficult. He had desired a fresh start, but it was evident that he would have to settle old problems first.

He exercised his freedom in visits to family and friends. He travelled to his sister's home. The emissary he had sent to inform her of his release found her in labour. By the time he arrived, she had already delivered a baby boy, a large shapeless bundle with its father's blunt features. Mafuta was overjoyed; she beamed with pride, the first hurdle cleared. She lay in hospital recuperating, getting attention for the damage inflicted on her by the bundle. She smiled through her pain, crying tears of joy over her brother's resurrection. She and Mafuta had had a big quarrel: She wanted to name the boy after Bat. Mafuta had wanted none of it. He wanted to supply all the names; it was his first child, after all. The child bearing the names of a man he disliked smacked of defeat, loss of face and authority. They had reached a compromise: she would provide one of two first names; Mafuta would give the baby its surname.

On arrival, Bat heard that he had acquired a namesake.

"I am overjoyed, Sister," he said, squeezing her hand and looking in her eyes.

"It is a very good coincidence," Babit remarked, wondering whether she was really barren. The sight of babies had started to hammer her with doubt and a string of questions. Bat's indifference to the subject just seemed to make it worse for her. She imagined the joy he would have felt had he come from captivity expecting a son. She imagined herself in Sister's place, flat on her back, propped by white pillows, smiling, receiving homage. The stark white room, with the green bed and the casement window, looked like a sweet cross to carry and get crucified on before entering the paradise of motherhood.

"I am so lucky to have a sister like you," Bat said loudly, as if addressing a big audience. "Calling Villeneuve was the most important move in the whole drama."

"I kept blaming myself that I had not done enough. I would lie here and curse myself for not being in the city trying."

"I knew you were doing your very best, Sister," he replied, squeezing her palm. Tears filled her eyes. For a moment he felt extremely close to her, as if he knew everything about her and would remain by her side forever.

"Brother-in-law, welcome back," Mafuta said, marching into

the room. "It is a relief to see you back." He squeezed Bat in an impromptu bearhug.

"I appreciate the effort you made on my behalf. A son is a fitting reward. Congratulations."

"Thank you. A historical baby in family terms," Mafuta said, glowing with pride. This was his creation, the best thing he had ever done. He was euphoric. All the pieces of his life seemed to have fallen into place. He seemed to have won a victory over Bat. He had a son, somebody like him; Bat didn't. He felt grateful for the moment. He wanted to stretch it out before gloom, competition, jealousy, tarnished and swallowed it.

Bat found the town small, uninspiring. It did not evoke any tender feelings in him. It was just another shapeless entity astride the road. Rural life bored him; it constricted him. It looked frozen, caught between the past and the future, as if afraid to advance or retreat. Having grown up among farmers, listening to their complaints about fluctuating crop prices, he now felt how cut off they were from the centre of power, government, decision-making. He had vowed never to find himself in such a predicament in the future. It was one of the reasons why he wanted to stay in Uganda. Here, he could move things; abroad, he would be on the periphery, a refugee trying to find a foothold. He always believed that the city and the big towns were the place to be. If they were dangerous and unpredictable, that was a fair price to pay.

Bat did not understand his sister's thinking at times. What did she see in this place? What if something had gone wrong with the delivery? Would she have made it to Mulago Hospital for surgery? Why she had chosen nursing puzzled him. Spending one's life with the sick, the injured, the needy, didn't look that appealing. That she could be so close to filth and still retain a smile on her face defeated him.

The days he and Babit spent in these mosquito-bitten backwaters visiting his family passed slowly, sodden with beer, flatulent with overeating, saturated with the same stories. He told his story and heard it retold till it became formless, almost unreal. It made his secrets seem very precious, close to his heart, privy to a handful of eyes. These people seemed to know him, and he kept thinking that there was a lot they didn't know. In some eyes he had already become a hero, somebody who had conquered death. The power of astrology had also been inserted into the saga. Some claimed that it had been Dr. Ali who had freed him in a dream. Bat found this curious, and he asked his brother why he had sacrificed the bull so openly. But then he understood the desperation caused by his disappearance. He decided to accept it all, although the glorification and mythicization bored and bothered him.

He realized that he was not fulfilling any useful purpose in these areas. He seemed to be getting in the way of his myth. His departure served everybody better. He would then love them because he would not have to deal with them. They would love him more because his myth would become more malleable, easier to forge into different shapes. They could then turn him into a politician, a fighter, whatever they wanted.

BAT SPENT his time preparing for his return to Britain. He had got his XJ10 back, even though he felt uneasy about driving it. Jobless, he felt he did not deserve to drive such a prestigious machine. He continued to use it only because soldiers still let him pass roadblocks unchecked.

Babit was both scared and excited by the journey. She wanted to see the other world, and thank the man who had helped free her husband, but she was afraid of losing the familiar. Uganda was still the font of her fondest memories, the cradle of the people she loved, the source of the hopes she cherished.

Her parents, on the other hand, wanted the pair to go away and get over the shock, and cement their love. They were afraid that if Bat stayed in the country he might get into more trouble.

"Every evil wind has to be given an outlet to pass," her father had said.

Bat spent an evening with Babit's family. They were farmers cultivating tea. They had been in the business for decades. From their earnings they had built a brick house, educated their children, and put something aside for their old age. They kept most of their political views to themselves, but let it be known that they had supported a progressive party and were ready to do so again when things changed. They expected Babit to set a good example for her younger sisters by marrying. Bat liked the contrast between Babit's parents and the people of his village. These people listened to his story carefully, asked questions, sympathized and were not out to create heroes. He left feeling quite close to them.

"Are we going to come back?" Babit asked that night, worried that like many people these days they might be embarking on permanent exile. They slept at a neighbour's house because traditionally it was improper for them to share her parents' house.

"We are going for a holiday, not to settle there, dear."

"Won't you be tempted to stay?" she asked, thinking that normally only rich people travelled or went for holidays. Finding herself in those circles frightened her.

"I know Britain quite well. I have no plans to spend the rest of my life there."

"But last time you had no money."

"Stop worrying, you will love it."

"I will start looking for a job when we return. What if the government throws us out of the house?"

"Don't worry about money. I will get a job when we return. If not, I can always borrow from Kalanda."

BABIT HAD BEEN RIGHT. Britain felt different this time. It had lost its power to bully and intimidate him. They had travelled to Kenya and caught a plane to London. Bat loved the luxury; Babit felt uncomfortable, always worried how much it all cost. She was not used to being served by white people and she felt insecure about her English.

"We are paying for everything, service inclusive," Bat explained. "If you want anything, just ask, even if it is something to vomit in."

This was the first time he noticed the difference in their academic backgrounds; before, it had been a joke. It did not bother him at all because he separated work from home, and if Babit was vulnerable, it was his job to take care of her. She seemed to believe that people noticed that she had never been on a plane before, that she did not know London, that many English accents baffled her. At this Bat laughed.

"The British don't understand their own accents. When the Irish talk Irish English or the Scots Scottish English, nobody understands them. You speak ten times more clearly than those people, dear."

The luxury and magnificence of the city sat in her mind like a bull in a hut. A taxi had driven them through the city to the Grand Empire Hotel, a magnificent affair with marble floors, glittering lifts and cathedral-like rooms. All traces of havoc wreaked by the IRA bomb were gone, blown away by money and technology. Anyone who did not know the story of those killed or injured there could never guess. It was the Western way: tragedy erased and carted away into library files where it lost bite, later coming off the page like a shadow, bland in its weightlessness, almost a figment of the chronicler's imagination.

"But you are paying a fortune for this!" Babit gasped in horror. "How are we going to relax in the midst of this?"

"Close your eyes and think. A few weeks ago you were looking for me in a heap of bodies. Right now we are moving in top circles. It is just life, dear," he said, patting her on the shoulder.

"Everything is happening so fast! Captivity! This! I guess I am too happy for words."

"That is what happens when a girl finds a good guy, and a guy finds a good girl. Leave it all to me. If you see a dress you want, we buy it. We are here to enjoy the best that is available."

During the first week, they did nothing but eat, drink, go out for walks and luxuriate in their surroundings. They loved cruising through the city in big cars, neon lights gliding by like a string of coloured balloons, lighted jewellery shops flashing icy diamonds. They loved the feeling of insulation from the city's mundane problems. It felt wonderful not to have to worry about their security.

During the second week, Damon Villeneuve got the time to see them. He was a Labour politician representing a poor London borough. He was a tall, thin, small-headed man with green eyes in a serious face. They found him in the hotel's restaurant. When he saw them, he rose, stretched out his hand and said, "Mr. Bat Katanga, I presume."

"You must be Damon Villeneuve, the rogue MP found with a crocodile purse on his head and a pipe in his hand," Bat joked, smiling from ear to ear. He gripped the proffered hand, embraced the man, and patted him on the back.

"And this must be . . ."

"Please meet my girlfriend."

Babit and Villeneuve shook hands, exchanged polite words, and the trio sat down. Babit found Villeneuve's accent hard to understand and wondered if he was Irish or Scottish. He seemed to swallow letters where she stretched them out. He understood her well, but the exchange remained laboured. This is our saviour, this is our saviour, this is our saviour, she thought. Before, it had been a faceless person, without a voice, without human qualities; now he sat in front of her, and she did not know what to do. She wanted to embrace him, to kneel in front of him, to rub his feet, but felt it would be highly improper.

Bat felt grateful, as grateful as he had ever felt in his life. For a moment he felt very close to Villeneuve. It seemed amazing that his only real friend at Cambridge had turned into his saviour. He remembered him in his house captain days. He had always been steady, reliable, capable. Nothing seemed to bother him. He lacked the charisma of a born leader, but he got things done. It felt strange to be this deep in debt to somebody. He felt incapable of repaying him. The words that came to his mind felt limited in range, jaded. "You saved my life, Damon. The noblest thing you will ever do. The biggest debt I will ever have. Thanks." At that moment he remembered that Damon used to love "I Can't Get No Satisfaction." He started singing it, right there in the restaurant, clapping his hands for time, putting in quite a bit of soul, stretching the "ooohs and aaahs." Damon first listened as if he could not believe his ears, then he joined in singing the higher notes. Babit looked on for some time with her jaw hanging open till she started clapping. Bat seemed totally free, floating, all inhibition gone. At the end, with Bat sweating and smiling and feeling very happy, they sat down.

"I will settle for that thank you. I haven't been serenaded in ages. It is good for a politician to be thanked once in a while. We mostly get dog pooh in the letterbox or on the lawn as a reward."

"You should have looked for a proper job," Bat grinned.

"Said my dad. But then you would be dead or still in detention. Hey, life has been kind to us. We can't complain."

"It is not every day that a Conservative MP is found wearing a purse on his head," Bat said, trying to imagine the dead honourable member with the garbage bag on his head.

"When I got your sister on the line, I thought, What a waste of life! When such a thing happens to somebody you know, it feels like a ton of newsreels dumped on your head. You start panicking and calling up people."

"I am sure you've got a huge phone bill waiting for me."

"It depends on how deep your pockets are."

"I am not too badly off."

"I can see where you are staying."

"I can make a donation to your office. Anonymously, that is."

"We need all the funds we can lay hands on. There are no bigger beggars in the world than politicians," Damon explained, smiling self-deprecatingly.

"By the way, I hope you still have that car you had at Cambridge. I want to buy it."

"Thieves took it a long time ago," Damon said, raising his hands palms-up in the universal sign of resignation.

"It is a shame. I wanted to take it back to Uganda as a memento."

"Have you explored London, Mrs. Bat?" Damon asked, turning to Babit.

"A little bit. It is amazing."

"That is the fun part. You should come and see the area I represent. Unemployment, poverty, riots, demonstrations, parades by the extreme right. We have it all."

"It must be quite exciting. Do you go around in armoured cars?" Bat jested.

"What is extreme right?" Babit said, looking at Bat, who wanted to burst into laughter.

"I can introduce you."

"Damon, please. We are here on holiday, not on a journey of exploration. You can save us the smell of your sewers."

"I want to meet them," Babit said with genuine curiosity.

"What do you want? Shit thrown in your face?" Bat asked angrily.

"We came to see London, didn't we?" she insisted stubbornly.

"Fine, fine, fine," Bat said defeatedly.

"Don't worry, it is only a circus," Damon said mischievously.

THE TRIP to the housing estates, which reminded her of flats in Bukoto and Naguru, made Babit realize how well they were living at the Grand Empire. It had in a way been too good to be true, lacking in the two-sidedness of life as she knew it. She had craved the familiar pressure of the world, the evidence of poverty, social unrest, the tension generated by different people living together. She had glimpsed some people sleeping rough, but there had been something fanciful, unreal about it. Faced with the baldheaded men, the dead eyes, the ugly black clothes sown with spikes, the outlandish boots, the sky-bound fists, she felt afraid despite being under police protection. They shouted abuse, spat, waved banners and placards, and raged relentlessly. Taking into account that they had never killed people in big numbers, they looked like cartoons of the State Research Bureau, who, Babit was sure, would frighten the ugly clothes off their backs. The cartoons looked more insidious only because they were more organized, using word to spread their message whereas the Bureau relied more on their guns and had no ideology to pass on to the next generation. In a few years the Bureau boys would be dead, whereas these cartoons would go on living, slowly consolidating their power. Babit did not fear or hate them. Having lived with the Bureau, nothing seemed able to touch her, and anyway she had no plans of settling in London.

"You don't look too impressed by our circus," Damon said with an ironical smile on his face.

"These boys don't have guns. They don't have powers of life and death. They can't penetrate my mind. If you've been terrorized by the Bureau, you can't be intimidated by the cartoons. In the past months I spent sleepless nights, fearing for Bat's life. I have come through it without losing my mind. I am not going to let anyone infect me with hate, fear, negativity."

"You are right and I will remember the word 'cartoons.' I like it."

On the way back, going through areas with small dirty shops with hardly any verandas or porches to speak of, making her think they were in Bwaise because of the presence of mostly black people, they went past a leftist demonstration, the two groups kept apart by mounted police. Babit liked the caricatural part of it: the banners, the fists, the shouting, the chanting, the laughing, which made it look as if the two groups congregated to entertain bored Londoners.

Later that evening Bat commented on how excited she was.

"London no longer frightens me. I just admire it. It is that part I want to keep."

"I am glad to hear that. After all, we came to enjoy ourselves."

"Is Damon coming back to see us?"

"He doesn't have time. He works more than twelve hours a day."

"Did you both learn that at Cambridge?"

"Not necessarily. Many Cambridgers don't want to work. We are just special people," he said by way of bragging. "By the way, what should we eat tonight?"

"Choose. You know London better."

"Snails, frogs and dog steaks, madame."

She just laughed.

"I can take you to a Chinese, Indian, Russian, Mexican or even Ugandan restaurant. It is all here."

"I told you to choose."

AFTER A MONTH Bat was already thinking about returning home. Things had started repeating themselves. He missed the discipline of work. When he discussed the idea with Babit, she agreed with him. They were sitting at the top of the Grand Empire, the Thames glittering in the distance, the city going about its evening business.

It suddenly occurred to him that if he was going back it would be nice to ask Babit to marry him. Without much ceremony he took Babit's hand, kissed it and asked her if she wanted to be his wife. She accepted. A moment of total silence followed. Bat was glad he had been accepted. He remembered that Kalanda had asked his wife to marry him in a bar. The Professor had done it in his house at the university. It seemed the place did not matter that much.

They sat and watched the lights in the distance. They did not make any solemn promises; there were no dramatics. He had a feeling that they had known each other all their lives, and this had been just an affirmation of a lifelong commitment. He imprinted that part of the city, especially the lights, in his mind. In the years to come they would return to commemorate the day.

"Look at those lights carefully, wife. They are my wedding gift to you. Carry them in your head from now on. After every so many years we will return, stand here and reminisce."

"Thank you, husband. This is the best night of my life," Babit said breathlessly.

He ordered champagne. They drank it in silence, looking at each other, and at the city, making wishes. He kept thinking that his fate had been redeemed here weeks ago by Damon, and that a new one had begun in the same city. After a very long time in which not much was said, they descended to their room. They drank more champagne, played some music and danced, and Babit asked him to sing "I Can't Get No Satisfaction" for her. She clapped as he sang, watching every gesture, enjoying every word, every inflection, every modulation. She told him afterwards what he suspected, that nobody had ever sung for her.

As they lay in bed, Babit expressed how happy and proud she was. She talked about informing her parents, her friends, people she knew. She talked about the wedding, the gowns, the guests, the ceremony, and Bat wondered if this was really what it was about. Then it occurred to him that this was indeed Babit's chance to shine, to occupy centre-stage. Somewhere along the line he expected her to talk about children, but she didn't. There was no use spoiling a beautiful occasion by going into a field mined with uncertainty.

In the morning he woke up with the feeling or fear that something had changed. Babit was already awake, watching him, covers up to her chin. They greeted each other cheerfully but did not say much; each seemed to be digesting the implications of the previous night. Bat was overpowered by a feeling of stability. Now he had somebody to take care of through thick and thin. And in turn there was somebody committed to him in the same way. At that moment he thought about Victoria and her obsession with him, and how strangely love operated. From now on I have to take the threats much more seriously, although I see no way of forcing Victoria to stop issuing them, he thought. In sickness and in health: from now on the threats have become health hazards I have to combat for Babit's sake. He sneaked a look at her. She caught him at it and said, "What?"

"Nothing," he replied, smiling. "You are my wife; don't I have the right to look at you from all angles?"

"Your look was communicating something. As if you were having second thoughts."

"Not me, dear wife. From now on it is you and me."

THE JOURNEY to Cambridge was like a pilgrimage; each knew more or less what to expect. Bat showed Babit around, explaining the functions of different buildings, and where he had done what in the past.

"It is not as bad as you made it sound in Uganda," Babit observed.

"It was the atmosphere I was talking about, not the buildings, dear."

"I was joking."

The last days in London were the best. They spent the biggest part of them indoors, lying in bed, taking long baths in the massive tub, or swimming in the common pool. For the first time, Bat thought about growing old and felt he knew what it would be like. He saw it as a slowing down, a liberation from urges, appetites. The years would flatten things out, till he and Babit became more or less like brother and sister. Then, and only then, would he stop working. Then, and only then, would he reveal his secrets to her, and to his friends. They might pout and call him paranoid, but he did not care. By then General Bazooka would be dead, or so he hoped, and his capers ground to oblivion. Those looking for Bazooka would find his name among those of

Amin's henchmen. Bat thought he would also ease quietly into oblivion; after all, bureaucrats thrived on invisibility.

On their last day in London they met Damon at his office in the House of Commons to say goodbye. They met his secretary, the woman who had made some of the phone calls and written the letters. Bat looked at the MPs who had signed the letters on a television screen. Blue, they looked like outlandish fish or rare birds flapping underwater. Trapped on the screen, it was tempting to dismiss them as clowns and overlook the terrible power they exercised in the world: the wars they rubber-stamped, the arms they helped pump out around the world, the garbage they let British companies dump. Dressed in suits and ties like sellers of insurance, and shouting "Hear, hear" like a family of monkeys when somebody said something funny, they did not look like men who had the power of life and death over millions of ex-colonials who were clinging to the apron strings of this nation. Damon, ironical, self-deprecating, with his small head and casual manner, was the proof of that.

Bat looked at the massive, history-laden House and at the dirty Thames outside and felt out of place. In the mass of nations yonder he could hardly see tiny Uganda. Momentarily, it looked as if he were pursuing an illusion, returning to virgin territory where he would have to struggle for every crumb of food, for everything. But that was where he wanted to be. He had no qualms about saying adios to London.

LITTLE HAD CHANGED; the government was still on its rubbery legs. It was as if Babit and he had not been away. There was no urgent mail waiting, calling him back to his old job or offering a new one. No government ministry had missed him. Rumours were rife in the city: Amin had been shot at; one hundred bulls had been castrated at the State House and their genitals thrown all over Entebbe; there had been another bloody rebellion in the army; the Vice President had had a car crash, broken his back, and had been flown to Libya; the Saudis had taken control of twenty islands in Lake Victoria; there was a shortage of petrol, a new curfew ...

The Professor seemed very surprised to see them back; he had assumed that they would stay away longer or not come back at all.

Bat told his friends about his impending wedding.

"Welcome to the fastest-growing club in the country after astrology. What kind of birds are you going to free on the day?" the Professor said acidly, still unable to reconcile himself to his friend's return.

"I remember my wedding to this woman," Kalanda said playfully. "Everything went wrong that day, but it was the happiest day of my life."

"It obviously would have been, wouldn't it, for somebody who couldn't cook and was tired of pulling his wire," the Professor teased, leading to laughter all round.

"At least I made a good choice," Kalanda said, winking at his wife. "How about you, Professor? Do you still have sex with your wife?"

The Professor took it well. "No, I don't. I do it with my wife's black-and-white pussycat."

"Boys, please," Mrs. Kalanda called, amused.

"There is nothing wrong with pussy, dear wife," Kalanda, who still enjoyed challenging his wife's prudishness, bellowed. "We should hear more about pussies coming from your mouth."

"Boys, boys, I thought we were talking about Bat's wedding."

"I will pay for the wrestlers," the Professor volunteered.

"I will pay for the professional eaters," Kalanda laughed.

"No, no, no wrestlers and eaters, please," Bat protested.

IN THE WEEKS THAT FOLLOWED, Bat applied for a job in the Ministries of Education, Planning, and Finance. The Ministry of Finance took him up as Bureaucrat Two. He was part of a team charged with the Herculean task of propping up a dying economy. The statistics were depressing: Foreign debt had soared to $3.8 billion, the trade deficit was $400 million, the shrink rate at which the economy contracted was a whopping 500 percent. Inflation was at 986 percent. Ninety percent of the citizens did not pay tax because of rampant black-marketeering, reversion to barter trade, and worthless earnings. The answer to every money shortage was to print more money, with the latest bills boasting pictures of the Marshal smiling benevolently, kissing babies, eating a lollipop, and shitting on the heads of Imperialists and Zionists.

The money Saudi Arabia sent in exchange for the islands was spent on defence. Amin's disrespect for economists was just getting worse. He liked to ad-lib on fiscal policy and not remain constrained by the stale ideas coming from imperialist countries. Even that wizard Colonel Robert Ashes seemed to have despaired on the economic front. Even God, Dr. Ali, had let Amin do what he wanted in that area. Both men had opposed the construction of an artificial lake in the city suburbs, which meant razing neighbourhoods to the ground, moving people around. But the Marshal saw the project as a future boost to the Department of Fisheries on the principle that two lakes yielded more than one. It would also ease the garbage disposal problem, he had added.

Bat did what he could, an effort that was like trying to dam a river with a few planks. His office was again on Parliament Avenue. In his free time he would think about the Parliament and its secrets. It would now and then give him the shivers, but he knew that his day would come to get back at the regime. Somebody was bound to turn up and show him a way.

The answer came during his wedding preparations. Amidst the bustle, with his people and Babit's mixed in an effort to make it a memorable occasion, his brother asked him for a word. The timing could have been better, what with all the expenditure for the wedding, but Tayari had a dream and could wait no longer. They went to the lake and sat on a rock facing the water.

"We need help," he said, turning to his brother.

"You and your woman?"

"Me and my friends."

"I don't seem to know any friends of yours."

"I am a member of a fighting group."

"Boxing, wrestling, kung fu . . ."

"A dissident group, brother."

"Don't you know that it is not good for your health and our well-being?" Bat asked, to hide his shock and excitement.

"Everything is a risk. You were not a dissident, but they took half a year out of you."

"What has that got to do with your group?"

"We are looking for sponsors."

"Who isn't? What are your plans? What have you achieved to merit my attention?"

"We spread Amin-Go-Away leaflets in the city. We now need money to buy radio equipment in order to spread the word nationwide."

"The word is already out, if you don't know."

"We are going to preach it even harder."

"Have you thought of the consequences? You are going to be on your toes all the time. Hunted. Do you like that prospect? Do you trust your instincts that much?"

"On the day the soldiers got powers of arrest, detention, torture, looting, the odds became clear. And as always it is the innocent who get hurt."

"I agree, but I still see no way you are going to have an impact."

"We are the civil wing. The military wing is in Tanzania. We need to pave the way for them. Like prophets announcing the coming of the Lamb," he said, grinning.

"A blood-soaked lamb. Let me remind you, brother. I don't want to be cited when confession time comes, you hear? Things are bad enough as they are. I don't want to go back to prison. I have Babit to look after."

"Calm down, big brother," the young man said. "The

moment we get the money, we disappear. My time as pyrotechnician is over. If I take up my fireworks again, it will be for another sort of celebration. Yours will be the last wedding I will do. I will of course keep on looking out for your best interests, but for the biggest part I will be out of your life."

"Is this really what you want to do?"

"It is my vocation."

Bat felt as though he were standing on a threshold, about to launch his brother into the world of dangers he courted. He was also aware that he had not been told the whole truth, but he felt in no position to stop the wheels turning. Let the young man face the world the way destiny cut for him. Maybe he would become a captain, a colonel or general, in the end. He seemed to have the dedication. All his life Tayari seemed to have been gathering himself to seize this moment. Bat felt a moment of intense excitement and closeness to his brother, his avenger. It felt as if he had plucked Tayari's secret and added it to his own little pile.

"It is a deal," he said, giving his brother a hand.

"I knew you would not let me down."

"I trust that you know what you are doing. I don't want Sister or anybody else blaming me later on."

"I don't like Victoria," his brother declared, as if he had not heard what Bat had said. "Did you know that she works for the Bureau?"

"What?"

"She is a member."

"How did you find out?" Bat said in an unsteady voice.

"Her story did not fit. I did a little homework afterwards."

"Why didn't you tell me earlier?"

"It was too late. You already had had a child with her by then."

"She has been threatening Babit."

"I know, that is why I decided to investigate her. I have been keeping an eye on her. If she does anything foolish . . ."

"They are empty threats," Bat said to defuse the situation.

"If they are empty, why is she still making them?"

"Harassment," Bat replied to hide the fact that he was alarmed.

"Did you know that she used to be General Bazooka's girl-friend? She was involved in a few nasty cases in the past, though of late she has been rather clean."

"Do you think that the General put me in because of her?"

"I don't know. It is possible that he planted her to go after you. You were one of his top employees, after all. But then again, maybe he did it for fun. Those guys are up to anything."

"How did you figure these things out?"

"I have friends who know people who know things. When you disappeared, I tried to use them to find out where you were, but they failed. Don't worry; my boys will be keeping an eye on Victoria. When did you last see her?"

"A fortnight ago," Bat mumbled, feeling dizzy. That his brother knew these things made him nervous, afraid, angry. Another stasher of secrets? How many was the bastard sitting on? Now he was doling them out.

"What did she say about the threats?"

"That they were harmless, that she was deeply in love with me. She kept calling me her saviour and miracle-worker."

"Don't worry. Go and enjoy the wedding, big brother. Leave the rest to me."

Bat was shocked to hear how mature and confident his brother sounded. He had fooled everybody with his silence, hiding his astuteness and toughness from the world.

THE WEDDING WAS MODEST in scale but very well done. The day began with the sort of rain which made a day in bed seem a seductive option. But the sun came out, created rainbows and dried the dampness off everything. There was a motorcade, dark cars tailed with colourful ribbons and flowers, slowly making its way past the golf course, the State House and the airport. Tayari exploded his last fireworks. The sound of music gently eased the evening into night. Babit glowed and beamed. All the people Bat cared about were present. It was a day that would haunt him with its beauty.

AS SOON AS TAYARI and his three friends got the money, they left the city and settled in the town of Bulezi, thirty kilometres from Kampala. One of them had inherited his late father's house a few years back. They opened a car repair shop at the front. Two operated it while the others organized things behind the scene. The idea of a radio station had been a fiction from the start. It had been the only way to get Bat to release the cash. They had guessed right that an intellectual would not be thrilled by the truth, thus the sugar-coating. In the violent world of spying which they had been part of for years, words without action counted for nothing. They were sure that not even the dissidents would have respected the radio plan. The culture had changed.

They knew that they could have gone back to their families, married, had kids, taken jobs and waited for the regime to fall. But the bug of the times had infected them. Without their doses of adrenaline, without moving closer to the flame, without the feeling that they held their lives in their hands, they would have felt useless. Only with the instruments of death and destruction in their charge did they feel safe, in command. Disarmed, incapable of action, they were civilians, kids, women, the very symbol of the defencelessness they had been taught to despise. Yoked to the obscure cause of liberation, their bombs would be double-edged swords, soothing their personal demons and bringing them closer to the day when the regime would fall. They didn't know what the fighters in Tanzania were up to, and what would happen when they came. They didn't know whether they would be alive in a year or two or less. They were just determined to be in a position where they could not be ignored or kicked about.

Over the years, during the mysterious disappearances, Tayari had become a member of a spy ring affiliated with the Eunuchs. They were supposed to investigate certain individuals, especially government functionaries for signs of self-enrichment. Tayari had learned how to fire guns, make bombs and defend himself in every way. He had proven to be a gifted bomb-maker. His handlers had allowed him to make fireworks shows as a way of honing his talent, raising funds, and getting closer to his quarries. It was much easier to get inside people's homes. It was much easier to see what they collected and how they showed off their wealth. Excited by the audience a wedding accorded, they often boasted about money, cattle, holidays, children in foreign universities . . .

In time, the ring had become very successful, and the army officers complained that as a result they spent too much time getting friends and family members out of the clutches of the investigator. They wanted the whole nonsense stopped. They had fought to bring the regime to power; they saw no reason why their families could not do what they pleased without the Eunuchs sniffing them out. When the Eunuchs were elevated to the status of a private army, Major Ozi, the new boss, disbanded the spy ring because Tayari and his friends were not Amin's tribesmen and could no longer be trusted. Major Ozi also used the chance to exact revenge for friends in the army whose relatives the ring had reported to the Eunuchs. Tayari and his friends were arrested and locked up for a week, with no food. It was at that time that they decided to cross over to the other side and make themselves useful before the dissidents arrived.

Behind the car repair shop they made plastic and fertilizer bombs. The first bomb to go off was planted in a car driven by a notorious State Research Bureau man. Tayari and his friends recognized well the licence plates allocated to security agents. Sometimes these people travelled in unmarked cars, which just gave them away. This car was parked outside a bar on Bombo Road in the middle of the city. On a warm evening Tayari placed the device underneath the car and walked away. Six minutes later the explosion happened. It lifted the car off the ground, scooped out its entrails, and left the shell to burn. A war of attrition had been declared.

The second target was a big shop in the city centre, owned by Major Ozi. The device went off, blew out all the windows, the merchandise caught fire and the building burned all night. The fire brigade was called, but the big red machines could not come because of lack of fuel. By the time Major Ozi had used his influence to secure fuel from the nearest military depot, the shop was beyond salvation. Nobody claimed responsibility. The men on patrol had seen nothing to arouse suspicion. The finger was pointed at the dissidents, and a promise was made to crush them with maximum force. More soldiers were deployed to patrol the city in Stinger jeeps, shooting whenever something frightened them. Far away from the city the quartet drank a toast to their success and debated what to do next.

The repair shop went nowhere, but that had been the intention from the start. The boys spent most of the time idling, pretending to work, preparing themselves for the next mission. Tayari felt a bit guilty about not telling his brother the truth. But he did not blame himself much because he knew that his brother wanted to get back at the regime and would probably sympathize. He only hoped that Bat was not spending sleepless nights over the current turn of events.

The boys travelled to the city and observed how well patrolled the city centre was at night. They decided to try an easier target: Jinja. They had operated there in their spying days, tailing the bosses of big factories. They loved the place, its roominess, the weather. They decided to plant at least five bombs and deflect attention from the city before attacking it again. A bomber needs luck to go along with technical skill because so much can go wrong; theirs held well. There were lots of targets to choose from and high-ranking officers in the area.

In one explosion, the fifth and last one, General Bazooka's wife lost an arm and was severely burned. She had gone to Jinja to visit the General's mother and a few relatives, one of whom worked for the Bureau. The only mistake she made was to borrow the Bureau man's car for the afternoon while hers got a tyre change. She always drove by herself, refusing to be herded like cattle by her husband's bodyguards. The recent explosions had convinced her more than ever that anonymity was the best way to escape trouble. The car exploded when she started the engine. There were no fire extinguishers around, and the ferocity of the flames kept every rescuer at bay for some time. She was finally pulled out of the wreck, the fumes almost choking her to death. Bystanders gave her just a few days to live.

GENERAL BAZOOKA WAS CONFRONTED with a unique situation. In all the preceding years he had managed to escape untouched. The few people he lost he never mourned. In fact, he did not know what mourning was. Life seemed to come and drift away. A real man, a real soldier, never let anything get to him. He had been in all kinds of shoot-outs, ambushes, and had come out on top. He had killed robbers, soldiers in purges, civilians caught in crossfires. He had ordered bodies thrown away or drowned, and it had never bothered him. All this just cemented his belief in his own invincibility. Above all, his family was out of the game. Even Ashes seemed unlikely to dare touch his dear ones. It was a border nobody easily crossed.

Then came the news he had never even dreamed about. His rage failed to protect and numb him. He was looking into the abyss of helplessness for the first time in many years. He was pricked by thorns of self-pity; he felt the chill of loneliness, utter isolation. He simply didn't know what to do. In the meantime, he received a message of condolence from the Marshal, who praised his wife as a woman the whole country should be proud of. It was as if the Marshal believed that she was dead. The language was so bombastic that somewhere in his heart, a small troublesome region now packed with intrigue and suspicion, he had the sneaky feeling that this might have been a plot executed with the Marshal's blessing. But why? Had somebody accused me of treason? If so, why hadn't they targeted me? Why have I heard nothing of it from my spies in the Marshal's office and among the Eunuchs? he wondered.

In his heart of hearts he believed that Reptile was responsible, using the cover of the recent bombings. It felt like Ashes, that reptile. He would not come out directly and shoot her on the street, or abduct her and pound her to death like he did to Mrs. Bossman. No, he had to hide behind something in order to show his tact, and then sit back and howl with laughter because nobody could link him to the deed. Reptile definitely knew who had tried to kill his wife. This was no random bombing, especially because my wife had been driving somebody else's car, the General thought bitterly.

General Bazooka had his wife transferred to Mulago Hospital for the best medical attention available and for proximity to her children. He planted guards on the hospital grounds and on each floor to protect her. In the hospital he was introduced to all kinds of deformity disease could inflict on the body. He saw cheeks blown out by boils, eyes runny with pus, lipless, legless, armless wrecks. He caught sight of patients with limbs caught in networks of pulleys and levers like flies in spider webs. He was especially troubled by children with single limbs playing in the hospital's corridors, lost to the stink of formaldehyde, and the crush of visitors, nurses, doctors, cleaners. He saw victims of fires and wanted to look away. He realized that the hospital was the worst place he had ever visited: It brought him too close to his own mortality. It dispensed with all the myths of invincibility he cherished. He was no longer possessor and flaunter of life-

and-death powers: the doctors and nurses were. He had to bow down to them, and listen when they talked.

On a number of occasions he had tried to commandeer the only lift in operation. It had not been worth the bother. It often transported corpses neatly covered in translucent sheets, or victims of car crashes bubbling in their blood, organs all over the place. He stuck to walking. He did it quickly, unseeingly, the burden of the effects of Marshal Amin's policies—poverty, lack of medicine—ambushing him on every floor. The load became heaviest on the sixth floor, and outside his wife's door. What if she was dead? Would his body be able to support the resultant rage? At such moments the country seemed to be full of enemies, conspirators, dissidents.

In the plain gaze of timid patients he seemed to detect fear and pity; the former because he could destroy them, the latter because he had come down from his high horse and, like them, he was dependent on doctors and nurses. It seemed as though they had seen the likes of him before and were ready to receive and outlast even more. Here at the hospital they used unsightly toilets, drank bad water, and could hardly afford to bribe doctors for treatment and drugs, and yet they looked at him as if he were already dead.

He suddenly remembered the artificial lake the Marshal had commissioned. An artificial lake to grow fish and dump garbage in! The bulldozers had huffed and puffed for two months, and now the project had crash-landed. No more money. Gaddafi had refused to finance it, even if the Marshal had promised to name it after him. Lake Gaddafi! All the money wasted! When he had asked for money to buy new dam equipment, he had been denied. All of a sudden, he felt disillusioned. He had been approached for help on two occasions by coup plotters. They were now dead. He felt he should have supported the second group. He suddenly wondered where he would be in ten, twenty years.

General Bazooka's stomach turned when he saw his wife

again. It occurred to him to shoot her and end her misery, but he didn't want her to go. He wanted her around, in whatever shape. Marshal Amin had sent his team of doctors to look at her; there was little they could do for her. He went to her bed, sat down, held her hand and talked to her. He told her stories of his youth. He reminded her of the day they met. He recounted the events leading to the birth of their first child. He talked about the future of the children and his plan to build her a mansion bigger than his mother's. He promised to buy her cattle, goats, sheep.

She could not talk, nor was he sure that she had heard him. She looked like a piece of cinder interrupted here and there by red patches and bandages. He brought the children to her and made them hold vigil, promising them to bring the criminals to justice. They had never seen their father looking so distressed. They had always seen him in his glory, in the glow of youth. Now he looked old, harassed, deranged. They knew that his future plans had been derailed, which meant uncertain days ahead. What if something happened before their mother got well? Would she survive a helicopter journey to the north? What if the helicopter was not available?

General Bazooka's mother remained his only rock. She consoled him and urged him to shoulder his burden and move on. She wanted him to take his wife to Arua as soon as possible. He, however, preferred to wait a little longer and see what the specialists could do.

IT TOOK THE QUARTET some time before they heard who was injured in the last blast. They celebrated but at the same time knew that they would have to be extremely careful. The stakes had risen to incredible levels, thanks to coincidence. General Bazooka had a reputation; he wasn't going to take this lying down. They suspended operations while trying to find out the counter-measures the General or the security agencies were going to take. During that time Tayari suffered bouts of hellish worry: What if Victoria sold him to the General? Wouldn't the General arrest Bat in order to make him tell where he was?

AT A STATE BANQUET a few weeks later General Bazooka could not bear the sight of Colonel Ashes any longer. He went over and confronted him. The white man was holding his favourite cigar while talking to a friend. He laughed loudly, a hacking sound that spread across the room, tipping his head far back to allow the merriment to gush out of him. It was this cocky, self-assured laugh that incensed the General so much that he feared he might have a fit. Ashes looked so inaccessible, a cut above every guest present. He continued talking and laughing even when he saw the General striding towards him as if he intended to go right through him. They were in the gardens of the Nile Perch Hotel, the city at their feet. The sun was going down with a dazzling display of deep reds and oranges set against a pale high sky. Colonel Ashes always made sure that he observed sundown because it was so dramatic and so quick. It made his spirits rise and he toasted it with a stiff drink except when he was at receptions where alcohol was forbidden.

"You will not get away with this, I can assure you, Colonel," the General spluttered, pointing his finger at his arch-enemy.

"I don't understand. Do you want a drink, General?"

"The cowardly attack on my wife . . ." he hissed, too furious to finish the sentence.

"It was a bloody shame what happened to your beloved wife," Ashes said, emphasizing "beloved," hardly able to hide his glee. The fact that fire was involved made it all the more delectable to him. How he would have liked to watch! "But you can take it from me that I had nothing to do with it. It must be one of those pathetic dissident groups you boys seem unable to take care of."

General Bazooka reached for his gun but remembered that it was empty. Nobody had been allowed in armed, even if it was only Marshal Amin's double in attendance. The Marshal's favourite double had been shot in the stomach a few months before, and ever since, the rules had changed. "You will pay for this, I can assure you."

"I don't understand you people. Some small guy lays a finger on your tit and you start screaming as if he were cutting off your nuts. My wife's house was attacked some time ago, but I never uttered a word. It is part of the game. You can't play a man's game with that boyish mentality of yours. You should have known that from the beginning, General. As one musician put it, 'Too Much Love Can Kill You.' "

General Bazooka was shaking with exasperation. His forehead was covered in beads of perspiration. He wanted to strike the Englishman, but he knew that it would be of little use. Many dignitaries at the party knew about the bad blood flowing between the two of them, and it would serve no purpose to fuel their gossip machines. "I—I—I . . ."

"If I were you, I would be in hospital holding my wife's hand instead of hanging around here drowning in self-pity. Men who have tasted the power of life and death should never degrade themselves with such sentimental pooh. It all makes me wonder whether you have ever been shot, General. I have, on a number of occasions. It hurt like hell, but proximity to death breeds fortitude. I have pain in my legs, but I don't complain. I love it. Why don't you try it? You could begin by, say, plucking out your sinning eye, as your Bible tells you." He grinned at the younger man, who looked totally confused.

The things the General wanted to do to this man were indescribable. He had, after all, auctioned his demise a long time ago. But wonder of wonders, the money remained unclaimed. It said a lot about his power and the state of the army. He spat a mouthful of soda in the grass near the Englishman's shining shoes.

"It is people of very crude origins who do things like that," Ashes said, inhaling a large volume of smoke from his cigar, as if to wipe away the insult. He looked disappointed. He saw how easy it was to destroy him. One word in the Marshal's ear and he would be dead. He realized that these men received too much power too early in life, before they had learned iron discipline and proper detachment. It was the reason why the country had gone to the dogs; it was full of dogs. The very fact that he could come in and take over, and make millions of dollars, showed how rotten the structure was. He was sure of one thing though: he would not be around when the edifice collapsed on these people's heads. He savoured his superior attitude with flair: this was the first time in his life that he worked with people he really despised. These men had given him little to respect them for. They were too predictable, the typical dumb soldiers who reached for the gun even if they only meant to take a piss.

He remembered the time that his wife's house was razed to the ground. He had suspected General Fart, but he had kept his head and said nothing. On that day he just kissed his wife, and they spent the day on the island hunting parrots, roasting fish and later on making love. Now he regretted that it was not his men who had bombed Geneal Fart's wife's car. He would have savoured it more, and the woman would be dead as a doornail. For all the tough talk these men spouted, he knew they were afraid. Of the Marshal, of himself, of Dr. Ali, of the future. There was a rift of weakness in them. A general who allowed his wife to go out unprotected didn't strike him as tough or sensible. In these times a general's wife had to go out escorted by automatic rifles and Shark helicopters.

"One day you will regret this, I can assure you," he heard the General, medals dancing, face swollen, eyes popping, say pathetically.

"We all have things to regret; it is the human condition, General. Maybe you more than I. I have one rule in life: I don't look back. That is how I have survived to reach this age. Somebody blasts me, I blast back. If I don't, I have myself to blame. If one day you become president, send a whole battalion of your sharpshooters to arrest me. If you send boys, I will kill them all, and you wouldn't want to begin your reign with burials, would you?

Otherwise, I don't give a bloody damn. If you do, then maybe you are in the wrong business, General."

"One day you will see . . ." General Bazooka uttered, feeling constipated by hate and ire.

"I live by the day, General. If I wake up dead one day, I won't regret it. I do my job chasing and burning smugglers on the lake. If you boys did your work on land, and in your ministries, this would indeed be the pearl of Africa."

Unable to stand it any longer, General Bazooka stormed off, trailed by his entourage. Few people paid attention; hatred among the top brass was as common as fleas on a dog.

FOUR STINGERS STOPPED at the front and the back of Victoria's block of flats, and soldiers rushed in to secure the corridors. People peeped through their windows to see who had arrived. Many suspected that somebody was being arrested by the Eunuchs, the Bureau or the Public Safety Unit. They waited in vain to see some subdued figure emerge caged in a phalanx of soldiers.

It was around eight o'clock. Victoria had just finished feeding her daughter, who was in a good mood. She was walking about pulling things, laughing, jabbering. She brought her mother a pink doll. She pulled her mother's hair, as if to make it as straight as that of the doll. Victoria's heart sank when she heard the crunching of the boots. The noise seemed to confirm her worst fears that somebody wanted to kill her. It did not help that she had had a big row with Bat. He had ordered her to stop bothering his wife. He had confirmed that their relationship was over. He had shown her the wedding ring. He had told her that he knew who she really was. He had made it clear that her dreams of salvation did not include him; at least not in the role she wanted. He had remained impervious to her offers of everlasting love. She had cried, begged, and tried to use the child as leverage, but failed.

"You don't understand. You performed a miracle. This child is a big miracle. You don't understand, but one day you will," she had insisted. He had then marched out of the flat.

In the meantime, she had decided to reconcile with her mother and family. She had spent a month looking for them in the villages but had not found them. Every time she found a promising lead, it crumbled. Had they changed names? Had they been swallowed by the endless cattle-rearing plains? Had they fled to Tanzania and joined the guerrillas? Her mother too! Had they died of malaria? The one aunt she had managed to locate refused to cooperate. Sworn to secrecy. Infuriated, Victoria had threatened to kill her, and the woman had said: "You see? That is the reason why everybody deserted you. You wanted to kill them. Your man sent soldiers to them. If they had not bribed them, they would be dead now." She had left with a heavy heart.

Now General Bazooka stood in front of her, medals glinting in the yellow light, swagger stick held stiffly in his left hand, gently tapping his right palm.

"I am very glad to see you, General."

"You don't look too happy."

"I am extremely happy," she said, kneeling down to greet him in the traditional way. A wench paying homage to her prince.

"Stand up, Vicki. I want to see your eyes."

"Yes, General," she replied, hardly able to stand straight.

"Did you hear what happened to my wife?"

"It was a very sad, cowardly act," she said, echoing the national radio word for word.

"Are you the newsreader? Whatever happened to your brain?"

"I am very sorry to hear what happened to her."

"As if you didn't hate her."

"I don't, General."

"Whatever happened to your sense of duty? I gave you an assignment, and instead of doing your job you fell in love with the goat-fucker. What does that say about you, eh?"

"It just happened, General."

"Did that man know that I had fucked you?"

"No, General."

"Stop calling me General as if I were a general store," he screamed. "Why did you betray me, Vicki? Was it a bleeding southerner conspiracy?"

"I couldn't get him to talk. He was too sophisticated for me."

"You could fuck him to death but couldn't make him open his mouth! Had he no family? Nobody of use? Where is your bloody brain? Is there nothing in that pumpkin on your bleeding neck?"

"You ordered me to focus on him. You said nothing about his family."

"I have just been told that there was a man who used to make fireworks shows. Where did he go?"

"I don't know."

"Do you know what all these negations mean? That we are paying people for nothing, that the Bureau is a smokescreen, a pile of shit. If the Bureau can't find this man, why are we paying you? Why don't we stage a firing squad and shoot you all in front of the public?" He was yelling and advancing towards her as if to ram the stick down her open mouth. "My wife lies in hospital blinded, burned, arm torn off, and nobody knows who did it. Dissidents are running free in the city, known to some of you, and you are helping them bring the government down."

Victoria kept quiet and stood very still, praying, hoping.

"Do you love that child?"

"Very much."

"Do you know whose child it is? It is mine. Next time I am going to rename it and introduce it to its true family."

"Yes, General."

"Start doing your duty, for the child's sake. Do you hear me? I am keeping an eye on you. Unless you pay your dues, you won't have any peace of mind. Not for one second. You know me well. I have spoken," he said, echoing the old kings. Dead kings. He suddenly asked himself why he was wasting precious time when he knew who the real enemy was. He would have peace of mind only when Reptile was dead. Without saying another word he turned around, collided with a bodyguard and left.

Victoria remained where she had been, near the thin sofa, the radio, the pot of artificial flowers. She had saved Bat's life once again. She had a crushing conviction that he was rightfully hers, and she, his saviour. She had to act quickly to make him hers, hers alone. There was only one person standing between him and her, and that was Babit. She had to go. From now on there would be no more phone calls, no more threats, no more words of advice. She had to go. The General's problems didn't interest her in the least. She had hers and it was called Babit. She had to go.

IN THE MEANTIME, cars continued exploding in different towns. People did not know what to do about it. There was a general fear of cars, and of shops and of crowded places. Bat wondered what was going on. He had waited in vain to hear the pirate radio broadcasting. His sister had never heard of it. The Kalandas and the Professor thought he was pulling their leg. They called it Lake Radio, meaning that it was a fiction, like the failed lake Amin had tried to make.

"How many people did the pirates move in order to start their broadcasts?" the Professor ridiculed.

Bat kept quiet about his brother and the money he had supplied. Too sensitive a secret. He gave Babit the task of tracking the radio day and night. She scanned the waves, turning the dial round and round, watching the pointer slide past numbers back and forth, amidst explosions of claptrap and the occasional clear sound.

"Why all this interest in pirates?"

"Aren't you eager to hear when the country will be liberated, and what kind of people are going to do it?"

"Do you know what I think? This radio station doesn't exist and you are just teasing me."

"Yes, indeed, but keep at it. I am tired of working for these idiots."

"What do you think about these car bombings? I sometimes think that you should stop using that car."

"My XJ10? You are joking. I keep it in the ministry garage. To get at it the bomber would have to shoot the guards first."

"It is evident that he is bombing cars and shops belonging to security agents. But suppose he mistakes your car for the two belonging to the generals?"

"Don't worry. Nothing will happen to me, dear."

"Why doesn't the group claim responsibility?"

"They want to keep Amin and his men on their toes."

"How can you be so sure?"

"I am a very educated man, remember?" he said, chuckling.

"Yes, Professor."

She was glad that things were going well. So often after marriage things cooled down and became boringly routine. She had had her fears, which had proved to be unfounded. She was glad that he had talked to Victoria and, as a result, there were no more threats. Twice a week he drove home for lunch. She enjoyed those days the most. They compensated for his absences and late homecoming. They were like two extra Sundays, days marked by anticipation and intense pleasure. She never fretted about money any more. It seemed he would never run out of work. All the ministries wanted him. They no longer interviewed him; they just hired him. One day the Englishman was bound to come. And maybe they would fly back with him, and sleep in the Grand Empire and eat all those strange foods.

Bat had hinted at visiting America. Babit noticed that he read more and more biographies of American sportsmen, film stars, politicians . . . She believed it was his form of gossip, a search for other people's secrets . . . It would be nice to go there. Maybe by then they would have children. If not, maybe they would go to a specialist and get her checked. By then she would have completed her teaching course. For now though, on with the search for the elusive radio pirates.

Three
In Limbo

There were days so fine, so suffused with bright light falling from high-domed skies, the beauty of delicate clouds, the perfume of gentle winds, the gloss of exuberant vegetation, the sheer delight of living in a bubble of peace amidst an inferno, that Bat felt totally in tune with life. He was not a religious man, but once a month he accompanied his wife to church. She chose the best suit for him, the darkest shoes, the best tie. For herself she picked the finest midi- or maxi-gown, matching accessories and a subtle, expensive perfume. They would emerge from the house and stand on the steps surveying the flower bushes, red and purple bougainvilleas; the towering thousand-year-old trees, majestic, their branches spread high above; the lake, a broken marble surface linking them to neighbouring countries in a fraternity of water; and the XJ10, the crown jewel, shining, ready to go. They would descend the steps and drive away.

At church they would mingle with well-dressed men and women who worked in the beleaguered civil service, the diplomatic corps, the remnants of the aviation service, and the armed forces. In mufti, the soldiers and the spies tried to make themselves as invisible as possible. Bat liked the fact that these days the church had turned into a human rights podium. Priests spoke out directly or indirectly against the disappearances, the killings, the abuses. The clergy had felt the bite of the bayonet, the sting of the bullet, and it made a difference. The words rolled off the priest's tongue with conviction, steeped in pain. Bat liked to sit there and think of good memories, his achievements, because his captivity had taught him how precious and luxurious the fine moments were.

On such days he liked to be surprised by uninvited guests who turned up to interrupt and enrich a day he had offered to the whims of time, to his wife, to leisure. If it happened to be his sister, they would talk about her son, her work, the state of the country. Living in a rural area, she would have a different view, a down-to-earth vision.

When his parents came, they talked about the past, who had lived where and done what. His father liked his job, a proper job, as he called it. He would mourn the fact that the coffee trade had been undermined by smuggling. His mother said little; she had always been a very reticent person. Your father talks for both of us, she used to say. His father had a bad memory now and he believed that everybody was ripping him off. Bat found it comical and would laugh.

"I always dreamed of seeing London and visiting the British Leyland plant," he revealed one day.

"Why didn't you say so before?"

"Where would you have got the money to take me and your mother?"

"Where there is a will, there is a way, Father."

"It is a dream I wanted to keep. But when your wife said there were parts like Naguru and Bwaise, I believed it was better that I had not gone."

When Babit's people turned up, he would drive them round the town, to the zoo, to the airport, to the Botanical Gardens, to the landing point at Katabi where food and fish came in from the islands. Standing there always reminded him that Entebbe was a peninsula, almost choked by water, which in places was just a few metres from the road to the city. It was not hard to imagine floods rising out of the lake or crashing out of an angry sky, submerging the town for weeks, and receding to reveal a new island or clutch of small islands. It often made him curious about Robert Ashes' island. During these visits Babit led the conversation, and Bat enjoyed watching her and her people interacting.

IN THE MEANTIME, the search for the bombers intensified. Numerous arrests had already been made by the Bureau, the Public Safety Unit and, not to be outdone, by the Eunuchs. The Ministry of Internal Affairs set up a team to hunt down and destroy these men. It was believed to be a big group organized into small cells. Bat heard about all these operations and wondered where his brother was. Why had he heard nothing from him for so long? He hoped that Tayari had nothing to do with the bombings, especially after General Bazooka's wife got injured. He did not believe that the bombers were responsible for the General's wife's fate. He believed it was the result of infighting, possibly sanctioned by Amin to punish the man for one reason or other. General Bazooka's current low profile seemed to confirm the theory.

AT AROUND THIS TIME Victoria disappeared. She moved from her flat without informing Bat. He suspected that she wanted more money from him, which was fair since he had not seen her for some time now. At the Ministry of Works head-quarters he was told that she had been transferred to Bombo, a town dominated by a military barracks on the way to the north. He decided to let her show her hand, as she eventually would.

Soon after, his brother's fate became clear. As Bat was driving home one evening, a man waved him down at a road junction.

He held a piece of paper out to him in the darkness. Bat lowered the window and took it, and the man walked away without saying a word. He parked by the roadside and read the note: "Abel, one of us killed. Radio failed. Sorry. Cain is alive and keeping watch."

Bat's suspicions were confirmed: his brother was involved in the bombings. He felt a jolt of fear. He felt exposed, open to attack from unknown forces. There were many questions he wanted to ask his brother, the biggest being whether he had targeted the General's wife in order to extract revenge for him. And if he had thought about the possible consequences. He suddenly felt very angry with him. He regretted having given him the money. He wished there was something he could do to make him renounce his campaign of violence. The fact that he was the only family member who knew what Tayari was up to made him feel like an accomplice. By giving him the money he had become one, but what was he to do now? It had been exciting to hear about Bureau cars exploding, but where would it all end? And who was the dead boy? Where was Tayari hiding?

The news that his brother was keeping an eye on him did not reassure Bat. Nobody could be reassured when a government's resources were turned to hunting somebody down. Luck always tended to run out. People tended to make mistakes as the pressure mounted.

Bat chewed the paper and threw it out the window. Did Tayari know where Victoria was? Where was his daughter now? In the barracks? He cursed himself and the circumstances for letting his child grow up in such an environment. Some mistakes seemed to carry incredibly harsh sentences, hurting everybody in the end, especially the innocent.

TAYARI'S COLLEAGUE HAD BEEN arrested with bomb-making equipment at a roadblock not far from the city. The quartet had earlier sworn that if caught, one should fight, hit a soldier in the balls and be shot to death on the spot. That was what happened. The boy had been travelling in the back of a van carrying pota-toes and cassava. The soldiers had refused the bribe and insisted on opening the sacks. As the potatoes flooded the ground, the boy saw his life slip away. He grabbed the head of the crouching soldier, raised his knee with all his might, and drove it in the man's face. The man collapsed with a curse on his bleeding lips, his rifle clattering on the tarmac. The boy reached for it, but before he could get off shots, two soldiers shot him in the chest and he bled to death.

FOR SOME TIME NOW, cars had stopped exploding. Specula-tion was that the bombing ring had been crushed or had run out of steam. Bat tried to keep his mind off the events. He was busy sifting data in preparation for the annual budget. For two whole months he put in twelve-hour days and could not find time to return home for lunch as agreed. But after the Marshal had blessed the budget and launched a new million-shilling bank-note, with a picture of him defecating on Europe, the pressure abated. The shortage of petrol continued, and Bat could only afford to return home for lunch once a week as the rations at the ministry were reduced further.

The people hired to keep an eye on Bat were very delighted with this turn of events. He had thrown them off the track for some time. Energized, they put final touches to their plan.

On the scheduled day, all the staff stayed away. Babit found herself with no cook, no gardener, no guard. When they were around, she hardly noticed them, because they worked well. Now that they were absent, she missed them. The cook was a widowed middle-aged woman living near the landing point of Katabi. The guard came from the town's police station. Since the government paid him, she had little to do with him. The gardener was a large man in his forties. He had been injured in a car crash and subsequently had lost his job as porter at the airport. Since then he had been tending gardens and mourning his fall. He was very talkative and sometimes he told her stories. She both pitied and liked him. She sometimes gave him money because he was always broke and wasn't ashamed to admit it. He was like a sad uncle, dogged by misfortune, unlucky in love. She noticed his absence more than the rest.

Shortly before nine, she went to the kitchen to decide what to cook. She wanted to prepare Bat's favourite steamed bananas with fish or meat. She had dry fish in the house but no meat. The prospect of going to town for meat made her change her plan. She decided to cook fish. She soaked it in water to make the flesh tender. She made everything ready for the fire.

Shortly before ten she went for a bath. It would do her good on this bright sunny day. She filled the tub and slipped in, enjoying herself but keeping in mind not to indulge herself too long because of the cooking. She started dreaming, stretching things out to their blurred edges. Somewhere in the corners of her mind, she thought she heard the sound of a car. Bat never returned home in between leaving for work and lunch. He never forgot things. If this was an exception, she did not mind him finding her in the bath. He would most certainly crack a joke about something or sing at least a few bars of the song which had become their song: "I Can't Get No Satisfaction." If a miracle had happened and he had been given a day off, he might join her, re-creating some of the magic of the Grand Empire Hotel. The cooking could wait. They might drink a glass of red wine or beer in the tub and listen to the birds outside. He was bound to get angry with the staff for staying away without giving notice, as if, before moving in with him, she would protest, she had never cooked, shopped, or cleaned. Things are different now, he would counter sharply.

She could see the future of their relationship. Bat had the upper hand now, and she loved it. But over the years she would gain more leverage. He had told her that he loved her most of all because he had found her open, not yet embittered or hardened by the world, not yet set in her ways. They would set together like aging doors.

Suspended halfway between fantasy and reality, she hardly had time to see her visitors. In her eyes the green overalls were just the blurred forms which accompanied a chloroformed patient to unconsciousness, sometimes to oblivion. The visitors were swift, economical. Their scalpels, magnified by her fear, were inflated to the size and brutality of machetes. They towered, hovered, pressed down hard, and applied the speedy efficiency enjoyed by the best in their trade. They disrobed without fuss, cleaned themselves, bagged their garments, and prepared to go. They drank the tea they found in a thermos flask in the kitchen. They washed the cups and the flask and turned them upside down to dry.

AT THE SCHEDULED TIME the XJ10 swept into the yard with a flurry and a crunch of pebbles. Bat leapt out, tie eased, two top buttons undone almost in one movement. He filled his lungs, exhaled loudly, and savoured those few seconds when the wind hit his exposed chest. He pushed the door open, called Babit, but the house returned only his own voice to him, spurned. He called again as he dropped the briefcase on the sofa. He walked to the bedroom. He feared every lover's worst nightmare: find-ing one's lover in bed with another; his was of finding her with Tayari. It lasted a few seconds, but it bit deep. The bedroom was empty. Her clothes, a blue gown with red lines at the neck, and a white shift, were neatly folded, the black shoes near the bed pol-ished, waiting. He felt his anticipation, eagerness, cooling and coagulating into something nasty. She knew how precious their appointment was to him; why had she betrayed it? What did she have to say for herself? Was this the beginning of another phase, the revelation of a Babit he had not yet had occasion to see? Why was he so angry? Because he had come to rely on her, and he wanted it to stay that way. Maybe she was sick; who said she would never fall sick?

He took a few deep breaths and walked out of the bedroom. He saw footprints, large, blurred, pinkish. He called out as he opened the bathroom door. He almost stepped on her head. The torso was in the bath, arms hanging limply on the sides, the wedding ring winking shatteringly in the light.

He did not know if he cried out or just stared. He did not know if he fainted or vomited. It was just clear that things would never be the same again. He could have phoned. It just never occurred to him. The place seemed grotesquely swollen, with an oppressing smell that seemed to emerge from the bowels of hell. He somehow made it to the police station. It was a miracle that he didn't kill anybody on the way.

At first they thought he was insane, the freshest apparition from the windy domain of psychosis blowing through the land. They got to see a few of those per week as part of the job. But this one looked way out on the extreme outer reaches. Had he killed a general, taken his XJ10, and come to brag about it? Had he also killed the general's wife? Finally, they got through to him, or he got through to them, and the investigative machinery was nudged into motion. They wanted to detain him longer, but they realized that he would be of no help.

He left and zoomed to the city at an average speed of 160 kilometres an hour. The car was just a green blur steered by self-destruction seeking a quick suicidal release. The soldiers, who were the uncrowned kings of the road, committing every aberration in the book, from pushing cyclists off the tarmac to ignoring speed limits and red lights, sat back and watched in surprise. At the Clock Tower a group of Stingers was escorting a high-ranking officer. Bat drove through them, and before the soldiers could raise their fingers to point and threaten, he was gone. He parked in front of the house, rested his head on the wheel and wondered what to do next. It seemed such a weight to get out and put the tragedy in words. It seemed impossible.

Mrs. Kalanda remembered seeing him standing in the doorway, drenched in sweat, on the edge of despair, with the look of madness and grief in his eyes. The stoic bureaucrat had died, leaving behind a strange incarnation. He released a number of mangled sounds which spelled out a tragedy, of what calibre and sort, she could not tell. He waded through her questions, went to the cupboard and put a bottle of Scotch to his mouth. She had to fight him physically to retrieve the remaining quarter. There is no dignified way to grieve, she thought. Grief makes us totter between childishness and beastliness. The saving grace of wisdom and strength comes later when the poison is drained. He lay on the sofa and groaned, a heart-rending spectacle. He was saying at intervals, "I killed her, I killed her."

"Why?" she said trying to hold him. "I don't understand."

She went to the phone and called her husband and the Professor. They arrived to find Bat sitting on the sofa. He was somewhat calmer and he told them what had happened, what he had seen.

"Head on the bathroom floor!" everyone exclaimed at once. Even in a country tormented by lunatics, even to a group that had trekked to the forest to search for him among the dead, this was gut-wrenching. It was personal in every way. They huddled together, grieving, and tried to make plans. There were people to inform, people who would be hurt by the news. Bat took on the biggest burden: he decided to be the one to inform Babit's family. Mrs. Kalanda wanted to do it, but he refused.

"It is my responsibility."

He went with the Professor because he came from the same area as Babit. Also because Bat needed company in case something went wrong on the road. The journey was uneventful. The two men looked grimly in front of them. The Professor had lost a brother. He thought he had a good idea about what his friend was going through. Tired of supporting his sickly wife and getting little in the way of pleasure out of her, he had wished death on her on a number of occasions, but now he believed he had never meant it. The idea of finding her with her head chopped off made him shiver.

Inside the endless Mabira Forest the speedometer shot madly forward. Everything seemed to darken, as if sealed in a green cloth thick as canvas. The Professor prayed that no suicidal cow cross the road, and no mad soldiers place impromptu roadblocks on the tarmac.

"I shouldn't have let you drive! Jesus," he moaned. "Do you want to kill us?"

It was the way the car entered the compound that told people that something had gone terribly wrong. And when the duo emerged looking like they had been exhumed from a landslide, the parents knew that the claws of grief had gripped the family. Bat broke the news slowly, steadily, each word having the effect of cutting, scalding. They all watched him, and for a delayed moment it was as though he were speaking about a disaster averted at the last moment by the intervention of a miracle. But the claws gripped tighter and people's faces crumbled, their lips disfigured with the heaviness of their sorrow. Bat would have paid any amount of money to be elsewhere, even in prison. He asked them for their forgiveness for "killing your daughter who was so dear to me." His father-in-law patted him on the back, as if to say everyone would apportion the blame according to their judgement.

"It is those soldiers; that curse walking this land like an eternal plague. As soon as they attacked the palace and forced the king into exile, I knew that this country would never have peace again," his mother-in-law declared.

"What should the son of man do about those animals?" somebody said, intoning a general sense of helplessness.

"They are not animals as we know them. They are beasts, demented creatures," another elaborated.

It was generally assumed that the State Research Bureau or the Public Safety Unit or the Eunuchs or thugs from the armed forces were responsible. Criticism was not often aimed directly at the Marshal's doorstep, for obvious reasons, but now people talked freely. Grief had given them recklessness.

The cautious ones ended the tirade by asking when the body could be collected for burial. The Professor talked about the post-mortem, the ongoing investigations, the delays that might crop up. Somebody asked if the head would be sewn on the trunk again and received only dirty looks. Another wanted to know whether the freezers in the morgue worked, for, the last they wanted was to bury Babit with flies in her wake. Bat looked on with bowed head, waiting for the tempest to pass.

The police investigations were fast and furious, chiefly because the wife of an important man was on the slab, and partly because of the curious fact that none of the house staff had been around at the time of the murder. The policeman had reported sick, and had been sick for the past few days. Due to a shortage of staff his replacement had arrived after the murder. The detectives concentrated on the gardener and the cook. The former could not be quickly located, but the latter was at home. As soon as she saw the police cars, she knew that there was big trouble or tragedy in the air. The nasty stares from the detectives chilled her. Police brutality was common. The caning of prisoners or of children delivered by despairing parents into police hands was standard procedure. A policeman was like a lion; he was a friend only when sated or out of the way. The woman babbled in fear.

"The gardener told me that we had been given a day off. I did not ask him why. He had to know because he talked a lot with the late Mrs. Katanga . . . I don't know anybody who might have wanted to kill her. She had no enemies. The only person who did not like her was Victoria, the woman with whom Mr. Katanga has a child. She used to threaten her on the phone . . . Apart from her I know nobody who might have liked to harm her . . ."

THE GARDENER WAS FOUND late that evening. "Somebody with a State Research Bureau identity card told me to inform the cook to stay away, because he said that there were investigations scheduled for the day, regarding Mr. Katanga's work, and they wanted nobody around . . ."

The remaining question was: where was this Victoria?

TAYARI APPEARED THAT NIGHT. He sent an emissary, who asked Bat to go to the lake and wait for him. As Bat walked through the trees to the lake, he felt the urge to escape the place. It seemed to ring with Babit's death, like a cave that multiplied the sound, bouncing it against its walls. The lake stretched out in front of him. He looked at its dark-grey skin caught in the moonless night and felt disgusted by its indifference, its perpetuity. It was as if Babit had never visited it, loved it. Nothing seemed to matter to it. He stood in one spot, shivering, wishing to go somewhere very far away, a place Babit had never been. Maybe to the islands to catch parrots and fish. He hated the house with its history of British governors, its pomp, its indifference to time. The last governor had abandoned it and built a bigger house, the current State House. Maybe the others before him had also suffered disasters in its walls, uncharted miseries written in their tombs. He wanted to leave this town and forget it all. He wanted it encircled by water and swallowed whole, with its airport, and the roads Babit had walked. He wanted it reduced to a memory, a flicker in somebody's mind.

"Brother," a voice said to him, "I am extremely sorry about what happened. Maybe if I had taken more care of you, this would not have occurred."

"I doubt that even you could have changed things," Bat replied hoarsely.

"I happen to know where Victoria is."

"You do?" The words seemed to echo endlessly.

"She is in Bombo. Do you have a message for her?"

"I want her to stay out of my life forever."

"I can plant a device in her house—of course, when the girl is out."

"We don't know whether she is the one responsible."

"It is crystal-clear. There is nobody else who hated Babit that much. The work was too clinical to have been unplanned. She is responsible. I bet my arm she is guilty."

"I don't want anything to do with bombs," Bat said, feeling extremely weary.

"Do you want her dead in another fashion? Just give me the word."

"I don't want to kill her."

"You don't! Do you want that creature to remain eating and breathing after what it did to your wife?"

"I don't want anybody's death on my conscience."

"The responsibility would be mine, big brother. I would do it as a favour, a show of gratitude. You have helped my group and the country so much."

"I can't kill my daughter's mother."

"But she has killed all the children Babit would have produced. Aren't you mad about that?"

"Yes, I am. But killing is not my line of business."

"Give me her legs. I will put her in a wheelchair for you."

"Listen to yourself, brother. You talk like those men you are fighting."

"I can't allow injustice to go unpunished. It is the very reason why this country is still dominated by soldiers. Everybody is afraid to do a thing against them. I have done something, and I am sure that it has helped."

"I never gave you money to make bombs," Bat mumbled weakly.

"The radio could not work. Those thugs have no respect for words. They respect dynamite. And fire. They are looking for me, but before they get me, I will put many in hospital."

"Where does all this violence come from?"

"I decided to offer myself to the nation. To die for the cause.

It is a vocation, like priesthood. You are lucky that I am here itching to avenge my sister-in-law's death."

"Don't touch even a hair on Victoria's head. The law will deal with her."

"Do you believe that? Do you really believe that, big brother? Is that Cambridge University talking or utter resignation?"

"The law will take care of her. That is how we do it. Babit was not a violent person. Nobody is going to die in her name."

Tayari threw his hands in the air with frustration. If he could, he would have thrown his brother on the ground and punched his face or made him eat wet sand. "The law! There is no law in this country, except the gun. The bigger the better. Soldiers have the licence to kill. I take that licence in my hands and I want to use it."

"You don't mean it."

"After letting you down, I want to do you right and let you know beforehand. It is the reason why I did not attack her secretly."

"Look here, brother. I want you to find the killers and put them in the hands of the police. They will lead the investigators to her, and the law will take its course."

"I don't understand you, big brother. Maybe I never have. But I respect you. You are educated, but you have balls. Coming back after Cambridge made me respect you. Coming back after detention made me fear you. Any other person would have stayed in London and fucked Uganda. It is the only reason why I am going to do as you say."

"I trust that you will keep your word. Take care."

"You too. Oh, by the way, were you not happy when you heard that my piece had taken care of the General's wife?"

"It doesn't help me now, does it? Babit is gone. Go and find her killers."

"I won't let you down."

With that he slipped away in the darkness. Bat did not even hear his footfalls. It was as if he had flown away. Should I have sanctioned Victoria's death? Wouldn't some of Babit's people have been happy to get the news of her killer's demise? I don't expect Tayari to understand my position. For him justice excuses everything, the way Victoria believes that love excuses everything. They are both on the run. One hunting the other, the other hunted by the security forces, Bat thought. That two women's lives had been destroyed because of him saddened him, the kind of sadness his brother could not understand because in his world there were no half-measures. Victoria, the love extremist, had now discovered that too much love killed, that it was a drug that needed dilution if the user was not to be killed by the poison of its concentration.

He looked at the house in the distance, reduced to a bunch of lights dimly penetrating the foliage. He had no wish to go back there. He had no wish to face the people, and the weight of the memories, and the night. He had no wish to smell the cooking, hear the voices, sense their sympathies. He wanted to walk into the lake and repose in its ageless bosom. Many had found eternal rest there. The more he considered it, the more attractive the prospect became. What more do I want to achieve? I have seen it all, at least as much as I can stomach, he said to himself aloud. As the temptation mounted, crashing in his chest, swelling in his head, making his ears sing, he heard somebody calling him. It was the Professor.

"We have missed you, you bastard. Let us go home. People are waiting for you."

THE SEARCH FOR VICTORIA was short but very dangerous. Tayari and his friends had to be very careful not to land in the hands of their enemies. Having committed the crime, Victoria had curtailed her movements. Reality had kicked in, destroying the euphoric inebriation of the deed. She had already paid the killers, butchers from a nearby town. She had got in contact with them through a friend at the Ministry of Works, for, having lost favour with the Bureau, she could not get anybody from there to do the job. The men had named their price and had promised to deliver. In style. On two separate occasions they had joked that people were animals, that when you got used to slitting the throats of cows, like they did daily, you could easily do a person. They had even asked if she wanted proof. A hand or fingers or something more intimate. The head on a plate would have served as a bonus as well as a warning; a bonus for its biblical dimension: Herod's daughter receiving the head of John the Baptist; a warning to keep her quiet if things went wrong. She had assured them that nobody could penetrate the protective wall she had around her: the might of General Bazooka. But they still felt that a warning was in order. One never knew . . .

The friend at the Ministry of Works had already told her how it happened, and how the police were hot on her heels. It was the same friend who had told the gardener to tell the cook not to turn up. He had warned her not to mention him if things ran out of hand.

Alone, Victoria felt the world contracting. Luckily for her, the butchers did not know where she lived. It slowly sank in that it would take a miracle for Bat to take her back. She still loved him deeply and wanted to be with him, but the way was now blocked by Babit's death. For the first time since the murder she thought of her daughter: what would become of her? In her terror she tried to reach for the only rock of certainty in her life: General Bazooka. She tried to call, but the phone was engaged. She wanted to go to his house and report the deed and ask for advice, but she was afraid of landing in police hands. She knew what the General would tell her: he would congratulate her and advise her to savour the moment, but she wanted to hear it all the same. It struck her again that if she failed to locate him, or if he turned her away, she was all by herself.

Two days later somebody knocked on her door at eight in the morning. Her heart leapt with fear. He knocked again, loudly, like the knocking of soldiers. "Fungua mlango," he barked in gruff Swahili. She threw the door open and saw a man standing in her doorway. He was dressed in the gear of a Safari Rally driver, with advertising stickers on his clothes. When she recognized him, her fears grew. Behind him was a rally car festooned with dark windows and big advertising stickers. It looked like there were people inside. Perhaps it was Bat with military policemen or guys from the Public Safety Unit. The thought of falling into their hands chilled her. They would take the chance to vent their hatred of the Bureau on her. Not too long ago there had been a gun battle between the two groups.

"We are going for a ride," Tayari said in a stern voice.

"I can't leave my child here by herself," she replied in a shaky voice.

"Do you want to bring her along? The clock is ticking. I hope you won't reach for a gun or do anything stupid."

"I don't have a gun."

"Every Bureau member is entitled to a pistol, but can always get an AK-57 rifle."

"I don't have one."

"You obviously prefer knives. My first love is dynamite. It is cleaner and more dramatic," he said, smiling maliciously.

"You can't kill me. I am the mother of Bat's daughter."

"Just hurry up, will you?"

They left the child with a neighbour. Victoria sat in front with him. He was a little surprised by her lack of resistance: she could have shouted and alerted neighbours, and maybe somebody would have called soldiers from the barracks. The car roared and then sped away. They were headed for the north. His plan was to follow the main road to Kakooge, Katuugo and, if necessary, continue to Nakasongola. If by then she had not told him the truth, then he would resort to other means. He would have preferred to use weathered back roads to bruise their backsides in the potholes, but the possibility of hitting livestock, cyclists or schoolchildren kept him away.

She sat in the car, beautiful, gloomy, her breasts heavy on her chest. He felt a small pang of regret. This might be her last journey, their last meeting. Personally, he did not care; he would do anything to get his brother out of his current state of grief. He remembered the first time he saw her. He felt outdone by his brother, who seemed to have it all: the education, the power job, the beautiful woman. But a lot had happened since. His stint as a spy had blunted his fantasies.

What mattered now was getting the truth. He would try to respect his brother's decision. Intellectualism bred guilt which bred gutlessness much of the time. He agreed that there were things he did not understand, intricate designs and logic his head could not bore through. Those were the things which held his brother in check. Less education made his own position easier to defend: he either did something or he didn't. When he decided to do something, he did not regret it. His father had more or less the same attitude.

Over the years, he had met many women like Victoria: women wanting to break out and doing it wrong. To rebel against their parents they married soldiers. To appear tough they hung out with Bureau men. To feel safe they joined the Bureau. They often ended up in the clutches of evil men who were infected with violence. They had children with these men, making the bonds of their oppression even tighter. They got blackmailed into staying or complying because they feared for their children. Sometimes they complied and the children got hurt all the same. He had helped a few to get out, but some had been so bruised that even when outside they felt unsafe, wanting to go back to what they knew. A few years ago he might have let Victoria off lightly, reasoning that the dead couldn't be brought back whatever one did. Now he was a different man, maturer, tougher.

The first fifteen kilometres were done in a matter of minutes. They overtook everything on the road. He played games with the Boomerang of an army officer. He would slow down, let it overtake him and get away, and then he would put his foot down, put on the spotlights, catch up with the bigger car and overtake it in one breath. He did that twice. The second time the soldier stuck out a hand and waved an automatic pistol at him. He was gone by then. The soldiers at the roadblock admired the car.

"When did you win the Safari Rally?" one asked, almost drooling.

"At the beginning of the year," Tayari lied, adjusting the visor on the helmet, feeling grateful to the friend who had organized the borrowing of the car and the gear.

"It was my dream, still is," the man said and waved him on.

The sun had come up but was kept out by the smoked windows. During the next twenty minutes, with top speeds of two hundred and above, Victoria's bowels gave way. Tayari was awakened from his trance by the stench. They were now in the endless grasslands of Katuugo. The giant grass, almost two metres high, formed thick walls on both sides of the road. When the wind blew, it felt as if the grass walls would collapse and drown the road and the car. He opened the side window, ground through the gears and stopped. He held his breath for some twenty seconds, savouring the deliciousness of adrenaline, the banging heart, the shaking knees, the tingling in his back. He got out and stood beside the car, breathing in fresh air.

"I want to know where the killers are," he said, leaning in.

"Let me first wash up, please."

"Hurry."

As she walked away, she remembered the military school where General Bazooka had sent her to become an agent, especially the big posters with the words WE LOVE YOU MARSHAL AMIN. She remembered her hair being shaved off; and stripping, walking naked with other women through a corridor to get military fatigues and boots; the old clothes and shoes burning on a heap through the night; the graduation parade wearing new clothes, a new persona; and membership of a new family. As she washed the filth off her body, she knew that it was time to become a full person again. But how and where?

Tayari smoked a cigarette. It was going to be a beautiful day, clear, warm, windy. It was very quiet here and gave the impression that the whole country was at peace, blessed with the serenity of a very small rural village. He wondered what he would do after the conflicts, the dynamite. Would he return to civilian life? Or spy for a new regime? The way things looked, the final war would be short and fierce. The regime had dislodged itself by virtue of its lack of order. The fact that they could not catch him, and that many believed he was a ghost, said a lot about the present state of affairs. His journey down this dangerous path had begun simply: with sibling rivalry. All he had ever wanted was to beat his brother and prove his worth. The weight of the political situation, and the fact that he would never catch up to his brother, had pointed the way to his destiny. He had enjoyed the secrecy, the silences which had covered his tracks. People had written him off. Then came the fireworks, the beauty of the weddings, the air of celebration, the release of the explosion. He sometimes missed the ambience, the smell of pilau, the dancers, the wrestlers, the beauty of the flower of dynamite fading in the air.

The sight of Victoria stumbling back broke his train of thoughts. He stood in front of her and watched her approaching. She dared not meet his eyes, preferring to look to the side or on the ground, which was for the better because he felt so much hatred for her that he did not want to see her as a full person. He wanted to see her as an object he could hate and, if given the opportunity, could smash and trample. His voice was an ugly croaking sound which carried the full impact of his feelings. "We can do it the easy way or the hard way. It is up to you. Start talking." Standing two metres away, her head turned to the side, her fingers playing with a cluster of blades of grass, her voice tremulous, she told him everything. From the way she talked, he knew that she was telling the truth.

"Get in the car."

The drive back was slower; he had got all the answers. She thought he was driving her home; instead, he took her to the small town where his friends were waiting. They debated whether or not to go and arrest the butchers themselves. They knew that the killers would be on their guard and would do anything to protect themselves. They knew that they were burly men, not easily subdued. Wisely, they decided to call the detectives working on the case.

THE NEWS OF THE ARREST of the main suspects in the murder investigations was broadcast on the evening news. Victoria had hit national radio. It was further reported that one of the suspects was in hospital with gunshot wounds sustained during his arrest. He had swung at the arresting officers with his machete-cum-cleaver and been shot.

THE BODY OF THE LATE BABIT was finally released by the coroner for burial. The torso had, mercifully, been reunited with its head, the whole embalmed, and enclosed in a gleaming mahogany coffin with genuine brass handles. During all this time Bat's mind was locked onto the encounter in the surgeon's office. He had gone there to sign some forms pertaining to the case. He arrived to find the man holding his wife's head by the hair, headed for the operating theatre. He remembered standing still to take in the scene. He might have shaken his head to clear the perplexity. The man was smoking a cigarette and humming Nat King Cole's "Coquette." He smiled when he saw him and said, "This baby is in safe hands. I am going to sew her up really well."

All that time he kept thinking that he had held that head in his arms, kissed it, laid it on his breast. He had liked that lifeless hair, and sometimes complained about the smell of the products used to keep it glossy. He had loved those eyes, now vacant, and knew those lips, now gaping, and that tongue, now lolling. He knew that neck, now abbreviated, waiting to be rejoined onto its old hinges; the taste of the saliva in that desecrated mouth; and the torso which lay somewhere on a slab, emptied of its organs. The essence had gone; the head now looked foreign, monstrous.

At that moment he was convinced that there was no resurrection of bodies; he didn't want the idea to exist. He had no wish to meet Babit in that body ever again. It would be too unpleasant an experience; there would be no joy in it. His mind would keep going back to the bathroom, to this office. He only wanted to meet her in ethereality, pure, liberated from bodily encumbrances. Sublimated. At the same time, he discovered another basic truth, that he had become a polygamist, just like any man who lost a wife in whichever way. Babit had become a trinity: there was the Babit he had courted and married; the dead Babit, whose head he found on a plate on the bathroom floor; and the ethereal Babit, the one he wanted to see again.

The scene played itself in his head through the wailings, the eulogies, the rituals of saying goodbye. The first shovelful of dirt to hit the coffin sounded like an old prison gate banging closed: how long would his incarceration last?

The family was reminded that it was an exceptional occurrence to lower the coffin when the culprits were already apprehended. There was a growing feeling that they could be the few who would benefit from the justice living a weak existence in an age of gun rule. This became the focus tempering much of their grief because, deep down, people were optimists, who wanted mistakes corrected, things back to running as they remembered them in the past. They waited for the court case as if it were unquestionable that the verdict would be in their favour. They could not allow anybody to crush that with pessimism; that would be like breaking open Babit's grave and throwing her body out of the coffin. Bat promised to hire the best lawyers money could buy and to give the killers the sentence they deserved.

What Babit's family did not know was that General Bazooka had been briefed about the case and had vowed to leave no stone unturned in the effort to free "a hard-working Bureau agent falsely accused of the murder of a common prostitute." It was just as well that they remained uninformed. In a country where there was no open prostitution, the word "prostitute" would have hurt too much, most especially because Babit had known only one man in her life.

BAT FOUND HIMSELF in a crater of despair he could not climb out of. His friends visited often, but because they knew him well, they knew when to stay and when to leave. With other sympathizers it was different. They kept streaming in from the village of his birth, from Babit's and Mafuta's families, and they kept the place buzzing even when he craved solitude, a moment of contemplation. People he had done favours for, lent money to, recommended for jobs, came to pay their respects. On one level the attention was good; on another it was counterproductive because grief is an individual emotion. But he still entertained his guests, men who now held him in high regard because of his education, and the fact that he had come back from the dead after being presumed six months in the morgue. He had become their man, their beacon. They could count on him to understand their problems.

They brought him chickens, multicoloured birds with legs tied together with banana fibre. They brought him goats, which had survived the roadblocks and the cooking pans of hungry soldiers. They brought him long-fingered cooking bananas because they had heard that they were his favourite food. They brought him sacks of beans, groundnuts, maize, millet. His home became a food depot, an abattoir, a chaotic holiday camp. In their goodness, their enthusiasm, they just made things worse. He would see them following him around, listen to their questions about the lawyers: Why had he not hired Saudi or Libyan lawyers who were most likely to exert influence because of their nationality? Why had he not hired people to take care of the killer? Why had he not removed his daughter from the hands of a murderess? When was he going to remarry?

In his present state of mind he could not concentrate on anything. He asked for a leave and devised ways of dodging his guests. He hid at the Professor's a few times. He spent nights at the Kalandas' and in the few still-functioning hotels. He spent long periods talking with his sister. They had become closer than ever now. She listened to his words, his silences, his mumblings. He listened to her stories, her indirect words of advice. They talked about the coming trial, the lawyers, the prospects. She cooked his favourite food, and they ate it with some degree of enjoyment. She devised a system whereby she spent a week per month with him. But he grew tired of waiting for her arrival and he acknowledged his growing dependence on her—a dependence that seemed to be eroding her relationship with her possessive husband. Although he still did not like Mafuta, he knew that he had no right to deprive him of his family life. He put a stop to his sister's visits.

One day he received a letter of condolence from Damon, which was also an invitation to go to London. They could go out and tour the country, revisit the past or do something new. He remembered the nights at the Grand Empire, the posh nights, his proposal to Babit. There was something very appealing and something very repellent about it at the same time. He wanted to retrace his time there with Babit, but he realized that nostalgia would be the death of him. A mourner who returned to the sites of happier times was either reconciled or devastated. He knew that London without Babit was no longer his London and would crush him just like it had done others before him. He decided to go to America for a month.

BAT'S FIRST STOP was an expensive hotel in New York. He liked the seclusion, the anonymity, and the newness of it all. He liked the aggressive thrust of the buildings, the dire extremity of a crowded skyline. He liked the freedom he had from the encumbrances of familiarity, for here he was a speck in this city of millions, a mote flying in the wind. In the bosom of the great city, he sipped his whisky, praying for peace of mind. He settled down and turned on the television, seeking refuge in the deluge of images and sounds.

It was not long before he met Marshal Amin, who had made a grand entrance into Hollywood, and into the world of comic strips. During his stint in Tinseltown the Marshal had made two hit movies, now available on cable, both portraying his mentor, Il Duce Benito Mussolini. The bulk, the shaven head, the jutting jaw, the heavy make-up, the fact that a black giant was portraying a white runt, made for wonderful comedy. Of course, Amin had had to lose weight, shaving off much of the bulky stomach in high-tech gyms and by inserting laxative pills in his rectum. To hide the scandalous height difference, he was filmed from the waist up. In the first epic, *The Rise of Il Duce: Il Duce's Triumph*, he dealt with the problems young Mussolini experienced on the way up. The pains of growing up on the fringes, his height, his criminality, the rigours of army life, the unfulfilled dreams, the sexual frustrations, the boiling urge to shine, then the coup and the string of victories in Bulgaria, Greece, Abyssinia, and the emergence of Italy as a major power. In the second hit, *Il Duce's Blues*, Amin dealt with his mentor's turbulent career as empire-builder and chronicled the way Europe and America conspired to bring his reign to an end. He showed his mentor's bravery at the front, the fighting methods he initiated but which were credited to Englishmen or Americans, his selfless tours of military hospitals comforting the wounded soldiers with his golden tenor saxophone and the artificial limbs he distributed, his unrecognized efforts to dethrone Hitler, his bitterness at not being universally recognized as a genius statesman. Then there was the demonization by the press, the wives who kept committing suicide, the failure of Fascism to become a household name like Nazism or Stalinism, and his heroic end. The two films had made Amin's name and were

already classics, towering achievements for somebody who did
not make his acting debut till he was thirty-nine. As a result, he
had become Africa's first truly famous film star.

Bat also discovered that here Amin had tried his luck as a sex
therapist and small-time political spin doctor, with little success.
Too many competitors. He had sent President Nixon advice to
gag, lock up, or torture the criminals involved in the Watergate
adventure. If they still wanted to fawn for the cameras, he
advised gangland executions of culprits and their entire families.
The financial invoice he sent Nixon was never honoured. Nixon
had other plans, and when he fell, Amin sent him a telegram
congratulating him upon his impeachment and the golfing time
at his disposal. He offered his services to President Ford, warning him to take a much harder line and avoid the pitfalls of his
predecessor.

Bat took to television channel-hopping. He concentrated on
sports. He watched American football, boxing and wrestling. He
would lie there and watch the scrimmaging, the touchdowns,
the charges. He took a liking to the West Coast Destroyers, the
Buffalo Blasters and the Dallas Tornadoes. There was a wealth
of information about both the teams and the players. It amazed
him how many small details the media knew about the players.
They knew how many bones somebody had snapped in his
career, the bruises suffered, the pounds he bench-pressed daily,
his daily calorie intake, the names of his pets, his hobbies, what
he did ten Christmases ago . . . He would sit there and play with
the data, multiplying it, dividing it, setting up bets as to who
would win . . . As long as he kept himself busy, and drugged himself with enough whisky, the Babit trinity left him alone. But
when he woke up late in the night, his mind would begin to wander. He would get nasty flashbacks, something that had not
occurred in Uganda. He would lie in bed shivering, trying to fix
his mind on something else. He rarely succeeded. He would
wake up, switch on the television, drink some tea and wait for
the day to break or sleep to return.

During the day he would venture out and visit a few famous

places. It was soothing to walk through the parks on sunny afternoons, feeling the tender grass under his feet. At one end of the
Village, away from the restaurants and residential areas, he discovered a place where extreme spectacles were staged. As a former sportsman, feats of strength, competition, expenditure of
energy, turned him on. He kept wondering what some of these
guys would be doing if they had been born in Uganda, and what
he would be doing if he had been born here. He watched men
with ten-foot boa constrictors and one-ton anacondas feeding
live alligators to their pets, which had names like Sweetie or
Popsy. He saw a man balancing a car on his head. There was a
young man juggling three raging chain-saws, and, hard by, rodeo
stars were riding snappy two-ton bulls, tasting ten euphoria-
laden seconds before the fall. There was always something spectacular to see, to take his mind off his situation, to tire him out
so that by the time he returned to his hotel he could sleep for a
few hours before the Babit trinity arrived.

After a week his urge to do something dangerous mounted
to insupportable levels. On television he saw advertisements of
street racing in Chicago. His love for speed kicked in like a fever.
He flew to Chicago to participate in the races. He watched the
plane rising, the Atlantic Ocean swelling, New York City shrinking and receding, and he felt relieved. He hoped that the nightmares would leave him alone and stay buried in the canyons
below him. He thought about his brother, and he hoped he
would renounce the violence before his luck ran out. He thought
about the Professor and how he would have loved to be here,
with the mighty city below him, headed for another one, well
away from his students and the tedium of teaching. He made a
mental note to give him a two-week holiday in America on his
birthday.

Chicago struck him like a dream, something he could have
planned mathematically. There was the captivating heights of the
skyscrapers, juggernauts with no competition in sight, then the
marvellous Great Lakes. Caught in the sunlight, they dissipated
like silver flashes into the sky, and seemed to stretch to infinity.

They made the city seem to float, a crowded ship manufactured by some delirious inventor and cut adrift to seek its destiny.

Bat installed himself on the hundredth floor of the Omniscient Hotel, where there was no day or night, where one washed one's face with clouds in the morning and dried oneself with the legs of the ubiquitous sun. Up there, he hoped to fool the night and mislead the Babit trinity into passing his suite by. He could look out for miles and feel like a bird flying over the lakes, or dodging in and out of the buildings and the clouds.

For a whole week he went each day to the racing track. There were limitless lines of scrap cars ready for sale with prices ranging from fifty to five hundred dollars per cadaver. You chose one, paid for it and filled it with petrol, then raced and crashed it at the end of the road. There was beauty in the demolition job, with iron tearing, tyres squealing, the crowds cheering, the smell of petrol overpowering, the mangled carcasses towed away, like dead bulls, to be crushed into balls of steel. He would crash four cars a day and return to his hotel bruised, purged, and sleep like a stone.

On the fourth day, however, he arrived at the track feeling down; the Babit trinity had located him and had terrorized him. He was more reckless than usual. The third car overturned. He was pulled out of the wreck with cuts to his face and legs. He was taken to a doctor on a stretcher, but his injuries were minor. He retired to his hotel. In bed, with the wounds and the leg smarting, he realized that he had been intending to cause himself damage for some time. Now that it had occurred, he felt better. He would stretch his leg and hear from muscles he had not heard from since Cambridge. He would turn and hear his body scream with pain. He now had enough distraction to keep his mind occupied. Coupled with the talk shows and sports on television and the whisky, he managed to get by reasonably well. The Babit trinity now visited for shorter intervals. He would wake up, stay in bed, and sleep again.

It was during this time that he saw an advertisement for hunting rifles and another for a shooting school, which claimed to be able to teach you within days. His mind flew back to his days in the Parliament Building and his wish to learn how to handle a gun. He made inquiries and was enrolled in the nearest shooting school, not far from his hotel. Military science and technology had never interested him as such because for most educated people soldiery and anything to do with it is the preserve of barbarians. He applied himself to the theory part of the lessons as if he were doing another degree course. He learned the history, the evolution, and the mechanics of guns. He concentrated on rifles and pistols, the most prevalent weapons in Uganda. The practical part was harder but also more fascinating. He could see his enemies, and what could happen to them after a bullet had entered their hearts. At the beginning the noise gave him headaches. But it was worth it, for a psychological barrier had been broken down. He could somehow empathize with his brother. There were moments when he forgot himself, feeling all-powerful, with the weight of the gun like a key to heaven or hell. It was an exhilaration that neared that of speed. Maybe that was what Tayari felt when setting the bombs.

These were his best days in America. Once a week he got on the phone and talked to the Kalandas, asking about the lawyers. Everything was ready; the trial was about to start. He spent one more week at the shooting school, made one tour of the city and prepared to return home and shoulder his burden.

THE DAY BAT ARRIVED was the day Dr. Ali left Uganda for the last time. The relationship between him and Marshal Amin had broken down. As far as Ali was concerned, he had no more work to do. The main bone of contention was Uganda's southern neighbour: Tanzania. Marshal Amin wanted to attack the country and neutralize the guerrillas who were now and then attacking Ugandan border towns. Dr. Ali had offered sacrifice and the omens had not been good. Despite that, the Marshal wanted to go on with his plan. Dr. Ali had aired his displeasure

and warned that Amin was digging his grave, but the Marshal
saw no other way out of the stalemate. Amin had then consulted
other astrologers, who had given him positive omens. He
believed that the Dream could be wrong this time . . . The parting had been acrimonious, with Amin accusing Dr. Ali of exploiting him. He had threatened to close the department of
astrology at the university if the astrologer left and to deport all
Zanzibari astrologers, but nothing could keep Dr. Ali in the
country. He did not mind if astrology disappeared in Uganda; he
had many followers elsewhere on the continent and abroad. As
his Learjet headed for Zaïre, the astrologer felt delighted; he
had played baby-sitter for long enough. Now he was going to sit
back and enjoy himself. Mobutu's chances were very good. He
had an iron grip on his country and no fear of guerrillas. The
astrologer kept thinking that Uganda was like a madwoman of
untold beauty; efforts to save her were bound to be doomed.
Lovers would come and go, breaking their backs trying to free
her from the bonds of hell, but it would finally be left to herself
to break the chains.

AS SOON AS BAT RETURNED, he knew that the coming
months were going to be tempestuous, to say the least. For the
first time he was obliged to get out of his XJ10 at all roadblocks.
He endured body and car searches and demands for bribes with
a stoic air. He would look at the rifles in the soldiers' hands and
feel like emptying magazines into the bastards.

A week after his return his lawyers withdrew from the case.
They were reluctant to give the reasons why, but he found out
that they had been abducted and their lives threatened by armed
men. Bat conferred with the Kalandas and the Professor and
they found other lawyers. This was a pretty distressing period,
but as one of the principal players in the drama, he had no way
out. He gritted his teeth and hoped for the best.

GENERAL BAZOOKA FOUND a new purpose in life when his old lover asked him for help in the murder case. He had always known that Victoria would return. They had been together for so long that the bonds, however aged, would be hard to sever. His original plan had been to engineer her escape from police custody and kill the trial summarily. A prince could get away with it, but his chief advisor, the self-effacing colonel, had cautioned him "to let justice take its course." He discovered that if he wanted to punish Bat properly, and to spit at the justice system at the same time, he had to let the trial go on. Thus he had let Victoria endure the humiliation of detention. He had nonetheless ordered the police to make life easy for her. She was given her own Nissen hut, where she could look after her child, prepare her own meals, and receive visitors.

He had renamed the child, calling her Samsona, claiming paternity on the technicality that Victoria must have carried his sperm in her body for years before it exploded into germination. He had convinced Victoria, who was not in a position to argue to the contrary, that this was a common occurrence among bears, and since bears, lower animals, could do it, what of humans? Whenever he came to visit, she would tell the child, "Come and greet your father, Samsona." The child would come and sit on the General's lap. He would make an effort to play with it before tiring of the games and sending it off. There was little conversation between the General and Victoria, partly because it had always been that way, partly because there was not much to say. The General usually came to instruct her what to do when the trial began. He had made sure that the State Research Bureau paid her salary on time, and in full, and gave her round-the-clock protection. This last provision did not sit well with the police, but there was little they could do about it; they had their lives and careers to think about.

Before the trial started, the General hired the best lawyers left
in the city and ordered the best tailors to design the most flamboyant garments for Victoria. The first time she appeared in
court, she was dressed like a Muslim pilgrim from Mecca. She
was wrapped in clothes so fine and so white that they looked
almost diaphanous. On her head she wore a thin cape which flat-
tered her features well.

Bat and Babit's family were scandalized. Since the first proceedings were highly technical, mere preambles, and since lawyers
spoke softly, most people in court paid more attention to Victoria's appearance than to what was going on. Bat had come
expecting the General to reveal his tactics, and from then on he
knew that provocation was going to be a regular feature of
the sessions. There were complaints from Muslims about Victoria's clothing in the only paper in business, but no apology was
offered.

The next time round, two weeks later, she came dressed as an
Egyptian queen, with flowing garments, a belt, huge gold bangles, rich eyeliner, a bottle of perfume radiating its entire intoxi-
cating content to every corner of the court-house. People got
headaches, stomach cramps, and violent attacks of nausea. The
judge became sick in his handkerchief and suspended the hearing for the day. It soon occurred to the General and his team to
dress Victoria as a southern princess. He immediately fired the
previous dressmakers, without paying them a cent, and hired
one who designed royal costumes out of barkcloth and cotton.
This time three hefty Bureau agents brought Victoria, with eyebrows in the sky like a haughty royal, to court in a resplendent
chair. The monarchists seethed with fury and vowed revenge,
but since the kingdoms were abolished, they had to take their
anger to bed with them.

The trial turned into such a farce that Bat walked out on a
number of occasions. He would lie in his bed at night, unable to
sleep a wink, and wonder what use the trial was. The search for
justice seemed futile. At the height of his despair he would see
his brother's irate face asking him why he had turned down his

offer to deal with Victoria outside the reaches of justice. "Is this what you wanted?" he would be saying in a hoarse voice. He would get up and walk about in the house to distract himself from such thoughts. He would think about Babit in her glory and in her desecration, and the determination not to give up came back. He no longer had nightmares, just waking dreams, feelings of longing, guilt, emptiness, loss.

On the days she was cross-examined, Victoria would put on her royal robes and arrive in a magnificent chair with long polished handles. Her lawyer made so many objections and wasted so much time that little work was done. Bat would lose patience with his lawyers, but since there were no others eager to take on the case, he could not push them too far. They were receiving death threats against themselves and their families but had refused to quit the case, and he respected them for that.

Many people, including Babit's parents, talked of dropping the case, if only to save Babit's name. They could not bear to hear her called a common prostitute. Bat knew that, these being rural folks, they might forget that history was ephemeral; it erased itself as soon as it wrote itself. Opening the case under another regime would not be possible. The case would simply vanish. Files would get lost or burned. They forgot that the next regime would have bigger problems than the aborted search for justice in Babit's name.

Babit's mother could hardly bear to look at Victoria. The fact that the same woman, a commoner passing herself off as royalty, had killed her first child made her physically sick, and many times she refused to go to court. She would stay home or come with the family and stay somewhere in town and wait for the reports at the end of the day.

GENERAL BAZOOKA SAVOURED the drama. He saw himself as an artist at work and he loved every minute of it. He would sit with his cronies on the veranda of his orgy mansion, drink and laugh and argue about the merits and demerits of certain episodes. He planned twists and turns, and the impunity of it served to take his mind off the pressures of work and the misery of having a wife hovering between life and death, her skin as brittle as a dry leaf. He still visited her, disregarding non-visiting hours if necessary, pushing doctors and nurses around, posting guards in awkward places. His chief advisor had urged him to vary his visiting hours for fear of attack by dissidents dressed as doctors, nurses or cleaners.

There had been plans to fly his wife to Libya, to the same hospital where the former Vice President stayed in his wheel-chair, but they were still on hold, for she did not want to leave her children behind. When he proposed sending the children along with her, she said that she would think about it. He remembered the way she struggled with each word, releasing it like a gummy drop of sap seeping from a wounded tree trunk. He could imagine the effort giving him an answer cost her. The doctors said that it was a good sign that she had begun to talk, albeit slowly, but he could not recognize her voice; it sounded like sandpaper on rough wood. Nowadays, whenever he brought up the subject, she would ask him to tell her a story, or to talk about the good old days, or to describe the weather outside the window. He had sensed that she was afraid to leave the country, afraid that she might get neglected, left on her own in a strange land. In his heart of hearts he knew that she wanted to die on the soil she had walked all her life. The idea of her death got to him. It trickled into the things he did. It insinuated itself in the way he behaved in cabinet meetings, the impatience he showed at traffic lights and roundabouts. It drove him into creating more spectacles.

He became obsessed with eternal life and Judgement Day. He noticed the abundance of marabou storks in the city. They seemed to be watching, waiting, stalking. It was as if they were waiting for his wife's carcass, and the flesh on his bones. There were several garbage dumps in the city where they congregated in the hundreds, in all sizes, the biggest large as a goat, the smallest not bigger than a rabbit. They looked like mourners frozen in their grief, or rather like very hungry people caught in the game of waiting for the next morsel. They infuriated him when they hovered above the city, coasting on thermal columns thrusting from the ground, almost without moving their wings at all, as though everything beneath them was theirs, ready for the taking. Every week he directed his chauffeur to take him to a different dump. He would take out his automatic rifle and fire, blowing off bills, ripping gizzards, crowning the garbage heaps with twisted carcasses of bleeding storks. Alerted by the shooting, the military police arrived on several occasions.

"Twisted," they said, going away. "Doesn't he have better things to do? A ministry to run?"

He would go away thinking that he had done something, but the next time the birds seemed to have multiplied by ten, as though out in numbers to mock their tormentor. He would feel his skin creeping with terror. At such moments he would remember his wife's question: "Are the bombers still busy at work?" Busy at work, as though delivering groceries? The power of that innuendo, that indirect criticism of his and his government's inability to take care of the problem, said without the least malice or animosity, could not be erased with the blood of a million storks, and would depress him.

THE TRIAL TRUNDLED ON to an uncertain end. The nearer the end drew, the more outrageously Victoria was instructed to behave. Nowadays she came to court escorted by ten Bureau agents dressed as court pages and behaving as such. On the penultimate day she came dressed like a Catholic nun, with a big glittering rosary dangling from her neck. A group of staunch Catholics took offence. They were dismissed because court rules were, everybody was allowed to dress any way they wanted, as long as it was not in miniskirts. Victoria's habit had fallen way below the knees and thus within the stipulation of the law. Out-

side court, one hundred indifferent people who had been collected off the streets, put on a lorry and dumped there, were
chanting her innocence. They urged the judge to dismiss the
case and stop wasting the taxpayers' money.

ON JUDGEMENT DAY Bat woke up very early. He had slept
very badly and the previous night's whisky had left him with a
big headache. He took a shower and prepared to pick up the
day's gauntlet. He had moved to the city, and now lived in a
quiet suburb in another government villa. As he sat on the bed
fully dressed, it struck him that he was alone, unfussed over,
unwatched, and that it was going to be a terrible day. It felt
almost as terrible as the day of the funeral. He could hear his sister moving about in another room. His nephew emerged first,
wearing a blue cotton suit with red shoes. His sister followed
and, seeing that he was not in the mood to talk, busied herself
with other things. He went into the garage and sat in the car
waiting for the Kalandas and the Professor. He had the urge
to drive away and leave everything behind, and return a day or
two later to hear what had transpired. His friends arrived ten
long minutes later. They exchanged greetings and in two cars
they drove to court. The morning mist did not lift the mood
either. Bat kept turning on the wipers, then off, then on, then off
again. His sister watched him from the corner of her eye, word-
lessly. They found Babit's family already at the court-house.
    Victoria came dressed as a princess with ten pages in tow. She
looked sombre though and did not leer at those she was meant
to torment. The proceedings were long-winded, as though the
judge had finally decided to assert his authority. Dressed in his
black robes and the ridiculous curly white wig, he looked like a
kettle with a white tea-cosy. The evidence, everybody heard, was
circumstantial, and thus not enough to convict. Victoria walked
free. The killers were slapped on the wrist. Victoria and her
team jubilated. The pages lifted her in the air, and she waved her

way out of court. Bat wanted to lunge at her, too angry for
words, but Kalanda restrained him. Outside, the princess talked
to journalists from the government paper.

"Justice has been done. Long live law and order and the spirit
of reconciliation it fosters. Long live the government of Marshal
Amin," she said, beaming.

Tearful faces raised curses at her. Angry fists were directed at
her. The strange thing about losing, even if it was in such a farci-
cal case as this, was that everyone looked embarrassed, as though
it was their fault, as though they had not done enough. They
found it hard to look each other in the eye. There were words of
consolation, which did little to soothe the burning sense of out-
rage surging in their breasts. Bat's father-in-law advised him not
to take the failure personally, and to avoid being destroyed by
the poison of bitterness. They all parted silently, as if to contest
the defeat at some later date.

BAT BURIED HIMSELF in work. The loss of the case seemed to
mark the end of an episode, and now he wanted to look ahead.
He wished to see his brother, and hear his voice, and know how
he was surviving, but he kept out of his way. It was a week after
the verdict that he sent a one-word message: "Bastards." It had
made him laugh; yes, bastards indeed. By now he knew that his
brother would not attempt to kill Victoria. It pleased him that he
had obeyed him. Maybe he was not beyond salvation, and there
were some lights of reason still burning in his head. He still
wanted him to yoke his bombing activities to a political agenda,
but he knew that the boy was a guerrilla, who fought his own
wars, his own way. Now and then, a car bomb went off somewhere. It amazed him how Tayari had eluded his pursuers. How
many cars had he blown up by now? How many army shops?
That he knew this person, and had known him all his life, also
amazed him.

Bat was aware that Victoria could have betrayed him and his

entire family to General Bazooka because of Tayari's activities.
She wasn't crazy, after all. If she was, then it was selective madness. Demented love, more like it. Obsession. Destroying lives.
He didn't want to see her again. And if it meant not seeing his
daughter, so be it.

VICTORIA'S FIFTEEN MINUTES of fame ended as dramatically as they had begun. As soon as the trial ended, General
Bazooka asked her to make her own security arrangements.
Many Bureau agents were angry with her for misusing and tar-
nishing the Bureau's name in a bid to clear herself of murder.
Others hated her because the General had made them worship
her and wear ridiculous costumes, beads and cowrie shells. Those
who had carried her in and out of court were furious because
they had been made to participate in a farce instead of going
out to look for the bombers, who were still putting many of
their colleagues in hospital or out of business. What did General
Bazooka and his slut think? That they were slaves or shit-eating
morons? Others were annoyed by the flagrant nepotism and
favouritism practised by the big shots, and the great leeway the
generals enjoyed. Southern agents, stool pigeons in offices, hospitals, schools, who had joined out of fear or for personal security, cursed her for spitting on royalty and for stirring local
resentment. They dreaded the possible rise of monarchist terrorists who might kill them and their families in the name of
the king. They were aware that many monarchists were ready to
die and kill for the restoration of the kingdoms. Afraid of what
might happen to them after the fall of Amin, some of them
thought of capturing Victoria and handing her over to the monarchists as a sacrifice to them.

Victoria realized that if she showed her face in Bureau circles
she would most certainly be killed. She knew that without the
General's protection, Tayari or some other assassin might come
after her with impunity. Very early in the morning she sneaked

out of the barracks with the sleeping child on her back and got on the bus to the west. She avoided the towns where she had stayed with the General in the days when he was still fighting armed robbers in the South-western Region. She followed her nose, cocksure that she would know when she had reached a safe town. The more she pushed west, the bigger the hills became, till they metamorphosed into mountain ranges, with one higher than the other, caught in the blue skies and the hovering mist and cloud, flaunting hanging valleys blessed with rivers. She was now in the region of the earth's tectonic plates. She could see the snow-capped Rwenzori lost in the clouds. To the north and south were a chain of breathtaking crater lakes. Nearby was a hot spring, and valleys carpeted with tea plantations. At around that time she seemed to cease to exist and she found herself observing herself from outside, just like in the period before Babit's head was cut off. Sunshine broke over the Rwenzori, sending columnar legs through cloud and mist. It hit her in the face as the bus turned. She felt a very excruciating pain. Her eyes seemed to explode and her hands flew to her face. She squeezed her eyes, not daring to open them, for fear of finding herself blind. Many kilometres on, in the town of Fort Portal, the pain slowly disappeared and she opened her eyes, trembling with relief. Here in the west, away from the city, with roads leading to Zaïre, to Rwanda, to Tanzania, anything was possible.

THE RIVALRY BETWEEN General Bazooka and Colonel Ashes raged on, fiercer than ever. Both men escaped death-traps on a number of occasions. General Bazooka believed that Ashes was the man behind the plots against him, although now and then he considered the possibility that some coup-plotting generals might be taking advantage of the confusion to get rid of him. Ashes, in his case, concentrated more on beefing up his security than on finding out who wanted him dead. The departure of Dr. Ali had only strengthened his position as Amin's top confidant, and that made many soldiers eager to cut his heart out. As far as he was concerned, there was only one person he had to keep happy: Marshal Amin. By the look of things, the Marshal needed him more than ever. He was lonely, stranded on the razor teeth of his crumbling power and massive paranoia. He was afraid of assassins, capture by the CIA, subsequent torture and incarceration. The fate of fellow dictators gave him sleepless nights. He remembered too well what had happened to Emperor Haile Selassie, who was locked up in a dank cell and starved to death. He had seen what had happened to Emperor Bokassa in exile in France. Heckled by the French press, false accusations of torture and murder thrown at him every single day. Water and electricity cut every other day. Dead pigs dropped in his yard every three days. Pictures of dead black babies mailed every four days. Refusal by Air France to transport him. Boycotted by all whores, black, white, latino.

"What did the poor runt do to deserve such disgrace? Has the world lost all sense of humour?" Amin would ask Ashes over a glass of whisky. "All the bastard ever wanted to be was Emperor Napoleon, and he was. Portraying him very well, including riding a white horse for his coronation. Now the French are rejecting him, saying that they can't recognize him despite the make-up!" Amin would burst into laughter and Ashes would follow suit.

"These are terrible times, Marshal. African leaders are being victimized for the sins of European leaders. Very soon people will be blaming you for Il Duce's mistakes."

Amin loved that one and he doubled over with laughter. He took a large swig of whisky and took another line of coke. "Well said, friend. It was the reason why I bought that princedom in Saudi Arabia. We Muslims tend to look after our own. The Saudis will take care of me for life."

"It is one of the best dreams you've ever had, Marshal."

"I am sure that some swine-eaters would gladly see me treated like Bokassa, pissed on copiously, for exploiting Il Duce to become world-famous, but they will never get hold of me."

"Not in a million years, Marshal."

"Friend, have you made any plans? Do you intend to hide behind the Queen's skirts or would you rather use Thatcher's bloomers as a cowl?"

They doubled over with laughter, but before Ashes could answer, the phone rang. Emergency. The dissidents had crossed the border into Uganda. With Dr. Ali's words of warning buzzing in his ears, Amin left to go and address the nation.

NOT LONG AFTER, an assassination attempt was made on the Marshal. He was cornered on the way to the State House. Bombs leapt and exploded in all directions. Rocket-propelled grenades hit the presidential Boomerangs and Stingers one after the other. The Eunuchs were mowed down as they valiantly fought back. In the confusion, Amin crawled away, and nobody saw him go. A bullet grazed his back, parried by his bulletproof vest. He made his way to the nearest compound and the petrified family gave him the phone. He called Ashes, who came for him in his helicopter. They spent six days together on the island.

The nation held its breath in suspense. Some said that he had been mortally wounded and was dying, and that the army was busy choosing a successor. Some said a helicopter had picked him up one hour after the attempt and flown him to Libya for operations to remove bullets in his arms and legs. Some said that he had fallen into the hands of dissidents and was being interrogated, spitting teeth and secrets. The sceptics simply kept quiet and waited.

In the meantime, the Marshal was enjoying himself, fishing, swimming in the dazzling waters of the lake, trekking deep into the island to look for parrots. He got the idea to catch a thousand parrots, train them to sing the national anthem, and make them the main attraction at the coming January 21 celebrations marking eight years in power.

"Isn't it a little bit too late, Marshal?"

"It is never too late, friend. We can send a battalion to comb all these islands and come up with as many birds as possible. The rest we can buy on the international market."

"At the cost of hundreds of thousands of dollars."

"Uganda is a rich country. If we can buy the most advanced Russian battle tanks, how about birds with curved beaks?"

Amin scrapped the plan a few days later, saying that the birds were too noisy and produced toxic shit. He went boating with Ashes, travelling hundreds of kilometres in speedboats with a helicopter combing the water and the air for enemies. Some-where in the islands they came upon a fisherman struggling to save a friend who was caught up in the nets of a capsized boat. Amin dashed out of his boat, cut the man free, helped him right the boat, and gave the men money to buy new nets.

"A civilian saved my life a few days ago. I have saved yours to thank God. In fact, I saw you in a dream; it is the reason why I was here in time. Come and visit me at the State House when you are over the shock."

The men were too overcome to say anything.

"You risked your life, Marshal, for some useless fishermen. What if they were dissidents?"

"So much the better. It would show them that I am fearless. And if anybody shoots at me, the bullet just bounces back and kills him."

Ashes enjoyed playing host; big occasions suited him well. He did everything with such dedication as to suggest that he would always follow Amin wherever he went. He was the only person on the island, apart from his guest, who was not on edge. He organized wrestling and boxing and eating competitions, mili-tary exercises, Amin's morning drills and afternoon strolls. The days drifted slowly, filled with relaxation and the faint sugges-tion that they might be the last days before everything changed. It looked like a farewell party, the last event before an institu-tion was closed and the buildings razed. Ashes screened Amin's favourite movies and video recordings. They watched *I Love Lucy*, joking about how much Lucy in the days when she was a stripper and aspirant actress reminded them of Margaret Thatcher. They watched romantic comedies and war films. They watched Amin's two blockbusters: his portrayals of Il Duce. They recited Il Duce's leitmotif: Better One Day as an Elephant Than One Hundred as a Pig. On Amin's tongue, the Italian words sounded like something very delicious.

Amin initiated Ashes into the difficulties he faced when making movies: the rehearsals, the repeated takes, wearing a wooden jaw, three-hour make-up sessions, the bickering and infighting of the supporting cast. He talked about Hollywood parties, the whores, the tubs of champagne; and he confessed that that was where he picked up his coke habit. Before Hollywood he had been a fan of marijuana. Now he could not imagine life without the magic powder. They watched his commercials for high-powered rifles and explosive bullets. He boasted about his ten wives, his fifty known children, the contributions he had made to the country's development.

"Uganda will miss me dearly, as dearly as I miss Dr. Ali."

Ashes talked about his youth in Newcastle, the endless fog, the chilly docks, the dirty factories, the pain of not knowing his real father, the shame of hearing his mother fucked by an impostor, the emptiness of school life, the beauty of the first fire he set, and the resultant fire fetish, the excitement of London's pre-war underworld, the seductive gangsters' wives and whores, one of whom took his virginity, his first kill, the war, and the thrill of landing in Africa. These were two men fantasizing, rewriting and reliving their history as it came out of their mouths, ruminating on their dreams, not people balancing on the razor edge of a country spinning out of control. They both agreed that paradise must resemble these intense moments of historical improvisation.

At the end of the holiday the Marshal realized that the country had drooled long enough with anticipation; it was time to reward it with the balm his resurrection would release. He left the island in his missile-proof helicopter. As it soared in the air, Ashes felt it in his bones that his time had come. It was a matter of waiting for the right hour. That night he heard the Marshal addressing the nation on the radio, refuting rumours that he was dead, or had been dead. He said that he had been to Saudi Arabia visiting the Holy Places, making sacrifices, praying to Allah to extend his rule for another fifty, only fifty years, during which rams would be fucking lionesses, and everybody would be driving around in an eight-door Boomerang. Ashes could not control his laughter. "He should have been a jazz musician. Such improvisation!"

GENERAL BAZOOKA WAS currently obsessed with one project: killing Reptile before the government fell. He knew a lot about his movements, how he now and then participated in hunting down and burning smugglers. With luck and diligence he hoped to lure him into the trap, or even to meet him at one of his famed bonfires.

At the beginning of the year the General detailed a group of his men to acquire boats and look for every opportunity to kill Ashes and his men. He had detailed others to seek employment with him and some had succeeded. With this two-pronged attack, he was guaranteed success sooner rather than later. It was now six months though, and Ashes was still alive. He was running out of patience. After Victoria's trial, with his wife's condition remaining diabolically unchanged, he had little to entertain him, apart from the parties. He further stood to lose his right little toe if he failed to get rid of Ashes within a month. A friendly general had challenged him at a party saying that he would never get the chance to finish off the reptile. General Bazooka had insisted that with his new plan it would take five months, at the latest seven. As a demonstration of confidence, the two men had exchanged toes. If Ashes died, the other general would cut off his own toe; if not, Bazooka would snip off his.

General Bazooka's men first posed as smugglers, then they discovered that their plan worked best if they provided security to smugglers operating in Ugandan waters. They staked their claim and sank boats which refused to pay upfront. From then on everybody did what they said. If they gave the order that nobody operate for a week, the lake stayed clean for that duration. That way they gained control over the waters, the ports, the islands, and waited for the chance to strike. They started provoking patrol boats, hiding on desert islands and shooting at them from the rocks with bazookas and machine-guns. Using powerful radios, they intercepted incoming messages, gave conflicting orders and lured patrol boats into traps.

Ashes resisted taking the bait. The territory under supervision was so vast, so treacherous, that he wanted to avoid costly confrontations. He still preferred to surprise smugglers, kill most of the men, capture the rest, sink the boats, and burn the captives as a lesson. Under pressure from their boss, General Bazooka's men decided to heat the water by sinking patrol boats with their crews. They started sending insulting messages to the Anti-Smuggling Unit, calling them cold-blooded murderers, cannibals, soiled sanitary napkins, gorillas, pigs' asses, and boasting how they were going to capture and roast every one of them.

Ashes responded by sending a helicopter to comb the lake and the shores. Soon after, two fishing villages frequently used by smugglers were bombed flat by helicopter gunships. That did not deter Bazooka's men. His chief advisor told them to spread rumours that the CIA was behind the recent acts of provocation. The CIA was a very feared entity in these parts. The presence of American warships in the Indian Ocean was enough to sow fear in anybody's heart. Ashes did not believe that the Americans were interested in Amin or in Uganda. He was still afraid that some crazy CIA boss might send his men to capture him just to kill boredom or to win a bet made in a brothel. After all, he was visible, white, outrageous. There was also the possibility that Interpol might ask the CIA to capture him for crimes committed over the years. Shaming him would shake Amin, and nowadays humiliating the Marshal had become a big pastime abroad.

Ashes proceeded with caution. His men were also becoming harder to motivate because, lacking information and analytical capabilities, they believed the CIA rumours and did not want to fight against Americans. He started going out with them more often in order to reassure them. However, his hand was forced when the Marshal got wind of the situation and asked what he planned to do about it.

"All-out war," he replied, lamenting the fact that Uganda had no battleships to grind the smugglers' hideouts to rubble.

The heart of the coffee-smuggling operations lay to the north and north-east of Lake Victoria. In that area the waters were full of islands, big and small, populated and bare, and the shores were rich with ports and potential landing facilities, bays, creeks. Some shores were massive, chopped, mean-faced boulders strewn with papyrus; some gentle sands and mud-flats alive with little fishes, leeches, and canoes. Sometimes forest crept near to the water, forming a thatched wall of trees easy to hide in. Sometimes one could move from the water and walk in short grass for miles. It was this variety, this unpredictability, this unevenness of surface, that made effective patrolling an impossible task. It would have taken a whole army to do a proper job. Ashes called himself "Admiral of the Victoria," but with the Kenyan government encouraging smugglers who, at the peak, also operated overland, he knew that his real power was limited.

At the beginning of his career he had chosen the most obvious option: patrolling the more popular waterways and stationing his men on the islands more frequented by smugglers. But his men had started taking bribes, and the smugglers had worked out alternative routes. More infuriating still, there were Kenyan islands two kilometres from Ugandan waters. The Kenyans would place gunboats just over the border and escort Ugandan smugglers to safety.

On the day the final battle was fought, Ashes had ten gunboats at his command. His plan was to attack with the boats and call in the helicopter to cream off the smugglers who tried to slip through the gaps. It would be nice to watch the helicopter toying with them, giving them a few metres here and there, and then taking them out in spectacular fireballs which would light up the night. The confrontation took place fifty kilometres from his island, in a waterway between two barren islands.

At around midnight the patrol spotted a lone smuggler. They challenged the boat to stop, but it took off at high speed. They gave chase in order to cut it off, but the boat managed to lure them into a cliff-faced creek. Five boats went after it, like mad hounds after a rabbit. It was a very simple but effective trap. As soon as the boats were within range, the machine-guns started firing. Bazooka's men blew up and sank patrol boats. The cries of wounded men were buried under the clatter of guns and the explosion of grenades. When Ashes started to withdraw his men, boats emerged from the blind side of the cliffs and opened fire. Ashes took a bullet in the chest area of his bulletproof jacket. He escaped with a cracked rib. When he called in his helicopter, an unfamiliar voice at the other end cursed him. At that moment he realized that Bazooka's men had overrun his headquarters and taken over his island. He had two options: to fight his way to safety and go to the nearest barracks for help, or to flee to Kenya and leave the country for good.

Escorted by two boats, Ashes made his way out of danger, sailed on and landed at the small port of Majanji. He hired a pick-up truck, which had come for fish, to take him to the border town of Busia. Two days later he crossed into Kenya on a false passport. At Mombasa he got medical attention and booked a place on a ship to Cape Town.

GENERAL BAZOOKA COULD NOT BELIEVE his ears. He had set the perfect trap, his men had overrun the island, and yet he had come away empty-handed. A day later his men arrested Ashes' wife, bringing her in with a black eye. It turned out to be somebody else. He released her, changed his mind, wanting to ask her a few more questions, but the men sent to go after her five minutes later lost her. The real Mrs. Ashes had, in the meantime, disappeared into the maze of villages.

A WEEK LATER the South African government bragged about offering political asylum to Amin's right-hand man.

AMIN UNLEASHED vintage invective against the racist regime for a whole week.

Ashes listened to his former employer's rantings from the safety of his farm, bought two years before. In the distance he could see the Table Mountains wreathed in mist. In his backyard he could see vines, laden with the grape famous for producing white wine. He could hardly wait to launch the harvest and his future career as vintner.

TWO DAYS AFTER CUTTING off his toe, General Bazooka received a summons to report to the State House. The Defence Council gathered and put him in command of the main force charged with driving the dissidents from south-western Uganda. Doing his best to disguise his limp and pain as the boot bit into the wound, he tried to find credible reasons for not complying. He had lost touch with the region. He wanted to stay and guard the city. His wife was, after all, in Mulago Hospital. Marshal Amin, who had been drifting away under hallucinations induced by whisky (disguised with Coca-Cola to keep up appearances as a teetotaler), cocaine and fear, seemed to wake up for the first time. All thirty eyes in the room turned to him, to scrutinize him for signs as to the fate of the errant general. There was a holding of breath among the congregated generals. Amin fixed on Bazooka a very meaningful stare. Disobedience? Wife? When the fate of the nation was at stake? The General felt chilly despite the fact that it was a hot afternoon and the sun was blazing outside. Amin had said nothing to him about Ashes and his involvement in the affair.

Under the cold stares of his colleagues, all of whom were grateful that Ashes was gone, General Bazooka accepted the order, but he asked for permission to take his wife with him.

"You must be mad. Do you want to give that patriotic woman to the enemy? Mulago is the best hospital in the country. It is where she belongs till you return with victory."

General Bazooka realized that mentioning his wife had been a big mistake, and the freezing looks from fellow generals and the hateful eye Amin fixed on him had unsettled him. Now he had to think very quickly of a plan to get her out. He had less than an hour to do it. He had last seen her the day before. He had once again asked if she wanted to go to Libya, and as a reply he had got the request to describe the smell of the air outside. Suddenly, he felt his dreams go sour, coagulating into heavy rotting lumps. He had got used to the visits, the sound of her croaking voice, the view outside the window. Without her and the children, he had little left. They underpinned everything, absolved every crime. Without them he felt hollow. He could see the winds from the south sweeping his achievements away, stripping him naked. Victory? Why should I be its guarantor? Maybe I should shoot the Marshal and die honourably, but there is no honour in suicide, except if committed to evade capture and betrayal of war secrets, he mused. He wondered what he should do next, but before he could reach any decision, the meeting was adjourned. He stood up, saluted and left with the rest.

Major Ozi, in his capacity as head of the Eunuchs, escorted him out and informed him that he, Ozi, was now in charge of the General's family's security and welfare. Ozi informed the bewildered general that he was not allowed to go to hospital to say goodbye or to collect his children from school. He was to get on the move to the south-west immediately.

Major Ozi enjoyed watching the signs of alarm on the General's face. He smiled as he watched him write out messages to his mother, instructing her to take charge of everything till his return. He had waited for this moment for a very long time.

He held all these generals responsible for the instability in the country and in the government. He held them responsible for failing to repulse the dissidents or to infiltrate their camps in Tanzania and wipe them out. He held them responsible for the death of his men in coup attempts, the last of which had cost him twenty men and left ten wounded, and for the bombing of his shop and shops belonging to some of his men. He hated them for indulging themselves instead of running their ministries and fulfilling other responsibilities on their shoulders. He hated Bazooka for wasting the taxpayers' money on capers, and especially for running Colonel Robert Ashes off, which had left Amin without a confidant, making him moodier, more paranoid, more dependent on drugs, and harder to protect. As a man whose job and life depended on Amin remaining alive and in power, Major Ozi hated these men for threatening his life, and the lifestyle of his men. What would happen to the wealth he and his men had collected? And on a more personal level, he hated the General for killing his friends while quelling revolts in the army.

In the past few years Major Ozi had done it all. The Eunuchs had risen to such power that everybody, including Amin's wives, was afraid of them. They had in fact organized a car crash in which one of the Marshal's wives died, and arrested another on suspicion of cheating on him. That had been the apogee; nothing could beat laying one's hands on the wife of the most powerful man in the land. The Eunuchs had also broken the Vice President's back. With these, and many more achievements bubbling in his head, he wondered what to do with this man. The Marshal had, literally, given his head to him on a plate. It was up to him to slice it off if he wanted. The Marshal had also given him this man's entire family. He wondered how to tackle them, whether to make it easy for them or to make their life extremely hard. He hoped that the remaining generals would learn a lesson from Bazooka's trials and tribulations. He dismissed the General with a friendly shake of the hands and wished him success in his coming campaign.

General Bazooka left the State House feeling sick. He was now head of troops he did not know and officers he did not trust. They carried out his orders woodenly, making no input whatsoever. On the way, he saw the nightmare of a disorganized army, with tanks in the wrong places, lorries full of scared soldiers labouring to the wrong destinations, orders lost on the way in a faulty chain of command, the wrong ammunition delivered to the wrong places. He could feel the glee with which the civilians watched, and he felt angry that there was little he could do about it. There were chaotic roadblocks which slowed the progress of both soldiers and supplies. The codes were messed up, and at times it seemed as if the dissidents were in charge. He suspected that some of these men were deliberately messing up things out of fear of engaging the enemy, praying that by the time their turn came the order would be given to withdraw. There were bodies along the road, civilians shot by soldiers, soldiers shot by soldiers mistaken for dissidents. And the fact that this was hardly two hundred kilometres from the capital dismayed him.

General Bazooka could not concentrate. During the first few days he got no chance to send a message home. The phones did not work, the radio messages were intercepted, the men were untrustworthy. When he finally sent men to check what was happening, they were waylaid and killed by the Eunuchs, leaving him in limbo. Over the years he had been looking forward to the chance to relive the adrenaline rush of the days before the coup. The incredible pressure, the fear of betrayal, the possibility of dying in action, the glowing beacon of victory. He wanted to explode and lose control for some delicious hours, and sow destruction with impunity. But now that the time had come, he found out that things had changed. There was no excitement, there was nothing to look forward to, no country to take over, no enemies to hunt down, no women to violate, no new experiences to be had. All he felt now was fear of the Marshal, and contempt and hatred for him. He looked down upon himself for landing in this predicament, for failing to shoot the Marshal, for obeying that terrible major and his killers. This was a lost war, because Marshal Amin had failed to keep things together. He had no plan, no talent for leadership. It had all along been a ride on the back of a mad bull, holding on for as long as possible.

He marched through the towns he had captured years ago and felt disgusted. The sound of guns offered no comfort, no solace, no signal to charge. They were scared guns. The hills had already been surrendered, the valleys a carpet for the invaders to walk on. The south-west was gone. He felt no desire to sacrifice these loathsome men just to give a lost cause a few more breaths of life. At any other time he would have enjoyed flogging them, maybe even wringing their necks. Now he wanted them gone, out of his sight. Many were deserting, disappearing in the night. They would rather risk capture and flogging or death than face the guns. He got on the radio to the Defence Council, but there was no one home on the hotline. At that moment he decided to go back to the city and rescue his family.

The city was unrecognizable: it was full of soldiers driving Stingers at breakneck speed escorting this or that fleeing officer, firing at buildings, shadows, vultures and marabou storks, looting, making themselves scarce. Everybody was hurrying or looking over their shoulder. The streets were deserted, strewn with hills of garbage. At the hospital he bounded up the stairs to Ward 6. The hospital stank, was full of empty-eyed patients searching for doctors, lying in the corridors of crowded wards, praying, consoling damaged children, women, the elderly. Ward 6 had lost its status: it was full of poor patients on soiled sheets, some on beds, most on the floor. His wife's bed was occupied by a one-eyed old woman. He rushed out to search for doctors. He learned that the Eunuchs had taken his wife away. He saw the name of Major Ozi on the release forms. He imagined how they had handled that fragile body and he shivered. The doctors knew nothing about his children or mother.

He tore through the city at top speed. The Boomerang took corners wildly, and at the roundabout it just sped through the stationary cars, horn blowing, full lights on. It climbed the hills of Kasubi at suicidal speed. All the houses formerly occupied by his friends were empty, looted, strewn with discarded paper, rags, and shit somebody or a group of people had diligently trowelled on the walls. His wife's home had suffered a similar fate: total desecration. The floors in every room had been dug up, so that one walked on chunky blocks of cement, the doors and windows pulled out and left hanging. He made his way to the basement in a daze, lower lip trembling, his stomach full of gas. There was a huge crater, coffin-shaped, where the gunny sack packed with fifty- and hundred-dollar bills had been. Millions. Gone. He felt something break inside him, an overpowering weariness that turned his legs to jelly. This, on top of all the other catastrophes! It was too much even to cry over. He knew that the Eunuchs had destroyed him and had left no clue as to the whereabouts of the fifty people on the hill.

It crossed his mind that they had all been killed. Fifty heads on a heap. And it was his fault. This civilian consideration shocked him. He had lived above the law for so long, out of bounds of civilian strictures, that it amazed him to look at himself and judge his actions according to the same. Could I have been betrayed to this extent? To the core of my identity? So fast? In less than ten days? he wondered aloud. The pain in his four-toed foot increased. The fact that he had honoured the wager, severed his toe, now struck him as a harbinger of a fall he should have foreseen. Normally, he would have laughed at the other general and compensated him with money or a cow or a car, but not gone to the extent of desecrating his body. Where had the man thrown his toe? He had taken it away in a polythene bag.

As he staggered from the empty house, he felt the final pangs of rejection: These hills, valleys, rivers, these people, had all rejected him, and pushed him back to where his ancestors had come from. He was already erased from memory. A new conqueror would soon be here, his minions cleaning and scrubbing, and filling the houses with household goods. His princedom had already gone, the bottom eaten out during the last ten days. Now he feared for his mother's business and for her life. In her house another sackful of dollars had been buried. It was his only salvation now. Without it he would be back to zero. The only reminder of his past success would be the ever-faithful Oris Autocrat on his wrist.

As he left the hill and the city, it struck him that there were eight, nine, ten children of his somewhere in these hills. Children with southern blood in them, children he had at one time craved but had ignored when they came. His legacy to the south, belonging nowhere and everywhere. He had met some of them, given them names, and coins to buy things. Others he had denied with impunity. What could peasants do to a prince? Before leaving the city for good, he found himself driving to two addresses where two of his children lived. He wanted to take these two, and their mothers, just in case. He did not want to leave empty-handed. He might learn to love them just to keep going. He might turn them into soldiers to empty their wrath on these hills at some later date. He needed them; they were his, after all.

At the first address, a house near the road, the place was deserted. Doors and windows had been knocked out, everything emptied. He felt himself grow faint. At the second address, he was informed by the landlord that the woman had left three weeks ago with her child. She had fled to a village about two hundred kilometres away. He suddenly felt very old and very weary. Pictures of men about to meet their death came to him: he remembered those who could hardly walk, dragging frail bodies which seemed to weigh a ton. He recognized the feeling; he could hardly move. Without looking the landlord in the eye, he trudged back to his Boomerang and asked his bodyguard to drive away. As he left, he felt that the south had repossessed everything it had ever given him.

In Jinja the face of destruction met him at his mother's home. The house had been reduced to rubble by fire. He made his way to the basement, his heart racing. The false floor had been lifted away. The money gone. In its place were piles of relatively fresh shit. He vomited. The Eunuchs. Major Ozi. He went to the barracks to ask where his family was. He asked a trusted officer, a tribesman; he said that he did not know. He went to the headquarters of the Eunuchs. In the compound were about two hundred men armed to the teeth, the majority wearing hundreds of bullets on chains. They stopped him at the gate. He was out of bounds. No information. No sign of Major Ozi. He tried to get in touch with the Marshal on the hotline. The line was dead. He knew that the Marshal was somewhere in this town, having fled the city a few days before. He felt his stomach sinking to his knees. He had grown up in this area, but there was no longer any place for him here.

He hit the road to the north; he missed his Avenger, whose whereabouts he did not know. This would have been the time to fly and make up for lost time. He pushed to Soroti, Lira, Gulu, Arua, hundreds of kilometres of devilish distress. Major disaster awaited him. His family was not there; neither were his fifty friends. It occurred to him that his wife and children had long been dead. The friends too. He got on the move. He spent the nights in the wild with three of his men, lying under the stars, winds sweeping over him. He could hear his wife's voice labouring through her damaged throat, asking him to . . . Reptile's revenge, he said to himself. Ashes, that vile reptile; only Ashes could plan something this diabolical. Reptile . . . He was always grateful for the break of day. It meant movement, the endless search for the ghosts of his family. Maybe they had lost their way and were wandering towards him on foot, emaciated, desperate. His right leg swelled from the pressure of activity and lack of proper medical attention. Tetanus bit into the wound; the rot started spreading upwards. When he heard the verdict, he did not wait. He put the barrel of a shotgun in his mouth and the explosion tore off the back of his head. Ashes, that reptile . . .

BAT LISTENED TO THE GUNS, the small ones answering the big ones. They seemed to expel soldiers and hangers-on by hydraulic action. There was wild shooting and looting as fleeing soldiers looked for money, civilian clothes, food, and medicines to sustain them on the long way north. Unlucky civilians were shot in revenge, frustration, desperation. He stayed inside his house, barricaded behind the steel gate. He made calls to his friends, and they called him to make sure that he was all right. There was a crescendo in the shooting and then the noise gradually died down.

The vacuum of power lasted a whole week. A new regime announced itself. There was relief, expectation, celebration. His brother paid him a visit one morning. He came with his two surviving friends. To thank him. He was very happy to see his brother, although he wondered how their relationship would be from now on. His sister also came. With a child, born during the last weeks of fighting. He got a phone call a few days later. He was offered his old job back by the new regime of former exiles. He knew some of them. He had been to university with a number of them. Professors, doctors, lawyers in army fatigues. He did not tell them that he knew how to fire guns. He accepted the offer. He was ready to relaunch his life.

He got into his car and surveyed the city, glad to see the high blue sky above on this clear windy day, and the people going about their business, picking up the pieces. A veritable sense of victory overcame him and he banged the wheel a few times. The Marshal, General Bazooka, the Zanzibari astrologers, had gone. The Libyans and Saudis had departed months before, their unfinished projects left gawking. He enjoyed watching massive statues of Amin being unceremoniously pulled down with ropes tied to lorries, and hacked to pieces. He drove to Kasubi. He had to see General Bazooka's house and make sure that he was gone. There were people walking about in the debris, commenting on the shit-smeared walls, cursing and laughing. He seemed to be the lone victor left after a vicious fight. He got back into his car and coasted down the hill, headed for his office opposite the Parliament Building.

During the last few weeks he had been plagued by dreams. The Babit trinity had appeared a few times. He had also had recurrent visits from Mrs. Kalanda.